BOOK OF SHA

THE
BLACK
TESTAMENT

A Novel

MICHAEL PENNING

THE BLACK TESTAMENT

First Edition. June 2024
ISBN: 978-1-7388551-4-8 (Paperback)
ISBN: 978-1-7388551-5-5 (Hardcover)

www.michaelpenning.com

For my father,
who always made time for my imagination.

Chapter 1

To Anna Jacobs, the cemetery was more than just a resting place for the dead; it was a hunting ground. Her grip on her knife tightened as she prepared for violence. She stood atop the ridge overlooking Boston's Copp's Hill Burying Ground, the full moon hanging high in the dark sky. Her thick black hair tumbled over her shoulders, mingling with the shadows, while her piercing blue eyes scanned the crumbling gravestones for any sign of movement.

The wind's haunting melody prickled Anna's skin as it whispered through the ancient trees. She shivered, not from fear, but from the chilly air. The bottom hem of her leather coat brushed against her boots as she wrapped it around herself. A thin mist had rolled in from the sea, cloaking the waterfront cemetery in its ghostly embrace. Anna breathed in deeply, taking in the salty brine and the scent of wet earth and rotting leaves that saturated the moonlit night.

Copp's Hill was a bleak and lonely place, with cobblestone paths winding through a labyrinth of graves and crypts. The old headstones, some over a hundred years old, were weathered and crumbling. This was a place of ghosts, of spirits of the past: the resolute souls who first braved the wilderness of America; the sailors who gave their lives at sea, fighting for their independence; the soldiers who fell in battle, their names etched forever in stone. Among the locals, there were tales of hauntings, of phantom figures that appeared at night, ghostly and translucent. Some claimed to have heard faint voices in the darkness, the whisperings of those who lingered somewhere between life and death.

Anna knew the ghost stories were true. She ended many of them.

Anna was anything but an ordinary eighteen-year-old. Her mother, Abigail, had taught her the forbidden arts of necromancy and the occult at a young age, initiating her into the secret realm of ghosts and monsters. Abigail had been a formidable occultist, having inherited her powerful grimoire, the ancient Book of Shadows, from a long line of notorious witches. But now, Anna carried the weight of their legacy alone. Her mother's body lay in a state between life and death, while her spirit waited beyond the Veil for Anna to do the impossible—to bring her back.

Anna's heartache deepened with each haunting she took on, intensifying the emptiness left by Abigail's absence. Their relationship had always been strained and tumultuous. Not long ago, Anna was so frightened of her own irresistible attraction to the darkest of magics that she tried to leave her life of witchcraft and violence behind. But now she had no choice. If she had any hope of restoring Abigail's lost soul, she was bound to continue her mother's secret work, fighting the forces of evil.

And if she was honest, there was nothing more pleasurable than killing to quiet the bloodlust that simmered within her eternally. Deep inside, she was grateful for the monsters she hunted.

Without them, she might be killing people.

Clouds gathered around the moon as Anna descended the ridge and crept between the gravestones. With one hand clutching the knife, she held an unlit torch in the other, prepared to ignite it as soon as the need arose. It was early April, and the night air was damp enough to penetrate her bones. Her boot-heels on the cobbled path echoed the rhythm of her heartbeat. It was a moonlit dance she had performed many times before, but tonight was different. Tonight she felt an unmistakable foreboding she couldn't ignore.

Anna's steps quickened when she spotted a faint trail of footprints in the frost-kissed grass. The tracks led her further into the heart of the cemetery, where the shadows grew deeper and longer. A gust of wind stirred the rotted leaves, drawing her attention to a mound of earth beside a nearby grave. It hadn't been left there by a gravedigger.

Something else had disturbed the eternal slumber of the dead.

The wet earth muted Anna's footfalls as she drew nearer to the grave. A repulsive stench greeted her, a reek of decomposing flesh that made her stomach churn. She pressed her sleeve to her nose as she knelt and ran her fingers through the disturbed earth. The dirt was loose, as if something had clawed it open from below. Anna dug deeper, her hands dredging through the soil until her fingertips brushed against the smooth surface of a bone. A ripple of revulsion rolled over her skin when she realized what she had uncovered.

A rotting head.

The corpse buried here was fresh. Moonlight played upon the empty eye sockets. Something had torn chunks of livid flesh from the skull, and there were distinct gouges left by sharp teeth, as if some rabid animal had gnawed upon the cranium.

Anna's adrenaline surged as she rose to her feet, the blade grasped firmly in her hand. She was wrong: nothing had crawled out of this grave, but something had clawed its way *in*. A corpse-eating ghoul had been haunting this cemetery, devouring the flesh of the newly dead. It would inevitably catch a taste for the living.

I won't let that happen, Anna thought. *I'm not leaving until I've killed it.*

The cemetery seemed to grow darker with each step she took, the silence becoming more oppressive with each heartbeat. Anna moved swiftly, her senses alert to even the slightest disturbance. She was the predator in this macabre landscape, and her prey was very close.

A low growl, full of ravenous hunger, rolled through the night. Anna spun around, her eyes scanning the gloom for the source. And then she heard it—the rusty moan of an open mausoleum gate creaking in the wind.

Anna tightened her grip on her knife, her breath locked in her chest. The stench of decay and freshly turned earth filled the air as she drew closer.

The mausoleum loomed in front of her, its stone walls chipped and worn with time. The sound of scraping and scratching coming from inside pricked Anna's ears, occasionally interrupted by slurping and gurgling sounds.

It's in there. Somewhere in those dark depths is the vile creature I've come here to kill.

Anna retrieved her tinderbox from her coat pocket and ignited the resin-soaked rag wrapped around her torch's head. A flickering flame blazed to life and danced in her icy blue eyes as she braced herself for the battle ahead. Her veins thrummed with the weight of her mother's teachings and her own burning desire for violence.

With a deep breath, Anna opened the creaking gate of the mausoleum. The stench of rot contaminating the stale air assaulted her senses. Her footsteps echoed unnervingly in the darkness, each step bringing her closer to danger.

The interior was a dark maze, illuminated solely by her torch. Its light heightened the tension in the air, casting distorted shadows over the desecrated tombs and cobweb-covered sarcophagi. The sounds grew louder now, resonating off the stone—a series of sickening crunches and snaps, like bones being shattered and tendons torn apart. Anna moved cautiously, aware of every subtle shift in her surroundings.

And then she saw it—a hideous figure, hunched over a fresh corpse, its elongated claws ripping through the flesh with a ferocious hunger. It turned toward Anna, and her torchlight lit its grotesque face. The creature's sunken eye sockets, once human, now held glowing orbs of malice. Deep wrinkles carved its gaunt features, as if it had survived centuries of torment. Its nose was a jagged protrusion, almost completely eroded by the ravages of time. Its bony fingers ended with long claws tipped with ragged, broken nails.

Yellow saw-teeth lined the ghoul's mouth, which seemed too large for its withered face. Dark droplets of blood stained its chin and dribbled onto its threadbare clothing.

It rose from its grisly feast, hunched and menacing, its emaciated frame covered in decaying rags. The creature's flesh was a sickly pale hue, tightly stretched over its bones, as if it were about to decompose. Each movement of its limbs revealed a patchwork of exposed tendons and sinew. The reek that emanated from it was overpowering—a revolting miasma of putrefaction that assaulted Anna's senses. She felt a wave of disgust as its rotten stench thickened the air, making her gag and reel in revulsion.

It lunged at Anna without warning, its bloodstained mouth stretched into a predatory grin.

Fueled by adrenaline, Anna raised her torch high and retaliated with a swift slash of her knife, aiming for the creature's heart. Her aim was off, but she still plunged the blade deep into its chest. Dark blood spurted from the wound, staining her hands as she grappled with the creature.

The ghoul's painful howl reverberated through the confines of the mausoleum. It lashed out with frenzied swipes, its long claws cutting through the air like scythes. Anna barely reacted in time, narrowly dodging the creature's first strike. But its movements were too fast. It raked her shoulder, tearing through her coat and leaving a deep gash in her flesh. She felt a searing pain as blood ran down her arm.

The monster sensed its advantage. It charged forward and sent Anna stumbling backward. Back-pedaling, she retreated through the mausoleum's rusty gate. The creature pursued her into the night and circled her, its glowing eyes fixed on her with unexpected intelligence. Most ghouls were cowardly and mindless, driven only by their insatiable craving for flesh. But this one fought with an unmatched ferocity—and it was far stronger than any she had ever encountered.

It pounced at her again, moving unnaturally fast, its clawed fingers grasping for her throat. Anna's instincts took over as she twisted her body, narrowly avoiding the ghoul's attack. She swung her blade in a desperate arc, aiming for the creature's vulnerable flesh. But the ghoul's strength was overpowering, and it delivered a bone-crushing blow that sent Anna sprawling to the frosty ground.

Pain radiated through her body. She struggled to regain her footing, her mind racing for a plan. The ghoul seemed to anticipate her every move as it circled her, its grotesque form blocking any chance of escape.

Anna's hand tightened on the knife's handle as she mustered the strength to stand. Her legs quivered under her weight. She couldn't afford to falter again. Summoning her courage, she lunged forward, slashing her blade through the air. The ghoul's rancid breath washed over her face as her weapon sliced through its flesh and notched into a bone with a sickening thud.

But the ghoul was far from defeated. It retaliated with brutal force, its agonized shrieks echoing through the graveyard. Pain shot through Anna's chest as it flung her body against a mossy tombstone. The torch escaped her grasp and rolled away, just out of reach. Blood flowed from a gash on her forehead, mingling with sweat.

Anna's vision blurred as she gasped for air, desperately trying to stay conscious. She rolled to the side, barely dodging the ghoul's deadly claws. More blood seeped through her torn clothing as she scrambled to another headstone, using it to haul herself to her feet. A strange fear crept into her gut. She had dealt beatings to men twice her size and survived battles with savage beasts, but this was one fight from which she might not walk away.

Could this really be the end? Was this the night she died?

And did she even care?

The creature's feral hunger blazed in its menacing gaze as it advanced.

The moment felt like time was slowing. Anna's training took over, perfected by her mother's mentoring. In one fluid motion, she dove forward, snatched up the torch, and swung it through the air. The fire ignited the ghoul's skin and it let out a blood-curdling screech, its body contorting in agony. The stench of its burning flesh mingled with the acrid smoke that billowed upward. The ghoul flailed and howled, its horrible cries reverberating through the cemetery.

Anna stepped back, her gaze locked on the dying creature. With her last ounce of strength, she delivered a forceful kick to the creature's sternum, propelling it backward into the mausoleum. Before it could recover, she slammed the heavy iron gate shut, sealing the burning ghoul inside.

With a desperate surge, the flaming creature flung itself at the iron bars, its claws shooting through as it reached for Anna. But she was ready. She sidestepped the attack and stabbed with her knife. The heat of the fire singed her flesh, and she released her grip as the blade met its mark, piercing the ghoul's heart. The creature emitted one last guttural groan before falling lifeless and smoldering to the ground.

Darkness filled the chamber. The silence descended like a shroud, broken only by the crackling of dying flames.

Anna leaned against the crumbling wall of the mausoleum, her veins thrumming with adrenaline and exhilaration. This is what she lived for now—the thrill of the hunt and the exquisite rush of pain and bloodshed that were her only vital signs. A chilling breeze swept through the air as she surveyed the aftermath of the battle. Her hard-earned victory would please the wealthy man who hired her to kill the defiler of his wife's corpse.

But there was no time to rest. The ghoul's ghastly shrieks would soon bring unwanted attention, and Anna had no intention of explaining her presence here. She retraced her steps, weaving her way among the headstones in the darkness, leaving a thin trail of blood in her wake.

A sudden crackling made her freeze in place.

Something felt wrong.

Anna's skin tingled with unease as the air thickened with an otherworldly energy. A fierce wind rustled leaves through the cemetery, and the ground beneath a weathered tombstone suddenly split apart with a slow groan. Anna's throat tightened as skeletal fingers pierced the surface of the earth. A gnarled and yellowed hand clawed its way out, followed by a bony arm in a tattered burial shroud.

Anna's heart raced as she witnessed something she never thought possible. She'd seen the dead walk many times, but corpses didn't just reanimate by themselves. Only powerful necromancy was capable of such a thing—or a spirit ancient enough to breach the Veil and possess the dead.

Moonlight seeped through the clouds, illuminating the

reanimated abomination as it rose steadily from the grave. Liberated by some unholy force, dirt and soil sloughed off its rotting frame. Its weathered bones were fleshless, and its empty eye sockets were windows into the abyss. A ghastly grin stretched across its skeletal face, its yellowed teeth glinting in the pale light.

Anna felt paralyzed by the sight of the creature lurching toward her. The battle with the ghoul left her drained and unprepared for such a confrontation. Fear and awe collided within her and she let out a gasp, barely audible in the night's stillness.

The corpse shuffled closer, limbs creaking with each step. Its eye sockets were twin voids that absorbed all light as they fixated on her, filling her with an unearthly dread. Its jaw hinged open, and a single word crawled out from between its yellow teeth.

"*Sévérité…*"

Goosebumps ran down Anna's skin. She recognized that hollow voice! Gideon, her spectral familiar, was bound to her at birth to be her guide and protector against the dark realm of the supernatural.

But why was he here? Anna had forbidden him from contacting her through the Veil, fearful of what else might slip through with him.

The mysterious single word he uttered lingered in the air.

Sévérité…

Anna's brow furrowed as her mind raced. "What does that mean, Gideon? Speak!"

But the familiar's power to revive the corpse was fading, his foothold in this world waning. Before he could croak another word, the corpse crumbled back onto the ground in a heap of bones.

Anna sensed Gideon's presence receding, his spectral energy fading away, leaving her alone to ponder her thoughts and questions.

Shouts of alarm echoed in the distance, spurring her into action. It was time to flee before they discovered her.

As she lost herself in the winding alleys of Boston's North End, Anna couldn't shake off the lingering sense of unease that gripped her. Gideon's unexpected appearance and cryptic message left her deeply unsettled. What did it mean? It had to be of grave importance for Gideon to disobey her and risk reaching through the Veil. Was it a warning? Was her life in danger? The spirit had unraveled a hidden thread, revealing a secret Anna didn't even know existed. Her footsteps reverberated through the streets as she replayed the encounter, the enigmatic word echoing over and over again in her mind.

Sévérité...

Anna felt the absence of her mother's wisdom and guidance more strongly than ever. Abigail would know what to make of this. Anna had a talent for breaking things, but it was her mother who knew how to put them back together.

The dimly lit streets only heightened her unease as time passed, leaving her even more unsettled. Anna changed direction and veered toward the harbor where taverns and whiskey could be found at all hours. The night's events had shaken her more than she would admit, and she suddenly didn't want to be alone.

The hunt was over, but the mystery had only just begun.

Chapter 2

The clouds hung low in the steel-gray sky as Judith Alden walked down the overgrown path into the desolate village. Wisps of mist curled through the deserted lanes, obscuring her way and deepening the already haunting atmosphere.

Buried deep within the dark heart of New Hampshire's White Mountains, the once-thriving settlement now lay in eerie silence, its buildings crumbling and overrun by nature's relentless siege. The villagers who once called this place home had long fled, leaving behind an empty shell of their former existence. The timber and stone cottages stood in ruins, their decaying facades and shattered windows now grim reminders of a forgotten time. Vines coiled their way up the weathered walls, strangling the structures in their embrace. Rusty abandoned carts with wheels half-buried in the earth hinted at a bustling past. The narrow lanes were muddy and rutted from the spring thaw. Weeds were already sprouting from the puddles, reclaiming their territory and obscuring any trace of human presence. The scent of decay and April dampness hung heavily in the air.

Judith's footsteps carried through the stillness. Silence reigned in this desolate place, broken only by the occasional hoot of an owl or a crow's screech. The wind through the naked boughs whispered a lonesome melody of abandoned dreams and lost hopes. Each crunch of gravel beneath Judith's worn leather boots was a chilling reminder of her isolation in this forsaken place.

A brisk breeze cut through the air, stirring up rotting leaves uncovered from beneath the melting snow. Judith shivered under the heavy cloak draped over her thin shoulders. Time had weathered her, etching lines of hardships and resilience onto her face. Once warm and bright with youthful dreams, her eyes were now deep and icy pools. Her chestnut hair, streaked with gray, tumbled around her shoulders. Her practical and unadorned clothes reflected the simplicity of her life—a faded dress covered by a worn apron, their colors as dull as the village's fading past.

Judith's senses sharpened as she ventured further. Her breath quickened with each cautious step, her heartbeat throbbing in her ears. A growing unease slowly crept up the back of her neck. Having sought refuge on the outskirts of the deserted village for nearly five years, Judith was well-acquainted with its empty silence. But after the unexplained horrors that plagued her family, the village now seemed alive with malice. A sense of foreboding gnawed at her, urging her to turn back and escape this dark and cursed place.

But first, she had to find her daughter.

Judith's mind seethed with frustration. How could Mercy be so foolish to sneak away again? How could her daughter still ignore the boundaries Judith had set for her own protection? Considering everything that had happened, didn't she understand the gravity of her actions? The image of Mercy wandering into the unknown, unaware of the potential dangers, fueled Judith's fury, making it burn hotter with every step.

Her eyes fell upon her destination as she neared the town square—the steeple of the dilapidated chapel pointed toward the heavens like a bony finger. Nestled beneath a gnarled oak tree lay the hallowed ground of the village's forgotten cemetery. The chipped and weathered tombstones bore the names of long-departed souls, their inscriptions barely decipherable. A shiver crept down Judith's neck, an icy finger tracing the contours of her flesh. The graveyard felt like a grim theater, with the dead as silent spectators to her unwelcome intrusion.

Judith hurried by and lifted her gaze to the chapel as she drew closer. Moss and ivy covered the weatherbeaten walls, masking the decay and wood-rot. The door stood slightly open as she mounted the creaking steps, inviting her to explore the darkness within. A sliver of pale daylight spilled through the gap, illuminating the dust-laden pews. The hinges groaned in protest as Judith inched the door wider, revealing a gloom that defied the sun's feeble light. She hesitated a moment at the threshold, but the overwhelming need to find her daughter propelled her into the unsettling silence of the sanctuary.

The air inside was heavy with a musty smell and an unsettling presence that made Judith's skin crawl. Aged pews with wooden frames lay overturned and in disarray on either side of her. The surfaces were tarnished and peeling, exposing the raw bones of pine. Empty gaps between the rows seemed to yearn for the warmth of a devout congregation.

Amid the gloom, the derelict altar stood in faded grandeur. Intricate motifs clung faintly to the rotted timber, and cobwebs draped the crucifix—a gossamer veil spun by patient spiders. Cold daylight filtered through the cracked stained-glass window above the altar, casting surreal fragments of color into the dust-filled air. The glowing hues of blues, reds, and yellows, once intended to inspire reverence, now lay like shattered glass over the timber floor.

A trail of fresh footprints led Judith's gaze up the aisle to a small figure kneeling before the altar. Her youngest child, Mercy, seemed unaware of her mother's presence as she remained with her head bowed and her back to the door.

Judith's toneless voice broke the stillness. "You'll find nothing in this place for you, Mercy."

Mercy spun around, taken by surprise. The twelve-year-old's porcelain complexion, devoid of pigment, seemed to emanate a luminous glow in the dim light. A cascade of pure white hair spilled down her petite figure, shimmering like strands of moonlight. Her contoured features were delicately shaped, with high cheekbones that emphasized her unblemished face.

Beneath her alabaster brow, Mercy's eyes were a strange duality. Both irises were different colors, each like a window into its own realm. Her right eye was a deep blue, as tranquil as the sapphire sea. But her left eye was a dreadful scarlet hue, like a crimson ember ignited by some infernal spark. A smoldering intensity lived within its fiery red depths, like a gateway to a dark realm where unholy cinders burned fiercely.

Judith saw in Mercy a young girl who transcended the ordinary with her ghostly complexion, silky white hair, and captivating eyes. But in the minds of others, the girl's appearance stirred fear and revulsion. Most considered her a monstrous abomination, and that vibrant scarlet eye of hers seemed to wither all who dared to meet her cursed gaze.

Mercy sprang to her feet as soon as she saw her mother's silhouette framed by the open door. "Mother! I... I'm sorry. I didn't—"

"How many times have you come here without my knowing?" Judith demanded. The timeworn floorboards creaked beneath her as she marched across the sanctuary to give her daughter the scolding she deserved.

Mercy dropped her mismatched eyes and stared at the floor as Judith loomed over her. "I am restless, Mother," she grumbled. "I cannot help myself. I come here sometimes for comfort. I merely wanted some sport—"

"Sport? Do you not remember the consequences of your actions? It has not yet even been a week, and yet here you are!"

Mercy's lip trembled. "I didn't mean for him to see me! How was I to know he would happen upon me so suddenly? I would have hidden, but there was nowhere to—"

"It is for these reasons that I forbid you to leave the cottage."

Tears filled Mercy's eyes as a sob cracked loose from her throat.

Judith's face softened, and she reached out to console her daughter.

Mercy recoiled from her touch. "Don't you realize what

you have done?" she cried. "You're forever damned for it! *That* is why I come here. To pray for your soul!"

Judith halted where she was in the aisle. "If it keeps you safe from those who would do you harm, then I will gladly endure the eternal fires of Hell. Mercy, you must trust in the righteousness of our actions, no matter how abhorrent they may seem—to *both* of us. Though it causes us great grief, we must suffer no one to lay eyes upon you. No one must know you are here. No one."

Mercy's tears spilled freely from her snowy eyelashes. She turned away, stifling her sobs, and directed her gaze toward the dusty altar. "What if they were right?" she whispered. "What if I *am* cursed? How can we hope to hide from evil if I carry evil within me?"

Judith went to her and wrapped her arm around Mercy's shoulders. "Don't say such things. Do you truly believe you were touched by the Evil One?"

Mercy remained silent, her strange eyes fixed on the shadowy figure of Christ obscured behind the veil of cobwebs. Dust particles floated through the air, catching the kaleidoscopic rays piercing the stained-glass.

Judith stared at her daughter expectantly. "Mercy? Answer me. Do you feel wicked?"

Mercy stayed quiet a moment longer. High above, there was a soft rustling of a bird somewhere in the rafters. "I have longings, Mother," she confessed at last. "Dark and sinful fancies that I dare not speak aloud."

Judith's expression softened as a flicker of understanding passed between them. "You are becoming a woman, my angel. Whatever immoral impulses assail you are naught but the wayward passions of youth. Such compulsions are natural for one your age. You are no more or less sinful than any child born and baptized." Judith traced a gentle finger along Mercy's snowy cheek. "This affliction is a test bestowed upon you by God. 'Tis a saintly burden that you bear. But like the saints who came before you, many will seek to persecute you. These are the ones for whom we must remain vigilant, the ones from whom I must guard you at all costs."

Mercy turned away from the altar, but didn't meet her mother's gaze. She was used to averting her cursed eye, even from her own family. "He was a priest, Mother."

"Aye, so he was. Don't you remember why we fled Penance Cove? Why we sacrificed everything to come to this place? It was men such as he that bore us the greatest threat. We must always be wary of the evil men do in the name of their God. Do you understand?"

Mercy gave a slight nod.

Judith folded her daughter in a loving embrace, then gently let her go. "Come, let's return. The others will worry."

They turned up the aisle just as the chapel door burst wide open, spilling light into the gloom. The frightened bird in the rafters erupted with a flurry of flapping wings.

Judith skidded to a halt in the middle of the aisle. Her heart skipped a beat, the sudden startle hitting her like a bolt of lightning. In a reflexive act of protection, her hand shot out to shield Mercy, only to relax when she saw the young man in the doorway.

"Kisosen…" she breathed the name with relief.

The man was an Indian whose presence exuded a serene strength. He had chiseled and defined cheekbones, and his eyes shimmered like obsidian. A prominent, noble nose stood beneath his brow, with its bridge slightly curved. A cascade of dark hair, as black as a moonless night, crowned his features and flowed down his broad back.

Wrapped around his strong and sinewy frame, his clothing reflected both functionality and his Abenaki heritage. A finely crafted deerskin shirt peeked out from under his heavy woolen greatcoat. The supple material clung to his torso, accentuating his physique. Intricate designs, adorned with vibrant beadwork and quillwork, told stories of ancestral wisdom and tribal legends. Deerskin leggings covered his powerful legs, offering both protection and agility. Fringes dangled at the seams, adding an element of kinetic energy to his presence. A necklace made of shells, bones, and sacred stones hung around his neck. Each piece expressed a connection to the earth, communion with spirits, and reverence for the land that sustained his people for generations.

The man wielded a sharp hunting knife in his left hand. He brandished a flintlock pistol in the other.

At the sight of Judith and Mercy, Kisosen tucked both weapons into his leather belt.

"You've returned early," Judith said, her heartbeat slowly returning to a steady rhythm. "I didn't expect you for another week, at the earliest."

Kisosen nodded. His voice was as calm as the wind rustling through the chapel's broken windows. "I was bringing fresh supplies to you when I heard a gunshot."

Judith nodded. "It was Susanna clearing the rifle."

Kisosen's inscrutable gaze flicked between her and Mercy,

his expression growing serious as he assessed the situation. "What has happened? Why are you here?"

Judith glanced at Mercy. "I must speak with Kisosen alone. Walk ahead but remain within sight. Take the forest path and do not stray. We will follow."

Mercy nodded obediently and brushed past Kisosen through the door, unable to resist flashing an impish smile at him as she went.

A somber hush fell as Judith waited until her daughter was out of earshot. The chapel's walls creaked around them, as if the spirits of the past were lingering, eager to eavesdrop on their conversation.

"We have been discovered," Judith said at last.

Kisosen's face hardened, his eyes narrowing. "Who? When?"

"Last week. Mercy followed us to sugaring and a missionary came upon us on the path." Judith hesitated, then took a deep breath. "I dealt with him the only way I could— as we agreed."

Kisosen's expression remained the same, his gaze unwavering as their eyes locked in a moment of shared understanding. "What brought him here? This missionary?"

Judith's brow furrowed as she frowned and shook her head. Through the open door, she caught sight of her daughter waiting at the edge of the cemetery. The fog outside the chapel continued to thicken, casting an unearthly gloom over the village.

"He was not the last of our troubles, Kisosen," Judith said, her tone darkening with foreboding. "I fear he was not alone."

Chapter 3

William Alden slogged through the dense undergrowth, his boots sinking into the wet soil as he followed the narrow trail through the forest. The branches of the towering trees intertwined above, creating a natural cathedral that blocked out the sunlight and cast a pall over the landscape. The earthy fragrance of moss and pine filled his senses. Only the rustling of leaves and twigs under his boots, and the occasional chirping of birds, disrupted the silence that surrounded him.

It was mid-afternoon, and William's choice to venture alone through the deep woods seemed foolhardy now. His conscience constantly reminded him of his duty as the man of the house in his father's absence. He tried to avoid thinking about the younger sister he had left back at the cottage. Without his watchful eye, what mischief would Mercy find? She was *his* responsibility, but after the dire consequences of her last disobedience, William trusted she wouldn't risk running off alone again.

Still, the specter of his mother's anger loomed like a dark cloud on the horizon. William dreaded the fury that awaited him if she found out he had left Mercy with their eldest sister, Susanna, while he went off into the forest. The fear of being discovered ate at his gut, threatening the fragile peace of mind he came out here to find.

But it was worth the risk; William needed to escape, even if just for a few hours. In the year that had now gone by since his father's death, his mind had become a tangled web of memories and disturbing images. Try as he might, he just couldn't stop imagining his father's last bloody moments. At just nineteen, tragedy had already given William a taste of the bittersweet fruit of adulthood. With no contact with the outside world, the isolation of his family's refuge only magnified the impact of his father's loss, leaving him feeling trapped and overwhelmed.

And now there were the dreams.

William couldn't escape the bewitching voice that plagued his restless nights. He barely closed his eyes when it whispered into his ears, creeping into his dreams. Its irresistible allure kindled a flame of desire within him, stirring up emotions he didn't yet understand. The voice, so enchanting and tantalizing, whispered sweet promises, weaving a seductive tale of release from his mundane existence. It tempted him to run away and escape this isolation, even if it meant leaving behind his only remaining family.

William often awoke startled and breathless, his heart pounding in his chest. Beads of sweat clung to his forehead as he lay in the darkness, longing for the comforting light of dawn. The lingering echoes of that voice entangled him like cobwebs, invading his mind and soul, impossible to ignore. Each night, the voice's spell over him grew stronger. In the light of day, reason reminded him that dreams were nothing more than fleeting illusions. Yet, when night fell and the haunting voice beckoned once more, its allure was so achingly real.

The unbearable weight of it all left William desperate for a respite from the darkness seeping into every corner of his life. Even if it meant risking his mother's anger, he had to calm his mind or it would crack under the strain of his daily existence. The mountains, so majestic in their beauty, always provided him solace, a temporary escape from the turmoil that engulfed him.

The forest grew more dense as he continued on, tangling the trail and obscuring William's view. Branches scratched his cloak as he pushed through the snarled underbrush, struggling to make out the murky trail ahead. Marked by honest toil and quiet resilience, his youthful face was still pale from winter's darkness. Tousled locks, the color of autumn foliage, flowed in unruly waves to his broad shoulders. His rugged jawline, coarse with the faintest trace of stubble, added a touch of burgeoning masculinity to his features. His eyes were stormy seas that revealed the hardships and sorrow of a soul far older than his years.

The forest seemed to resist his presence, its gnarled trees reaching out with twisted limbs, as if trying to ensnare him. Shadows lurked among the trees, casting phantom shapes that danced in the corners of his vision. At last, William escaped the suffocating woods and ascended to a rocky promontory. A panoramic view of the White Mountains in all their grandeur revealed itself before him.

It wasn't the first time William had come to this place, but it still filled him with awe. A ghostly mist covered the peaks, their snow-capped summits like a sublime crown against the gray sky. William could almost feel their ancient presence, as if they held secrets that transcended time itself. The wind whistled across the craggy cliff where he stood, and a sense of profound solitude settled over him. Sturdy and lean, his frame stood tall against the breeze. Every muscle, shaped by the arduous work of hunting, felling trees, and cultivating rocky soil, suggested a strength forged in the crucible of the wilderness. A tattered woolen cloak speckled with traces of woodland earth hugged his form to ward off the biting wind. His worn and patched trousers were victims of the unpredictable whims of nature.

William carefully retrieved charcoal sticks from his satchel, being mindful not to break them. He then opened the small journal Kisosen had gifted him after one of the Indian's trading trips to the north. As he sketched, his mind drifted away from the chaos that had consumed his life. His calloused hands, strengthened by countless hours of labor, possessed an innate grace. They were equally skilled in nurturing the land as much as capturing the interplay of light and shadow in his artwork. The landscape came alive with every stroke of charcoal as the silence of the mountains called to him. He pictured himself alone on one of those summits, gazing at the expansive view, free from the disturbing events at home. For a time, he immersed himself in the world of lines and shadows, reminding himself that darkness and light could coexist and that beauty would always endure.

But as the landscape took shape on the page, William's mind wandered further, led astray by the rhythmic scratching of his charcoal. Even as he tried to forget his mother's terrible deed, he couldn't escape the guilt that gnawed at him. When he closed his eyes, William could still hear the young priest's desperate pleas as he begged for his life. The image of his mother's bloodstained face haunted him with frightful clarity. The horror of the young man's last moments was now a constant reminder of the danger lurking in William's own home. He could still feel the dead weight of the headless corpse Judith had made him dispose of. He had always relied on his mother's love and protection throughout his life. But now that foundation had crumbled, leaving him feeling adrift and untethered. The one person who should have provided him comfort in this wretched wilderness was no longer there for him.

How much longer can I keep that truth hidden? he thought. *How long can I keep up the illusion that I still love her?*

With the final touches added to his sketch, William lowered his hand and admired his work. The mountains stood before him on the page, their grandeur captured in delicate lines and dark shadows. In that moment, William once again felt a sense of release from the troubles waiting for him back home. But the sensation quickly faded, swept away by a wave of sadness. The beauty of the mountains he had captured on the page only brought into contrast the ugliness that lived within his family. It was a cruel irony that the world's breathtaking beauty hid such unimaginable darkness.

William closed the journal and returned it to his satchel. Lost in his creative trance, he hadn't paid attention to the gradual shift in the atmosphere. The air had become colder, and a haunting stillness settled on the promontory. The day was growing late. Evening approached, a presence William felt behind him like an unseen gaze penetrating his back.

He could put it off no longer. It was time to return before Mother noticed his absence.

William's footfalls were light on the decaying leaves and moss, creating a hushed rustling throughout the forest. Pushing through dense undergrowth and swatting away cobwebs, a peculiar sensation tugged at him, a tingling unease that prickled his neck.

Something was wrong.

The wind had died. The forest was strangely still, as if its heart had suddenly stopped beating.

William swallowed and shivered as he pressed on. Soon, the foliage parted unexpectedly, unveiling a secluded glade filled with dappled gray light.

In the center of the clearing, a barn owl hung nailed to a towering oak.

Revulsion shot through William's veins, freezing him where he stood. His flesh shuddered with dread as he took in the scene. The owl's glassy eyes stared into eternity like two ink stains on the white moon of its face. Its wings were spread wide and impaled on the trunk in a cruel mockery of flight. A shallow incision had been sliced into the bird's abdomen, exposing the glistening viscera. Blood matted its once pristine plumage and dripped down the tree bark.

Strange symbols were carved into the ground with meticulous precision. The melted stubs of candles lay scattered about, and tattered scraps of black cloth clung to branches like mourning banners. Remnants of decayed offerings—bones, feathers, and dried plants—littered the ground beneath the owl.

William's heart pounded in his chest. As he approached the crucified owl, he felt the earth beneath him alive with whatever unholy power had been unleashed here. The smell of blood and rotting leaves filled his nose, and he had the unsettling sensation that the forest was closing in on him. He halted just a couple of feet from the bird. With its wings outstretched and nailed to the tree, it seemed massive. William's fingers trembled slightly as he reached out, a mix of horror and curiosity guiding his hand. He gently brushed his fingertips against the owl's outstretched wing. It was cold and stiff.

A sudden gust of wind tore through the clearing, extinguishing what little warmth the sun offered. An unnatural twilight fell upon the forest, turning the trees into sinister silhouettes. The shifting light caused shadows to flutter ominously around William, their forms shifting and contorting. The forest remained still, as if holding its breath for the unimaginable.

One terrifying question after another raced through William's mind. Who had done this? What dark forces had been conjured here? And what consequences would he suffer for having stumbled upon this grim scene?

Above all, one undeniable truth became clear to him, chilling him to the core. The evil he had only imagined was no longer a myth.

She's still out here. The witch that killed Father is still alive. And she's getting closer…

Fear whispered in William's ear, sending his thoughts into a swirling vortex of what-ifs. What if that vile hag found him here? What if she turned her attention toward his homestead and loved ones?

It was a terrifying realization, an understanding that his family's remote sanctuary was no longer safe. The isolation in which they had found solace was now an accursed prison, trapping them with an unseen menace in the woods. Scenes of bloody rituals and unspeakable acts formed in William's imagination, feeding his horror and fueling his urge to escape. He glanced around, his brow slick with a cold sweat. Did unseen eyes, filled with malice, lurk in the depths of the encroaching forest? Were they watching his every move? His whole being screamed for him to escape this cursed place and erase the memory of what he witnessed.

Yet an unexplainable curiosity scratched at his consciousness, making it impossible for him to look away from the grisly sacrifice in front of him. He needed to document the scene so that he could show Kisosen what he had discovered. Maybe the young Indian could make sense of this when he returned from his time among his people.

William's hands quivered as he took out his journal and a stick of charcoal from his satchel. As he sketched, he felt as if the air was growing heavy with a malevolent presence. He tried to convince himself it was all his imagination, but he couldn't be sure.

The images flowed like blood from his charcoal as William etched the details of the scene onto the parchment. He captured the elaborate symbols and sigils that adorned the circle of trees, feeling an uncanny sensation in his fingertips as he traced their intricate patterns. He had almost finished his hasty sketches when something curious caught his attention.

Something was moving inside the incision in the owl's chest.

Icy tendrils of fear coiled in William's stomach, but he couldn't help himself. He leaned closer to investigate as a cold breeze ruffled the leaves. Goosebumps prickled over his flesh, but he fought the urge to turn and run from this dreadful place.

Closer…

Closer…

His face only inches away…

William's breath caught in his throat.

The owl's small heart was still beating.

Its head snapped up without warning.

William stumbled backward, the forest swallowing his cry. The pages of his journal fluttered in the breeze as it slipped from his grasp.

The owl's blood-curdling screeches filled the hollow as it clung to life. It writhed and struggled against the tree trunk, struggling to get to William but restrained by the nails. Its huge black eyes spun wildly while its hooked beak darted and snapped at him. Its razor-sharp talons strained to tear strips from his flesh. The owl's body contorted, wrenching free from the nails that kept it impaled. Its wings unfolded with a sickening crack.

William skittered back and instinctively reached for the hunting knife strapped to his belt. His hands trembled as he unsheathed the blade just as the ghastly creature flew at him with a tremendous whoosh of air. Driven by sheer adrenaline, he aimed the knife at the owl's throat and thrust hard. The point sank deep, slicing through feathers, flesh, and bone, and severing the bird's head from its flailing body.

The owl's corpse spasmed uncontrollably as it plummeted to the forest floor, its head rolling away.

The hollow grew dreadfully quiet. William remained where he stood, panting heavily. With his body drenched in blood and sweat, he spun in a slow and cautious circle, gripping the knife tight as he eyed the woods nervously.

Nothing moved.

Yet.

William's blood throbbed in his ears as he swiftly snatched his journal from the ground. With the owl's tormented screeches still echoing among the trees, he quickly backpedaled and escaped into the forest, intent on distancing himself as far as possible from this cursed hollow.

Chapter 4

Susanna Alden stood alone, seeking refuge near the fireplace's warmth at the heart of the dimly lit cottage. Her hand traced the surface of the cracked and weathered stones. Shadows played hide-and-seek on the blackened hearth. The flickering flames struggled against the dampness in the air and danced with a subdued brilliance, casting an amber glow on Susanna's drawn and pallid face.

Above the mantle, a few faded porcelain figurines added to the melancholy atmosphere. The keepsakes didn't belong to the Aldens; the family that had deserted the house decades ago had left them behind. The figurines' vacant eyes stared at Susanna as she gazed into the flames. Two pegs protruded from the stones above the mantle where her father's rifle would normally hang to keep its powder dry. That space was empty now, the rifle laying on the dining table in the cottage's humble kitchen. Dust particles swirled in the air, lit by faint rays of cold daylight that filtered through the gloom.

The worn-down cottage stood as a mere ghost of its former self, barely holding onto the memories of its splendor. Time had stripped the keeping room of any semblance of comfort, leaving it austere and barren. Patches of moss and mildew crept along the crevices of the stone walls. Cracks in the structure now acted as pathways for cold drafts that whispered and creaked when the wind brushed against the aging home. The dark forest loomed beyond the dingy curtains hanging in the small windows, like an ominous secret waiting to be discovered.

Susanna's faded gown hung limply from her slender shoulders. Strands of auburn hair slipped out of her bonnet, framing her face. A stray lock still clung to her tear-streaked cheeks. She shivered, not from the chill in the room, but because she dreaded her mother's fury.

Susanna had never seen Mother so furious. She couldn't escape the relentless loop of self-reproach that echoed in her thoughts. How had she been so careless? How had she failed to notice Mercy sneaking away? She replayed the events in her mind, each moment eating at her conscience. Lost in her own thoughts and worries, she had been preoccupied and oblivious to her sister's whereabouts.

Susanna was filled with regret as she recalled her mother's angry glare upon returning from the sugar house and realizing Mercy was gone. She dreaded the anger Mother would unleash when she returned from the village, the simmering tension that would linger long after the confrontation had ended. Every passing second was like an agonizing minute, and the creaks of the cottage and rustle of the wind outside only increased her apprehension. Her mother's fury hung over Susanna like an impending storm, threatening to shatter the fragile peace she desperately clung to as her baby's birth approached.

Susanna's plump lips curved into a bittersweet smile as her gaze shifted to her belly. She placed a gentle hand on it. There were still no outward signs of her pregnancy, but she found comfort in imagining the soft flutters of life beneath her touch. The promise of motherhood was a fragile joy nestled deep within her, but sometimes it felt like a burden too heavy to bear. Soon, she would have to confess to Mother about her pregnancy. But for now, it fueled her determination to survive and protect her unborn child in this desolate place.

A gust of wind rattled the windows. Susanna jumped, thinking Mother had returned. She cast an anxious look toward the entrance, her hazel eyes darting, before shifting her attention to the rifle resting on the table within sight at the far end of the keeping room. The worn planks creaked underfoot as she left the fireplace for the kitchen. Frayed rugs, threadbare and weary from years of footsteps, lay scattered over the uneven floor and the trapdoor that descended to the cellar. The kitchen seemed to sag under the weight of neglect, as if somehow absorbing the loneliness and isolation that surrounded it.

The surface of the dining table bore the scars of countless meals and halfhearted maintenance. Water stains and burn marks marred its once smooth finish. Rickety chairs with missing or broken legs stood askew around it. Susanna drew one back, and the worn seat creaked as she eased herself into it. She wiped the last of her tears from her eyes and took the Kentucky rifle in her hands. Its long barrel gleamed with a dull sheen in the gray light as she inspected it. Mother wanted the weapon fired and reloaded regularly after the priest had caught them by surprise last week. There was no telling when they would need it again.

Susanna reached for a powder horn and a leather pouch of lead balls on the table. Just as Kisosen had taught her, she carefully poured black powder into the pan and down the muzzle of the flintlock mechanism. Her trembling fingers smeared the fine grains in the gloomy room. The distinct smell of gunpowder filled the stale air, blending with the musty odor of damp wood. Susanna retrieved a lead ball from the pouch, pressed the ball into the muzzle, and rammed it firmly against the powder. After priming the pan, she closed the frizzen, readying the rifle for its deadly purpose. The metallic click resonated through the quiet cottage.

Susanna's fingers clenched tightly around the worn stock as she raised the rifle to her shoulder. The weight of the gun in her hands reminded her of the life it had taken. Would she have the courage to use it herself if necessary? Her free hand caressed her belly as she lowered the rifle, instinctively protecting the fragile life within her.

The moment was shattered when William burst through the front door and stumbled into the foyer. He was panting hard and his cheeks were flushed from running. Sweat matted his hair and his clothes were streaked with dirt and blood, as if he had fought his way through the wilderness. He clutched his satchel against his chest, the contents hidden from view.

"What is it?" Susanna asked, startled by the panic on his face. "William, what happened?"

"An abomination… In… In the woods…" William gasped for air.

Susanna's hands naturally went to her belly. "William,

what are you talking about? You're scaring me."

William finally gathered his breath and found a voice that shook as he recounted the nightmarish scene in the hollow. The crackling fire cast eerie shadows that danced in Susanna's mind as she listened, heightening her growing sense of unease. After he was done, William's trembling hand reached into his satchel and retrieved his tattered journal.

"These symbols were carved into the earth." His voice grew darker as he thrust his sketches toward his sister. "Candles and animal bones, and… and the owl, Susanna. It was unholy. We're not alone here. The witch that murdered Father is still out there. Mother said she killed her, but she's still *out there*."

Susanna's eyes flicked to a grimy window. The brooding forest stared back at her, a constant reminder of the untamed wilderness just beyond the cottage's door. The gloom only magnified her sense of isolation and vulnerability. Her spine shivered as she heard the distant rustling leaves and the mournful howl of the wind. The branches reached out their bony fingers, as if eager to snatch away whatever illusions of safety she still had left.

It wasn't until then that William realized their younger sister wasn't there. "Where is Mercy?" he asked with a rising sense of apprehension.

Susanna lowered her eyes. "She ran off. I went outside for but a few minutes to fire the rifle, but she was gone by the time I returned."

"Does Mother know?" William asked, dreading the answer.

Susanna nodded, her lips pressed into a grim line. "She has gone to the village to search for her."

Susanna saw her brother's face crumple, the wind going out of him as if he'd been punched in the gut. His heart sank, and a heaviness settled upon his shoulders. Susanna knew how he felt, the guilt weighing on his conscience, suffocating him with a sense of impending doom. Mother's anger wouldn't just be limited to William. He was the one who had deliberately disobeyed her order to not let Mercy out of his sight, but Susanna herself had agreed to help him do it.

"Will you tell her what you found in the woods?" Susanna asked.

William sighed and shook his head. He paced slowly back and forth, his steps echoing through the room. "I don't know. I fear her sanity unravels by the day. She killed a *priest*, Susanna. I saw it myself. She was merciless, even as he begged for his life."

Susanna shuddered, not wanting to hear any more. "William—"

"The strain has been too much for her with Father gone. You must admit you have seen it for yourself."

"It has barely been a year," Susanna argued. "It's grief that makes her act so—"

"No!" William stopped his pacing and faced her. "Listen to me! She had me leave the man's corpse for the wolves! Answer me this, Susanna: what happened to Father's body? Was he given a proper burial? Or left for the wolves as well?"

Susanna's face darkened. "Mother would never have done such a thing."

"I'm not so certain of anything anymore."

"Then what would you have us do?"

"Leave this place before it's too late. We cannot stay here

any longer. The same monster that took Father may come for us next."

Susanna frowned and shook her head resolutely. "Mother will never allow it."

"Then we'll go with Kisosen. You and I and Mercy."

"And leave Mother here alone? She will surely die."

William's expression remained impassive, and Susanna realized he had already considered the idea and made his peace with it.

"She crossed a threshold from which there is no return, Susanna—for *any* of us." William motioned around the dreary room as he stepped closer. "What kind of life is this? We're barely surviving, our own lives slipping away with each passing day. We've become prisoners in this desolate place, while something dreadful stalks us and draws closer with each passing night. We could find freedom in the outside world. Pursue our own dreams. Maybe even find a way to help Mercy. It's a risk worth taking."

Silence weighed heavily in the room as the siblings stood face-to-face, their conflicting emotions laid bare.

After a moment, Susanna shook her head. "No, William. We came here for a reason. We must protect Mercy from—"

Without warning, a woman's distant cry rang out from somewhere outside the cottage. "Bonjour!"

Startled and alert, their gazes shot toward the nearest window. Through the cracked pane, they glimpsed a dark figure in the distance, moving along the path that cut through the forest from the deserted village.

Susanna was the first to dash across the room. She still grasped the Kentucky rifle—the only defense they possessed against the intruder. She whipped the door open, and they hustled outside into the muddy pasture that stretched between the cottage and the woods.

Adrenaline shot through Susanna as her finger quivered on the trigger of her weapon. The silhouette of a figure broke through the tree-line and she raised the rifle, prepared to defend themselves from the unknown threat.

It was a young woman, likely the same age as William. She was a haunting figure with midnight-black hair that fell in loose waves around her face, spilling over her shoulders and down her back. Her intense, piercing blue eyes gleamed like twin shards of ice. The depth of her gaze was accentuated by her long, dark lashes. But despite her attractive features, the rest of her appearance was that of a woman dragged through hell.

Dressed in garments suitable for a long and arduous journey, her clothes now bore the marks of a harrowing ordeal. She wore a dark woolen skirt that reached her ankles, paired with a loose-fitting chemise embellished with delicate patterns. Clinging to her lithe figure like a second skin, her clothes were now tattered and spattered with dried mud. A brown leather coat protected her from the weather. Dark and fresh stains caked the fabric, telling a tale of spilled blood and unspeakable horror.

The woman approached with a faltering gait, casting fearful glances over her shoulder as if the shadows were poised to strike. Her blue eyes flickered with fear, like a candle in a tempest. They darted wildly, scanning her surroundings warily as if haunted by visions only she could see. Her lean and agile body showed signs of a violent struggle. Bruises marked her wrists and one cheek, and her fair complexion was pallid and weary.

"Ah! Dieu merci! Pourriez-vous m'aider?" The woman spoke in French with a heavy English accent.

Susanna aimed the rifle at her chest, deadly serious. "Stay where you are."

The young woman skidded to an abrupt halt, startled at having the gun leveled on her so unexpectedly. She raised her hands in surrender and peered at the pair with a mixture of apprehension and curiosity. "You are American?" she asked, dropping her French.

"Why are you here?" Susanna demanded.

"I—I need your help," the woman pleaded. "My coach was attacked. They… They killed my coachman. I—"

"You cannot remain here." Susanna's tone was low and firm, her eyes two hard stones as she peered down the barrel of the rifle.

Susanna's heartless rejection left the young woman looking bewildered. "Please, I have nowhere else to go." Her voice quivered with pitiful desperation. "Those men may still be out there. There must be someone here who can escort me north to Montreal."

"There is no one," Susanna replied flatly.

"Then my fiancé will come looking for me when I don't arrive. All I ask is that you allow me to remain here to wait for him. Perhaps some food and water if you can spare it. He is wealthy. Once he finds his way to this place, I promise you a reward and we will trouble you no further." Tears welled in the young woman's eyes now. "I swear I mean no harm. I am alone, frightened, and in desperate need of aid. If you find it in your hearts to offer me sanctuary, I shall forever be grateful."

"Our answer is no," Susanna replied. "And we insist you leave this—"

William reached for the barrel of the rifle and gently pressed it downward toward the dirt.

"Come now, Susanna," he said, ignoring his sister's astonished glare. "We cannot possibly turn away a woman in such a dire state. Come…" He gave the woman a warm smile and motioned for her to follow him.

"Oh, bless you!" she exclaimed as she hurried after him.

Constructed with rugged, weathered stones, the saltbox cottage appeared to blend effortlessly with the granite bedrock of the mountains. It was a squat, two-story structure. Nature's relentless embrace left its scars on the rough surfaces of the stones. The mortar that held them together had eroded over the years, leaving irregular gaps and crevices. The lower portions of the walls were covered in a carpet of mossy green, a result of the dampness and age. Tendrils of ivy clung to the stone like curious fingers. Both floors of the cottage's facade featured small, rectangular windows. Rotted wood and peeling paint framed the clouded glass panes, which were speckled with age and reflected the somber forest.

The roof of the cottage sloped downward and was covered in decaying wooden shingles. Some had succumbed to time's relentless assault, leaving noticeable gaps. Others held on tenaciously, their warped and weathered surfaces giving the roof an uneven appearance. A lone chimney, standing tall against the twilight sky, projected from the roof. Wisps of smoke curled from its top, hinting at life within the isolated cottage.

Susanna scowled disapprovingly but held back her protest as she followed closely behind William and the young stranger. What was her brother thinking? If Mother returned while this woman was still here, there was no telling what she would do. Why was William knowingly risking this woman's life? Better they turn her away now and let her take her chances in the woods.

"I must apologize for the rifle," William said as he escorted the woman into the cottage's dusky keeping room. "As you have so tragically learned, this is rough country, and we have good reason to suspect outsiders."

"I assure you I take no offense, Mister…" The woman paused, waiting for William to offer a name.

"Wolcott," he lied as he offered her a chair at the dining table. "William Wolcott. And this is my sister, Susanna."

Susanna gave the woman a curt nod as she returned the loaded rifle to its place on the pegs above the fireplace mantle. Her face remained stony, her stomach knotted with anxiety while she lit a beeswax candle and pressed it to the wick of a tarnished oil lamp. A warm glow filled the room.

"You truly are an answer to prayer, Mr. Wolcott," the woman said as she eased into the creaking chair. "I despaired I wouldn't find a soul here once I discovered the village deserted."

The woman's gaze trailed after Susanna as she placed her lit candle on a windowsill. William had left his journal open on the table and the symbols etched on the parchment caught the stranger's cool eyes as she refocused her attention on him.

"What is your name?" William asked. He closed the book

41

and brushed it aside as casually as he could.

"Colquitt," she replied. "Beatrice Colquitt."

The lie came easily enough.

Anna never gave her real name either.

Chapter 5

The mist wrapped around Mercy like a gossamer veil, obscuring her vision. Her boots sank into the soft carpet of decaying leaves as she walked the muddy trail. Pockets of snow still lingered on the ground around the giant trees that loomed over her. The absence of birds and rustling wind created an eerie stillness that played on her nerves.

Mercy shivered and wrapped her woolen shawl around her slender body, the dense fabric unable to fully protect her from the cold. She had ventured through these woods in secret many times before, but the sinking sun and twisted branches now made her stomach curl with unease. It was as if the forest was cradling her, guiding her deeper into its murky depths. Each breath she took seemed to grow colder. She cast a furtive glance over her shoulder. The heavy fog made it impossible to see Judith and Kisosen following at a distance, but she still heard their muffled voices. Their presence comforted her. She would never admit it, but something about these woods had her spooked. Her instincts, honed by a lifetime of standing out and feeling different, warned her of imminent danger.

It's just my imagination running wild, she thought. *There's nothing truly sinister out there in the gloom.*

But as much as Mercy tried to convince herself otherwise, her mind still conjured ghostly figures with hollow eyes that penetrated her soul. The memory of her father's murder in these dark woods resurfaced in her thoughts.

What if that evil hag wasn't alone? With if there are others like her hiding in the fog, craving flesh and blood?

Mercy's thoughts drifted to the deserted village. What made the villagers abandon it so many years ago? Was it because they were afraid of something in this vast and dark forest?

As she ventured further, Mercy noticed a faint clinking echoing through the foggy woods. She slowed and detected the slow, rhythmic patter of liquid against metal. The noise grew louder with each step, drawing Mercy toward its source. She emerged from the mist and came upon a large grove of maple trees, all tapped for sap. The rows stretched out before her, their trunks laden with tin pails.

Mercy halted, that feeling of apprehension now squirming around in her stomach. She knew this place. She had been here just last week when she shadowed William and Mother as they tapped the trees—the dreadful day the young missionary happened upon her while she strolled along this very path.

Mercy couldn't stop replaying the events of that horrific morning in her mind. She remembered the moment they crossed paths, her peculiar appearance laid bare for him before she could even think of concealing herself. She desperately wished she could turn back time, to reverse whatever dark twist of fate had entwined her life with his. But reality offered no such reprieve. When she was alone and lost in her thoughts, Mercy was consumed by feelings of remorse. Her appearance was already an affliction of its own, but now she bore the heavy burden of a man's death at her mother's hands.

Before her family had fled to this godforsaken place, the villagers of their hometown had believed her cursed and touched by the Devil, as if her very presence would bring them misfortune. Ever since her father's murder, Mercy became convinced that those suspicions had become a reality. Wherever she went, disaster followed. As the days crawled by, she desperately sought absolution, yearning for a way to ease her guilt. Her inner turmoil was a constant battle, her mind plagued with questions she couldn't answer. Why did her presence always seem to invite tragedy? Was she truly a harbinger of death, as the villagers had believed? Her feelings of isolation intensified, making her long for an escape from the smothering confines of the homestead that served as both her refuge and prison.

It was this longing for release that compelled Mercy to follow the haunting voice that whispered to her in the night. It seemed to emanate from the very walls themselves, beckoning her to the village—a voice Mercy would never dare tell Mother about.

A metallic *plink* drew Mercy's attention toward the nearest maple tree. She peered at the tiny spigot and the dented tin pail that hung beneath it. Within seconds, another droplet of maple sap oozed from the tap and dripped into the bucket. *Plink!*

Mercy cast a quick look behind her, her ears pricked. She could no longer hear Kisosen and Judith. Had they fallen behind? Taken another path? She was sure this was the right one to the homestead.

A sense of foreboding tightened its grip around her as she kept walking. The forest felt like it was closing in; the trees growing taller and denser, blocking out the sky. Before long, she noticed an unusual scent wafting through the air, a metallic tang that tickled her nostrils. Mercy's pace faltered as she passed through the maple grove, her mismatched eyes narrowing. She peered through the gloom, searching for the source of the strange smell.

A solitary red droplet on a maple sapling caught her eye. Mercy drew closer, her breath held in anticipation. Her heart skipped a beat when she realized the liquid wasn't the golden sap she had expected. It was a viscous, crimson substance that glistened like…

Like fresh blood.

Mercy's skin prickled with a mixture of dread and morbid curiosity. Her hand trembled as she reached out and touched the droplet. The warmth and stickiness disgusted her and she stumbled back. Her hand flew to her mouth to stifle a horrified cry as she looked around.

More crimson droplets were dripping from the spigots now. Every drop fell into the tin pails with a resounding *plink* that echoed in the quiet forest. The metallic reek of blood filling the air overwhelmed Mercy's senses. Fear gripped her, but an insatiable curiosity urged her forward. The mist clung to her like ghostly hands as she peered into the nearest pail. The contents made her throat constrict.

The blood inside the pail churned, as if alive with a dark energy. Dread fell over Mercy like a suffocating blanket. The blood from the trees flowed faster and faster, cascading like rivulets of crimson tears, overflowing the pails and painting a ghastly tapestry on the forest floor.

Mercy's chest tightened with panic, urging her to flee. She let out a horrified cry and bolted from the macabre maze of bleeding trees. Abandoning the path, she veered straight into the murky forest. The woods seemed to contort and twist, forming a labyrinth of gnarled branches and dark recesses. Looming shadows transformed into grotesque figures, leering from the corners of her sight.

Without warning, a root snagged her ankle. She pitched forward and crashed to the forest floor. Her fragile frame shuddered with the impact, a jolt of pain shooting through her limbs. She lay there, momentarily stunned, her ivory hair spread like a halo around her delicate face. There was a throbbing ache in her hip as she scrambled to her feet and sprinted onward. She paid no attention to her direction now, looking back over her shoulder fearfully until she collided with something big and unyielding. She rebounded and nearly hit the ground again before powerful hands grasped her and kept her upright.

"Kisosen!" Mercy gasped for air and struggled for words as the young Indian caught her in his arms. "It—It has happened again…"

Judith's face was hard and grim as she caught up to them, panting heavily after chasing her daughter through the woods. "Again? They bleed?"

Mercy nodded, her chest heaving.

Kisosen remained motionless with his pistol in hand, his senses keen. The bloody pails were far out of sight now, lost somewhere deep in the fog. But there remained something dreadfully sinister about the gray and silent forest. A sense of menace filled the air. Something hungry was watching them from the forest.

"Kisosen, please see that Mercy returns home safely," Judith said. "I will see these trees for myself."

"No! Don't go!" Mercy threw herself on her mother's arm.

"It would be best if we remained together." There was an uncharacteristic unease in Kisosen's tone as he eyed the shadowy mist. He gestured for Mercy to follow, but she resisted, her fear turning into anger.

"No! I can't stay there any longer!" she cried. "Look what is becoming of me! You'll have me go mad if you keep me so confined!"

"Mercy! Enough!" Judith warned.

"No, Mother! I will not be silenced so!" Without warning, Mercy whirled and dashed away into the woods.

Kisosen was about to go after her, but Judith stopped him with a hand on his shoulder. "Leave her a few moments of solitude," she said with remarkable patience. "She is becoming a woman—and I fear a willful one."

The pair remained quiet and brooding as they followed Mercy's trail to the forest's edge. Twilight painted the sky with a tapestry of dusky hues over the isolated homestead. The cottage stood cloaked in shadows at the far end of the muddy pasture. The corners melted into the encroaching darkness, adding a touch of mystery and seclusion to the place.

There was a tilted, rundown chicken coop on one side of the pasture. A goat pen stood nearby, surrounded by a rickety fence of rusted wire strands that struggled to keep their form. Some sections sagged low from years of exposure to the elements. A single goat with white and brown fur paced anxiously in the pen.

The hulking carcass of a weather-beaten barn stood on the near side of the pasture, closer to the forest's edge. The timber was gray and splintered, the telltale signs of decades spent weathering storms and seasons. Portions of the siding had come loose, exposing glimpses of the barn's skeletal structure. A sagging gambrel roof crowned the dilapidated structure, the shingles warped and weathered. Many were missing, revealing beams that reached like bony fingers toward the sky. Lichen and moss grew on the remaining shingles. The barn's double doors stood slightly ajar. Their rusted iron hinges creaked mournfully as they swayed in the evening breeze.

Judith found Mercy standing at the edge of the tree-line, staring across the pasture at the cottage. Her pale face was dark and deadly serious.

"What? What is it?" Judith asked.

Her gaze followed her daughter's, and they both saw the single candle flickering in a small window of the cottage. Its flame cast eerie, shifting shapes on the worn window sill.

It could only mean one thing.

"The warning signal…" Judith gasped. "Someone is here."

Kisosen's palm dropped to the pistol tucked into his waistband. "Go. You know what you are to do. My presence here will only raise more questions. I will remain with Mercy in the barn."

"No!" Mercy exclaimed. "Mother, please…"

"Go with Kisosen and get to hiding," Judith insisted.

"Will you kill them too?" Mercy's strange eyes brimmed with angst.

Judith hesitated.

"Mother? Will you?" Mercy pressed.

"I will do all I can to avoid it," Judith replied. "Unless they lay eyes upon you, there is no reason they cannot continue on their way."

"Promise me."

"I swear it! Now hurry!"

Judith watched Kisosen lead Mercy toward the barn. "Mercy…" she called after them.

Mercy paused at the barn door.

"Be silent, my sweet. Do not reveal yourself, not for anything. No matter what you may hear."

With a timid nod, Mercy faded into the darkness as Kisosen shut the creaking barn doors.

Chapter 6

Anna sipped the strong coffee William gave her and tried to understand why Gideon had sent her here. After that night in the Boston cemetery, she didn't dare summon the familiar again for fear of what else she might invite through the Veil. The insidious spirit of Anna's own great-great-grandmother, Rebecca Hale—the innocent woman who sold her soul to the Devil on the eve of her hanging in Salem—haunted Anna's memories.

She and Rebecca were intertwined while Anna was still in Abigail's womb, and Rebecca now coveted her young descendant's flesh to escape Hell and live again. Her dark spirit came close to succeeding that night in Burlington when Anna called upon her dreaded ancestor in a moment of supreme desperation. Since then, Anna had sworn off necromancy. The danger was too great, the consequences potentially deadly—and she didn't trust herself to resist the enchanting power Rebecca's malign influence again.

"What more can you tell us about these highwaymen?" William asked. His curious gray eyes studied Anna from across the dining table.

Anna had spent days searching through her mother's collection of supernatural volumes in her arcanium until she finally deciphered the cryptic meaning of the word Gideon had uttered. After connecting it to Sévérité, a remote settlement near the Lower Canada border, she hired Chauncey Beck, her mother's longtime coachman, for the trip deep into the White Mountains. The arduous trek felt like a foolish and impulsive thing to do on such a thin hunch, but Anna could think of no other course of action. Gideon understood the tremendous risks of contacting her through the Veil. She had plenty of ghosts and monsters to hunt in Boston; he wouldn't have sent her here if it wasn't of the gravest consequence.

But now that she was here, Anna was no closer to understanding why. The only thing she was sure of was that this nervous pair of siblings couldn't be trusted. They were hiding something. But what?

"They… they were ruthless," she stammered. Keeping up the pretense of a helpless woman in distress, her voice deliberately quivered with fear. "We were traveling along that desolate road, the moon barely visible through the trees. The night was silent, but then, before I could comprehend what was happening, they were upon us."

Anna's white-knuckled hands clung to her earthenware coffee mug. "They were masked and armed, surrounding the carriage and demanding our valuables, our lives seemingly worth nothing to them. The coachman, a kind soul named Chauncey, bravely refused to surrender, vowing to protect me until his last breath."

As she spun her tale, Anna's keen eyes never ceased their secret dance from one corner of the room to another, silently mapping out the layout of the house. She paid close attention to the positioning of doors, windows, and escape routes. The first floor was one unbroken rectangle wrapped around the imposing stone fireplace. Anna noted the distance from the small foyer into which they had entered, and through the keeping room to the kitchen and dining area where she now sat. Her gaze focused on a back door, partly concealed, with a damaged latch that would serve nicely for a quick exit. While passing through the keeping room, she had mentally noted the location of an ornate fireplace poker next to the hearth. With its heavy weight and pointed end, it was an ideal option for an improvised weapon. Next to the fireplace, a slender staircase ascended toward the bedrooms on the second floor. Another bedroom and a pantry occupied the opposite side of the house.

Anna forced tears into her piercing blue eyes, as if fighting to keep her composure. "It happened so quickly. The sound of gunfire echoed through the night, and I saw Chauncey's body crumple to the ground." In truth, Chauncey Beck was alive and well and safely ensconced in an inn three hours to the south. At noon each day, he would wait at the spot on the road where he had left Anna until the day came when she met him to go back to Boston.

"I—I don't know why they spared me," she whispered, her voice barely audible above the crackling of the fire. "Perhaps they thought I had nothing of value. Or maybe… maybe they intended to…"

Her voice trailed off, as if overwhelmed by memories of the

traumatic experience. While her hosts listened, her fingers traced the edge of the wooden table at which they sat. She subtly memorized its dimensions, recognizing its potential as a makeshift barricade should the need arise. She took a deep breath, trying to steady herself, and continued her harrowing —and entirely fictional—tale.

"My heart shattered, and instinct took over. I knew I had to survive. I managed to crawl through the carriage window, desperate to escape the clutches of those monsters. The night was my ally, providing me with a cloak of darkness. Every sound sent jolts of terror through my veins, but I ran… fled into the woods. I can still hear their wicked laughter echoing behind me, haunting my every step."

She shivered, clutching her coat and inhaling. "I hid in the woods until the first light of dawn, terrified they would find me. When I finally emerged, I wandered aimlessly through the mist, certain I would perish, until I eventually happened upon that deserted village and saw your chimney smoke."

Anna didn't miss the furtive glance that passed between the young man and his elder sister. It deepened her suspicion, adding another strand to her ever-growing web of intrigue.

A strong wind suddenly gusted through the dreary interior as the front door swung open. A hard-looking, middle-aged woman entered the foyer. Her eyes flicked around as she swept through the keeping room—first to Anna, then to the rifle hanging above the mantle. It was the most fleeting of glances, but one Anna didn't fail to notice. She saw the woman's demeanor shift as she approached the dining area. Suspicion gleamed in her eyes as she looked from face to face, searching for answers to unspoken questions. Anna intuited that her presence had disrupted the family's carefully maintained isolation.

"Who are you and why are you in my home?" the woman demanded, her words laced with an undercurrent of hostility.

William rose from his seat at the table. "Mother, this is Beatrice Colquitt."

Anna gave a polite nod and her most disarming smile. "How do you do?"

The woman pursed her lips and seemed to swallow her aggravation. She forced a pleasant face as she neared the table. "Pleased to meet you, Miss Colquitt. I am Judith Wolcott."

Anna had spent a significant part of her eighteen years being mentored by the most cunning characters in Boston's seedy underbelly. She was an expert at reading people, and this woman, like her son, had just given her a false name. Why?

"Please, call me Beatrice," she said pleasantly.

"Beatrice was traveling to be with her fiancé in Montreal when she was set upon by highwaymen," William explained. "Have you seen them?"

"Highwaymen? Here? No, I have not," Judith replied tightly. "We haven't our share of strangers out here, Miss Colquitt. Perhaps two or three a year—trappers and traders, mostly. I am certain I would remember encountering anyone, most notably a gang of miscreants."

"Yes, I suppose you are right," Anna conceded. She leveled her gaze at Judith, testing her, probing for something. "If you will forgive my curiosity, might I inquire how you came to settle this close to the border of Lower Canada? This was French land, was it not?"

Anna sensed Judith's instincts immediately going on the defensive.

"My husband believed it immoral to take lands from the Indians without proper compensation," Judith explained. "Such a defense of the ungodly was not viewed favorably by our Puritan minister in Haverhill. Even so, my husband would not be silenced. We were banished for it, left to wander the wilderness until we came upon this village, long abandoned for Indian raids."

Anna studied her for a moment. There was something about Judith's story that didn't ring true. It was too clean, rehearsed. "I have acquaintances in Haverhill," she lied, intent on goading Judith into a trap. "Reverend Higginson must be the minister you speak of, yes?"

Judith furrowed her brow and shook her head. "Higginson? No. Bradstreet was his name."

Anna frowned and shrugged. She had no idea who the reverend in Haverhill really was, but even though Judith didn't fall for the trap, it didn't mean she wasn't lying; she was just more adept at it than Anna had expected. "I see," she said. "Might I ask how long have you endured this solitude?"

"This summer will mark our second year."

The room fell into an uncomfortable silence, the tension growing until William's voice broke the stillness. "Surely we can offer Beatrice food and shelter for the night?"

Caught off guard by his offer, Judith shot William a scathing look.

He returned his mother's glare, bold and unflinching. "It will be nightfall within the hour, and these woods are no place for a woman after dark. 'Tis only proper that we offer her our hospitality before I see her safely to her destination in the morning."

Judith's eyes smoldered with impotent fury, knowing she was powerless with Anna as a witness. She put on a fake smile, biting back her anger. "Of course. Any less wouldn't be Christian, wouldn't it?"

She motioned to the iron cauldron hanging above the fire. "Susanna, please see that our guest has some stew. William, would you kindly help me with the firewood?"

As she watched mother and son venture out the door, a sense of unease simmered within Anna, an intuitive inkling that something was amiss with her hosts. Whoever they were, they were guarding a deeper, darker truth. Maybe Gideon had sent her to find out what it was.

* * *

Judith wheeled on William the moment the cottage door closed behind them. Her fingers dug into his arms as she grabbed him and slammed him against the stone wall.

"What do you think you are doing?" she hissed.

William's eyes burned with youthful defiance as he glared back at her. "We can't just turn our backs on her, Mother. We can help her while still protecting ourselves. We must at least try."

"Help? Have you any idea of the danger you have placed us in?" Judith shot back.

"What of the peril we already face? The evil that torments us is still out there!" William described the desecrated owl and the unholy scene he had come across in the hollow.

"Have you ever considered that perhaps the witch is after Mercy? What if—"

The blow came without warning. Judith's hand lashed out with a sudden, violent motion, and struck her son across his cheek. "There is nothing wrong with Mercy!"

The sharp slap hung in the air, followed by a moment of silence as William recoiled, nursing his reddened cheek. He glowered at his mother, his eyes narrowing to sharp points. He had grown accustomed to her tirades, but she had never struck him before. This was something new, another line crossed.

"We cannot simply *trust* this stranger, no matter how desperate she may seem," Judith insisted. "We know nothing of her true intentions, and to invite her into our home is to invite the unknown into our lives. Do you not remember why we are here? Why we sacrificed everything? Do you truly believe it is a coincidence that the priest happened upon us *here*?"

William's expression grew somber as he grasped her insinuation. "He came looking for us?"

"What if he did?" Judith replied. "What if that woman tells others about what she sees here? Do you know what they will do to your sister if they find her?"

William didn't answer.

"Tell me, William! What will they do if that woman lays eyes upon her?"

William gave in and told her what she wanted to hear. "They will hang her for a witch."

"Precisely. How could you be so careless? Must you oblige me to kill this woman, too?"

A bitter silence fell between them. Tension hung thick in the air as mother and son stood face-to-face in the gathering gloom.

"With your father gone, the responsibility has fallen to me to protect you and your sisters," Judith said. "My actions do not require your approval or understanding, but they do demand your acceptance. Is that understood?"

William pinched his lips together, biting his tongue.

"What is it?" Judith demanded. "Speak your mind."

William's stare remained bitter and defiant as he met her gaze. "You speak of being our protector, but who will protect us from *you?*"

He brushed away the hand that pinned him against the wall and wrenched free from his mother's grip. He started walking away, but stopped before reaching front the door. "Do as your conscience sees fit, Mother. But I'll have no more to do with it. If you kill her, you may bury her corpse yourself."

* * *

Kisosen and Mercy huddled in the barn's darkness. Moonlight filtered through the cracks in the dilapidated walls and gaping holes in the roof. The jagged ends of the broken ceiling planks cast claw-like shadows across the ground. Cobwebs hung in intricate patterns from the beams, their delicate threads catching the silver light. Mounds of rotting straw covered the floor, its golden hue now a tangled brown mess. Rusty tools rested against the walls, and empty animal stalls lined one side of the barn, their wooden partitions rotting and collapsing.

Kisosen peered through a gap between the barn doors, his gaze fixed on the cottage across the moonlit pasture. The flickering candlelight in the window cast eerie shadows on the curtains and sparked a whirlwind of thoughts in his restless mind. What was happening in there?

The arrival of a mysterious stranger in Sévérité kindled Kisosen's imagination. Countless sinister possibilities played in his mind. As the minutes dragged on, his resolve wavered under the weight of doubt. Was he doing the right thing, keeping watch from afar? Judith had already shown her competence in handling encounters with strangers, but what if this situation was different?

Mercy sat next to Kisosen with her back against the door, knees drawn up. Her mismatched eyes focused on a piece of straw that she twirled absentmindedly between her fingers.

"She will kill again, won't she?" she asked, her tone grim.

Kisosen's lips pressed into a line. "William will find a resolution. He is becoming a man."

He strained his eyes, searching desperately for any sign that might relieve his apprehension. Was the stranger a threat or merely a lost soul seeking shelter? How could he be certain without risking Mercy's safety? Only the necessity of keeping her out of sight kept him from acting rashly.

"He has you to thank for it," Mercy said. "With Father gone, William now looks to you to show him the ways of manhood."

"Many years ago, my father swore an oath to protect your family." Kisosen's words flowed with a measured cadence. "In his name and honor, I am bound to care for you all."

"Bound? Is it truly such a chore to see to our protection?"

Kisosen glanced at her sideways. "Some are less a chore than others."

Mercy tossed her piece of straw aside and climbed to her feet to join him at the door. "You love her, don't you? Susanna, that is?"

Kisosen's face turned bitter. "It is forbidden. My people would cast me out—and I would not betray your mother so."

"'Tis a pity. I would do anything to have a man want me in such a way."

Kisosen shot Mercy another look and saw her crimson eye glinting with unspoken desire. She stepped closer, her hand reaching out for him. Her lips pursed ever so slightly, her intentions clear.

Kisosen withdrew abruptly, his eyes avoiding her gaze as he resumed his vigil at the door.

The rejection stung. His silence fell heavily upon Mercy, and an icy knot formed in the pit of her stomach. Her gaze dropped to the ground in shame. A burning flush rose to her pale cheeks as she retreated a few steps. Her chest tightened, and tears welled in her eyes, threatening to spill over. In that moment of vulnerability, her imagination played tricks on her, and the moon's pale light transformed the barn into something hauntingly surreal.

With a deep breath, Mercy tried to compose herself, wishing she could erase the mortifying moment from having ever happened.

What came over me? What was I thinking, believing Kisosen would ever be attracted to me? I am an aberration, clearly not worthy of winning his heart.

Frustration and anguish mingled with the ache of her shame, and Mercy felt a surge of anger building within her. Anger at herself for giving in to such an impulsive act; anger at Kisosen for making her feel this way. The pain and disappointment morphed into a burning fire of resentment, fueling her determination to prove herself worthy of his affection. She straightened her back and wiped the tears from her eyes, refusing to let him see her wounded.

"Do you believe it possible to be evil and yet not know it?" Mercy asked after a moment, her voice small. Her open and yearning heart now quivered with fragility.

"My people believe we are all made of two spirits, one good and one evil," Kisosen replied, relieved at the change of subject. "Such is the way the earthly balance is maintained."

A moment passed in silence as Mercy considered his words. "I miss my father, Kisosen. I am lonely here without him, lonesome to the point of despair. I fear I cannot bear this place any longer. Were it not a sin, I would take my own life to escape it."

A simmering anger flickered to life in Kisosen's dark eyes, one that Mercy had never seen before. "My sister chose such a path," he said. "You would do well to mind your tongue."

The weight of his revelation left Mercy stunned. She hadn't known Kisosen even had a sister, let alone that she had died by suicide. A deafening silence filled the space, punctuated only by the sound of Mercy's own heartbeat echoing in her ears. For the second time in minutes, her cheeks flushed with shame, and she felt the weight of her embarrassing words pressing against her chest.

"I—I am so sorry," she whispered, her voice quivering. "I

didn't... I didn't mean to say those things. Had I known, I never would have uttered such a callous thing."

Mercy's eyes remained downcast, unable to face that scornful look in her guardian's eyes. Kisosen's hard gaze pierced through her a moment longer before he swung his attention back to the cottage and said no more. The wind whispered a lonesome song through the nearby trees.

The scream shattered the silence just moments later.

Chapter 7

A damp rush of warmth spread between Susanna's thighs, saturating her worn-out skirt at her crotch. Droplets of blood leaked down her legs to her calves and pooled on the floor where she stood. The steaming bowl of stew she was carrying crashed to the ground and shattered to pieces as she doubled over and let out another sharp cry, clenching at her abdomen.

William sucked in a sharp breath while Anna and Judith stared in stunned silence, trying to make sense of what was happening. Before anyone could react, Susanna dashed from the room, her face twisted in pain and flushed with humiliation. Panic propelled her up the creaking stairs, her hand trailing along the splintered banister. The flow of blood didn't stop. It trickled down her thighs and left drops with every step, creating a crimson trail leading up to the second floor.

Judith's chair clattered across the floor as she shot up from her seat at the table and went after her. She bounded up the stairs two risers at a time, her heart racing, and swerved into the small bedroom Susanna shared with Mercy.

The moon's pale light seeped through the moth-eaten curtain, illuminating the bed where Susanna lay curled in a ball on the worn mattress. Beads of sweat dotted her pallid brow. Her delicate features contorted as she clutched at her gut and moaned in anguish. A long trail of blood smeared the tangled blankets from the foot of the bed to where she lay.

"This will pass, my child." Judith tried to keep her voice from quivering as she knelt by her daughter's side and smoothed the hair from her face. "Whatever ails you will pass. I gave over four babes to their graves to sit by the side of God in Heaven before He saw fit to deliver you to me. He will not take you from me now."

Fighting against her rising panic, Judith forced herself to think clearly. Were it not unthinkable, she would swear Susanna was in the throes of a miscarriage. But that was impossible. Her daughter couldn't possibly be with child.

She reached out for Susanna's hand, only to recoil as if stung. The warm touch of her daughter's palm had transformed into an icy grip, draining the warmth from Judith's own flesh. Fear slithered up her spine.

There was nothing natural about this affliction.

Warm candlelight spilled into the room and grabbed her attention. William and Anna crowded the door. Judith's expression soured at the sight of the stranger. "You should not be here," she said with a scowl.

"I understand," Anna said, feigning meekness. "But I thought perhaps I might be of help." She offered a bowl of water and a clean rag she had brought from below and stood waiting for Judith's permission to approach.

Judith was about to refuse, but a glance at her stricken

daughter forced a change of heart. Blood soaked the mattress beneath Susanna's hips now, seeping from between her clenched thighs and staining the fabric.

"There is too much blood," Judith said with a note of panic. "It won't stop."

The wooden floorboards creaked beneath Anna as she took a hesitant step toward the bedside, her gaze fixed on the frail figure lying curled on the mattress. The water was cool as she soaked the rag and pressed it to Susanna's sweat-soaked brow.

Judith fought back tears and held her daughter's hand, watching her writhe in agony beneath Anna's touch. Susanna's slender frame shuddered on the coarse bedsheet with each tortuous contraction of her stomach. Despite the cold compress, sweat still dripped from her forehead, mingling with the tears flowing down her cheeks. The room reeked of blood, but there was another smell in the air as well. Judith was only dimly aware of it, something sweet and woodsy, with a subtle hint of spice she couldn't quite name.

William stood frozen by the window, his hands trembling anxiously. Helpless to ease his sister's suffering, his eyes darted around the room. The quivering light of his candle threw grotesque silhouettes on the walls.

Susanna grimaced in pain and opened her eyes. She saw her mother kneeling by her side and raised a shaking hand, motioning for Judith to draw nearer.

"Mama, make it stop!" Susanna's voice was a mere whimper, barely audible between her moans. Her eyes were full moons, her face ashen and frightened.

Judith was painfully aware that her daughter hadn't called her *Mama* since she was a little girl. Her heart shattered, and she pushed aside her own mounting dread. She clasped Susanna's frigid hand in her own, desperate to do anything she could to ease her daughter's suffering. "Hold on, my dear. Mama won't let anything harm you."

But what terrified Judith the most was a haunting inner voice that whispered the undeniable truth: her daughter would die if they didn't find some way to stop the bleeding. She felt the crushing force of impending loss, extinguishing any glimmer of hope.

Susanna's face contorted, her brow furrowing. She grimaced and whispered through clenched teeth. "There is something inside me. I can feel it there, coiled like a snake."

Seized by a sudden spasm of agony, she threw her head back and let out a blood-curdling scream.

* * *

Kisosen's blood froze as the horrifying screams shattered the serene night. They came from the farmhouse. He tightened his grip on the pistol, his muscles becoming taut.

"What is happening, Kisosen?" Mercy's whisper quivered like a leaf caught in a gale, and fear filled her mismatched eyes. Her delicate frame trembled against him as they stood huddled at the barn door, staring through the crack into the darkness.

"I do not know," Kisosen replied, his voice low and filled with worry.

More tortured cries rolled over the pasture, and all thoughts of protecting Mercy deserted him. Fear shot through him as Susanna's screams clawed at his soul, leaving him shaken. He exchanged a glance with Mercy, her wide eyes mirroring his own apprehension.

Without a second thought, Kisosen flung open the door and bolted from the barn. His moccasin-clad feet hardly made a sound on the muddy earth as he sprinted across the pasture. Mercy trailed after him, her feet barely touching the ground as she ran. A cold breeze whispered through the night, chilling them both to the bone.

Susanna's screams grew louder, cutting through the darkness like a scythe.

The door to the cottage stood ajar as they approached, swinging gently on rusty hinges in the breeze, inviting them into the horrors that awaited them.

* * *

Anna sensed an evil energy pulsing in the room, the air tainted by a supernatural presence. She knew instinctively that the young woman's life was in danger, but she still had no idea what was afflicting her or how to stop it.

An unseen force suddenly snuffed out William's candle, engulfing the room in complete darkness. Outside, the wind howled like a pack of ravenous wolves, rattling the windowpanes. The curtains fluttered and moonlit shadows danced across the walls.

Susanna released her white-knuckle grip on her abdomen and twisted flat onto her back. She let out another harrowing shriek that died suddenly on her lips. Her mouth remained gaping wide open, and from somewhere deep within her, a low, guttural growl erupted.

Anna's heart skipped a beat. She knew what was wrong.

This young woman was possessed.

But by what? A dark spirit? Or something worse? Her eyes darted warily around the darkened chamber. Shadows converged, forming a shapeless mass, seeping into every corner of the room.

Judith caressed her daughter's sweat-soaked face with shaking hands. Tears streamed down her face as she whispered soothing words. But Susanna's anguished cries only intensified, her body arching in a paroxysm of pain. She couldn't possibly go on like this.

"We have to do something!" William's desperate voice cut through the darkness.

Anna jabbed a hand into her coat pocket and seized the silver crucifix she carried with her at all times. The metal felt cool against her skin as she pressed the cross to Susanna's breast and recited the incantation.

"Spirits of the departed, I offer you a chance at redemption, a path toward salvation…"

"Leave her be!" Judith cried with sudden alarm and lunged across the bed for her.

Anna's free hand struck like a viper, gripping Judith's outstretched wrist and wrenching it back hard. Judith gasped in pain, her knees weakening. Anna hardly wavered in her incantation. She closed her eyes, delving deep into the recesses of her being, and summoned her connection to the otherworldly realm beyond the Veil. A surge of power pulsed through her veins as she whispered, "You have suffered for far too long, trapped in this cycle of torment. But there is still hope for you. Embrace the light, relinquish your malice, and find peace in the realm beyond."

The serpentine words of magic slipped from her lips, and the walls seemed to quiver as her voice filled the air, its resonance intertwining with Susanna's moans of pain and terror.

But as confident as Anna was in her witchcraft, a creeping realization soon dawned on her—it wasn't working. Susanna was slipping further away from salvation with every passing moment.

Despair and uncertainty ate away at Anna's confidence. As Susanna's agonized cries grew louder, the dark energy that consumed the room seemed to mock her, its sinister tendrils seeping into her consciousness, whispering of her impending failure. Her incantation faltered and her hope sank. Dread washed over her as she realized she had mistaken the true nature of her adversary.

Susanna wasn't possessed. This was something else.

Just when Susanna could take no more, everything changed.

With another terrible shriek, she planted her palms into the mattress, arched her lower back, and thrust her hips high into the air with her knees spread wide.

A torrent of blood spewed from between Susanna's legs and splashed across the floorboards at Anna's feet. At the same time, a metallic tinkling filled the room, like coins clattering across the floor.

Anna skipped back in horror and she gazed at the assortment of old pins and nails scattered in the bloody puddle around her boots.

All at once, Susanna's contorted body dropped back to the

mattress like a marionette with cut strings. Her screams came to an abrupt halt, and she went dreadfully still.

A shocked silence filled the void. No one moved until Judith stumbled to Susanna's side. She clutched her daughter's shoulders and shook her frantically.

"Susanna? Susanna! Open your eyes, child…"

It was no use.

"*No! Open your eyes!*" Judith cried. She cradled her lifeless daughter, her mournful sobs echoing through the room.

William stood frozen and unblinking. The walls felt like they were closing in on him as he grappled with the horrifying reality of Susanna's shocking death.

A grief-stricken wail pierced the unbearable silence.

Judith whirled around, her eyes swollen with tears.

Mercy and Kisosen were at the door.

Anna saw them too. She gaped at Mercy in amazement as she got her first look at the girl's strange complexion. Mercy's silver hair reflected the moonlight like the bleached bones of long-dead animals, and her one crimson eye burned like a candle's flame in the darkness. Her pale skin glistened, as if her ghost-like complexion gave off its own eldritch light.

Kisosen let out a choked gasp and absorbed the macabre scene while Mercy wept beside him. Susanna's blood-spattered body lay sprawled on the bed, arms and legs contorted in unnatural angles, eyes wide open and mouth frozen in a silent scream of terror. A raw cry of anguish and grief escaped Kisosen's throat. Rooted in place, he remained frozen in time, as if Susanna's shrieks still echoed through the old cottage.

Judith was the first to react. Lunging across the room, she

snatched the pistol from Kisosen's nerveless grip and leveled it at Anna's head.

The move caught Anna off-guard. Still shocked by her failure to save the young woman's life, her eyes flew wide with surprise. She raised her hands and retreated a step. "Wait!"

Judith cocked the hammer, ready to fire.

"Hear me! Hear what I have to say!" Anna shouted.

Her pleas had no impact. Judith's finger found the trigger.

"Mother!" William yelled.

"I've been sent to help you!" said Anna.

"Mother! Don't!"

"I know what the symbols are! The ones in your son's journal!"

Judith squeezed the trigger.

Chapter 8

The flintlock roared. In the same instant, William lunged and swatted Judith's hand aside just enough to knock her shot off target. Anna dodged to her left, narrowly evading the bullet that tore through the air and ricocheted off the stone wall with a spray of sparks.

One shot remained in the double-barreled pistol. Judith's eyes gleamed with a dangerous fire as she cocked the second hammer and aimed.

"Mother, please!" William leapt forward, inserting himself between her and Anna. His voice trembled, but his expression revealed a fierce determination.

"Move aside, William," Judith snarled, her face flushed with fury and betrayal.

"No!" William motioned to Susanna's bloody corpse, unable to hold back his tears. "Look what has become of us, Mother. Look! We can no longer go on like this. We can no longer ignore what has been happening to us. Even here, evil has found us. Some ungodly terror is bent on our destruction. We cannot hide from it. If there is even the slightest possibility that this woman speaks the truth—that she can somehow help us—should we not at least give her a chance to explain herself?"

A myriad of emotions danced across Judith's face. The pistol quivered in her grip as her eyes darted between her son and Anna. A tense silence filled the room, broken only by Mercy's gut-wrenching sobs as she wept by Susanna's side.

Drained of energy, Judith appeared to shrink in that moment, as if burdened by a weight she could no longer support. She lowered the pistol with a deep, shuddering breath. It hung at her side while she fetched a wool blanket from atop a chest. Her eyes glistened with tears as she gently unfurled it. Her movements were slow and deliberate, filled with a sense of reverence and finality. With quivering hands, she carefully draped the woolen blanket over Susanna's lifeless body. The soft fabric settled over her like a shroud, offering a fragile layer of warmth and protection. It was an act of love and motherly devotion, an attempt to shield her daughter even in death.

"We will bury her at dawn," she said, her voice a pained whisper. Her focus shifted to Anna. "Bring her."

Kisosen marched Anna out of the room, the sound of their footsteps echoing down the creaking stairs. When they emerged into the keeping room, Anna kept a watchful eye on the rifle above the mantle as they crossed the room to the dining table.

Judith aimed the pistol at her and gestured for her to sit. "Speak," she commanded. "Who sent you here?"

"I will explain everything," Anna said. "But first, perhaps it is time you told me why you are really here?"

Judith raised the barrel of the pistol just a little higher, aiming at Anna's head. "You are in no position to be making demands."

Anna exploded forward with the speed of a viper. Her hand whipped out to snatch the barrel of the pistol, her fingers clenching around the still-hot metal. Gritting her teeth against the heat that seared through her palm, she corkscrewed her body, using her momentum to rip the weapon from Judith's grasp. Without breaking her stride, she spun at William. The steel of the pistol flashed in the candlelight as she pressed it to his head.

"One more step and I'll blow open his skull," she growled at Kisosen, who was already striding across the room with his knife drawn.

The Indian froze where he stood, his dark eyes smoldering with fury.

Anna held her ground. Her sharp gaze remained fixed on Judith, who gaped back in shock.

"After this night's events, I'd venture that you are no longer in a position to *refuse* my demands." Anna's voice was low and laced with deadly warning as she held the young man hostage.

The pistol glinted ominously in the firelight. Anna's jaw clenched, overcome by that old, familiar bloodlust. She imagined the bullet exploding through William's head. The vision was intoxicating, a potent cocktail of power and retribution.

"If you value your lives, you will not threaten me again," she warned through clenched teeth. "I am more than capable of slaughtering you all and leaving you here to rot—including you." Her frigid blue eyes flashed to Kisosen. The raw desire to strike back against her aggressors seethed within her veins like poison. Still, beneath the wave of vengeful longing, a faint remnant of reason persisted. She was a survivor, but she was not an executioner. Her strength lay not in succumbing to her thirst for blood, but in rising above it.

Anna relaxed her grip on the pistol, feeling its weight slip away as she exhaled. "But killing you is not why I have been sent here," she said. With effortless grace, she released her hold on William. She kept a wary eye on the others as the young man staggered away and spun around to face her.

Anna reversed her grip on the gun and returned it to Kisosen, who accepted it with surprise and thinly veiled suspicion. It was her way of showing goodwill, a strategy to earn their trust and prove that she posed no threat. Given the awful tragedy that had unfolded just moments ago upstairs, it would be foolish to leave them with no means to defend themselves.

But secretly, part of her didn't trust herself with the weapon. She feared what she might do with it if provoked again. She thought of how close she had come to putting a bullet in William's head, the frightful mercilessness that had nearly overwhelmed her. From where had that wrathful compulsion come? It had been months since she experienced something like that, not since freeing herself from the corrosive influence of her great-great-grandmother, Rebecca Hale. As Anna had grappled with her inner demons, she believed she had finally conquered her violent urges. However, what she was experiencing now surpassed anything she had ever encountered before. It was more than just a desire for violence, but a consuming bloodlust that controlled her every thought and action.

"Sent?" Judith scowled. "By whom? No one knows we are here. You are desperate. You'll say anything to save your own skin."

"You have already lost one child," Anna countered. "I can see that you do not lose another. Please, let me help you."

"How?"

"Begin with the truth. Your name is not Wolcott, and you have been here for far longer than two years, have you not? Now tell me, why are you here?"

Judith was visibly torn as she contemplated revealing her long-held secret. Her grief collided with a sudden overwhelming impulse to reveal years of hidden truths.

At last, the dam broke within her.

"Please, sit," Judith murmured, gesturing to the rickety chair at the table.

Anna obliged, her face dark with curiosity and suspicion.

Judith took a deep breath, summoning the courage to relive the onslaught of memories she had fought so hard to lock away. "Our name is Alden," she said. "And we come from a costal village named Penance Cove on the shores of Maine. It was founded by Puritans who fled north from the witch trials in Salem—but they didn't leave their ignorance and superstitions behind. The villagers were devout, but their faith had warped into something wicked. My daughter Mercy was born in that forsaken place."

Judith's gaze wandered to her youngest child, the tender warmth in her wan smile unmistakable. "She was never like other children. The villagers saw her as a cursed child, a creature to be feared, and they sought to destroy her. They whispered she was a witch who consorted with demons, that she was capable of dark sorcery. The whispers grew louder, the accusations more vicious. They left threats on our doorstep, dead animals hung from trees—anything to let us know we were no longer welcome. They claimed Mercy brought illness and misfortune to the other village children—and they demanded her blood for their own salvation."

Judith's voice quivered with suppressed emotion as she continued her tale. "It was a Sunday night in May when the mob came for her. Reverend Finneran himself led them. She was only six-years-old—just a child. I don't know how many men—perhaps more than a dozen—much more than my husband, John, could defend against. They dragged Mercy from her bed to the yard and stripped her naked before beating her and scratching her with pins until the blood ran down her flesh. The bloodletting was supposed to weaken her power as a witch. John struggled against them, but they knocked him senseless. It was only by some divine intervention that Kisosen arrived before they could drag Mercy down the rocks to the seashore to dunk her, else she would have surely sunk and drowned. They outnumbered Kisosen, but the mob lost their courage after he shot Thomas Braybrook dead."

Anna raised an eyebrow and her gaze flicked to Kisosen. "You killed a man to save this girl?"

Kisosen stared back at her and remained silent.

"I couldn't let them ever take her again," Judith whispered, tears trickling down her gaunt cheeks. "I couldn't bear to see my sweet Mercy suffer at their hands. We fled Penance Cove under the cover of darkness that very night, leaving behind our friends, our neighbors, and everything we once knew. In his time as a trader among the Indians, John had befriended an Abenaki chief—Kisosen's father. For a time, we found refuge in the wilderness until Kisosen led us to this abandoned village near his tribal lands, far from the zealots' reach. With his help, we made this house our own and planted crops. We even deceived ourselves into thinking we could forge a life for ourselves out here…" Judith's voice trailed off.

"But that is not what happened, is it?" Anna prodded after a moment's silence. "Where is your husband, Mrs. Alden?"

Judith opened her mouth, but a lump in her throat choked her voice.

It was William who answered. "He was murdered by—"

"William! Say no more!" Kisosen interjected suddenly.

"Let him speak, Kisosen," said Judith.

"No!" Kisosen shot back. "The *skadegamutc* is none of this woman's concern!"

"Enough!" Judith's hand slammed the table, the sharp crack of her palm on the wood reverberating off the walls and ending the argument. "Kisosen, please take Mercy and set yourselves to preparing Susanna for burial."

Kisosen's gaze bore into her, filled with anger and defiance, before finally giving in and stalking up the stairs.

William waited for the Indian's footfalls to quiet before continuing. "An evil sorceress murdered my father after Kisosen's tribe cast her out for practicing black magic. As is their custom, when the elders discovered what she was doing, they exiled her to the wilderness to meet certain death."

"Except she did not die," said Anna.

William shook his head. "She lived on in the woods near to here, prowling among the trees, waiting to feast on human flesh and slake her thirst for living blood until the day—"

"Until the day she killed my husband and I ended her life," Judith said, her expression a stony mask.

Anna leaned forward in her seat. "Tell me what happened."

"He had gone to tap the trees for sugaring," Judith replied. "I followed his trail, bringing him pails, when I came into a clearing. And then, there it was—the wretched scene…"

* * *

In her memories, Judith carries a stack of tin sugaring pails. The damp chill of the early spring seeps into her bones as she follows the crude trail through the forest.

Suddenly, she stumbles upon it—a hatchet, well-worn and speckled with rust. It lies partially buried under a tangle of underbrush at her feet. It's John's hatchet, of that she is certain. Its wooden handle bears the marks of countless hours of labor. The blade, though pitted from heavy use, still looks sharp and menacing.

But what is it doing here? Did John happen to drop it on his way to the maple grove?

"John?" Judith waits, her call echoing among the trees.

No response. Nothing at all. Only an eerie silence.

She continues on, slower and warier now, gripping the hatchet tightly. Her eyes trace the shapes and shadows between the trees as she scans the underbrush, searching for any sign of her husband. She has walked this winding path countless times, but today it feels different. Sinister. Her senses stay alert, honed by the unnerving silence of the forest. Birds should be singing, and the rustling leaves should be mere whispers in the breeze. But the woods lie in a strange, oppressive hush. Nature itself is holding its breath.

Judith turns to look over her shoulder. Her eyes dart among the shadows, seeking the source of her unease. She finds nothing. The trees loom, their branches swaying as if taunting her, inviting her to imagine wicked faces in the bark. Her steps quicken, taking on an urgency she can't explain. The pails clang and clatter together, echoing like a mournful bell tolling in the oppressive quiet. Her skirts gather twigs and fallen leaves as she trudges along, her heart pounding like a drum.

She knows the stories Kisosen's people tell about these woods, the legends they have passed down from generation to generation. The forest is haunted. They whisper of mysterious disappearances, of cries that echo through the trees in the dead of night, and of those who wander into these woods never returning. Judith always dismissed such tales as mere superstition, but now she can't help but feel a shiver of fear.

She casts another glance over her shoulder, her breath misting in the cold air. There is still nothing to see—just the trees, their gnarled branches now resembling sinister, outstretched fingers.

She hears the sounds first.

Grunts. Chewing. Gnawing.

A rapturous moan, a low and guttural sound, carries through the misty air. It's a sound that sends shivers through Judith's bones, a sound too disturbing to be produced by any creature of the forest.

The awful sounds are coming from somewhere just ahead.

Steeling her courage, Judith takes a cautious step forward…

Then another…

Soon, the forest opens to a large maple grove.

A corpse lies sprawled at the base of a giant tree.

Judith can't make out who it is. A hunched-backed figure straddling the body obscures her view as it feasts hungrily. The hollow crunching of bones being devoured makes Judith's innards squirm around inside her stomach.

Unaware of Judith's presence, the figure remains engrossed in its vile task, feeding on the corpse. Its hair is a wild tangle of graying strands.

Judith raises the hatchet high over her head, ready to strike as she creeps closer…

Closer…

At last, she gets her first glimpse over the figure's shoulder, revealing the full horror of the scene.

John's dead and vacant eyes stare back at her. His corpse lies sprawled on the ground, his clothes in tatters, his body mutilated and bloody.

Draped in a tattered cloak, the hunched figure has torn his chest cavity open. Its gnarled fingers plunge into his intestines with ravenous delight. Steam plumes into the air from his still-warm entrails. The sickening squelch of organs and the grotesque slurping of blood fill the grove, making Judith's stomach spurt bile into her throat.

A gasp claws its way from her throat, tearing through her as she stands, paralyzed by the nightmarish scene. The tin pails hit the ground with a clatter.

The figure's head swivels around, revealing a monstrous hag. Her skin resembles desiccated leather, and her wrinkled face is smeared with John's blood. She has the dead-white eyes of a corpse, and there's an unholy hunger gleaming in them as she fixes her feral gaze on Judith.

Judith's limbs freeze, unable to move as the hag grins. Her teeth are broken fangs, sharp like shards of shattered glass. Her lips curl back like rigor mortis, and she lets out a fearsome shriek, her bony fingers flying out for Judith.

Judith's scream tears through the gloomy grove.

WHACK!

Her hatchet slices through the air and bites deep into the hag's neck—but the blade doesn't hack through all the way. Blood flies in spurts as the hag recoils, screaming in agony, her unearthly wail reverberating through the trees.

Before Judith can strike again, the hag twists, ripping the hatchet's handle from Judith's grip and knocking her to the ground. The impact jars Judith's senses, her vision blurring for a moment. The enraged hag flies at her, scrabbling across the ground on all fours, the blade of the hatchet still wedged in her neck.

Judith scrambles backward over the dirt, but the hideous creature is too fast. She feels the hag's weight on top of her now, her foul breath hot against Judith's cheek as she shrieks and claws and bites. Judith fights with all her strength against the creature's relentless assault, desperate to break free. Her hand shoots out and gropes the ground blindly for anything with which to defend herself. Her fingers brush against cold steel and she doesn't care what it is. Her palm closes around the handle of John's flintlock pistol. A flicker of hope ignites within her. Without hesitation, she raises the weapon and aims it at the hag's grotesque face.

BOOM!

The explosion tears through the grove. With a mighty blast of sparks and smoke, Judith's shot blows the hag's head apart. Her skull erupts in a spray of blood and bone, and her lifeless body collapses onto Judith's frail form, bleeding out in gushes. Judith lies pinned beneath the weight, blood seeping into her clothes, mingling with the leaking insides of the hag's ruined skull.

Judith wrestles her way out from beneath the corpse and staggers to her dead husband, where she collapses again at his side. Only now is she struck by the full shock and horror of what has just happened. Cradling John's mutilated body in her lap, she gives herself over to grief-stricken sobs and moans.

Across the hollow, an enormous crow swoops low and lands on the hag's corpse. It's soon joined by another. And another. Their shrill cries punctuate Judith's sobs as they feed, ripping through skin and stripping flesh from bone with their sharp beaks.

* * *

Judith closed her eyes and inhaled a deep, shuddering breath, as if she could still smell the blood and gunpowder in the air. "In the year since the hag killed my husband, we have been tormented by a scourge of afflictions."

"What manner of afflictions?" Anna asked.

"A string of sinister phenomena, each more terrifying than the last. The trees bleed living blood when they are tapped for sugar. Animals are found mutilated in the most horrific of ways. And now, there is Susanna…" Her voice trailed off; the grief was still too raw.

"We are haunted, Miss Colquitt," William said. "It is as if some malign force has set itself upon our undoing."

Judith leaned forward in her chair, resting her elbows on the table, and fixed her gaze on Anna. "I believe you have now gleaned all you need to know about my family, Miss Colquitt. For years, we have lived with these secrets, revealing them to no one. I have been ready to kill to protect them if necessary. Now tell me… how can you possibly help us?"

Anna chewed her bottom lip, the truth slowly piecing itself together like fragments of a shattered mirror. "Mrs. Alden, I am about to reveal two truths that you are unlikely to accept. But if you entertain any hope for your family's survival, I urge you to consider these truths carefully."

Judith eyed her icily. "Go on."

"The first truth is this: Kisosen and his people are correct in their beliefs. There *is* a world beyond our own, one inhabited by spirits and monsters caught between realms. Once you have accepted this truth, you may be ready to embrace the second."

"Which is?"

"That I am not what I seem," Anna confessed, her words hanging heavy in the air. "My real name is Anna Jacobs. I am a ghost-hunting necromancer, a wielder of ancient witchcraft to protect innocent lives from the evils that lurk beyond the Veil of the living world."

Anna grabbed William's journal from the table and flipped to the cryptic symbols he discovered in the forest. "This is powerful black magic. Where did you find these?"

"Inscribed around the corpse of a crucified owl in the woods," William replied.

Anna nodded. "Nailing a bird of darkness like an owl to wood is part of an ancient hex."

"A hex?"

"Indeed. Someone performed this ritual to bring great harm to your family."

"Who?" Judith's brow furrowed. "We are alone here."

"Clearly, not as alone as you think. Someone here has been practicing witchcraft."

Silence descended upon the room, broken only by the crackling of the fire. Judith stared at Anna, her expression a mix of incredulity and mistrust. "Ghost-hunting? Witchcraft? How can we trust you?"

Anna returned her gaze. "I understand how unbelievable this may sound, but I assure you I have walked the thin line between the living and the dead. I have seen horrors that would haunt your nightmares—and I have slain them all." Anna's eyes glittered with an unwavering intensity. "Darkness has taken root in this village, Mrs. Alden—in your very home. And I am here to end it."

Chapter 9

The wind whistled through the tall pine trees, their branches creaking and swaying as Anna made her way through the dense forest. The moonlight barely lit the path and filled it with jagged shadows. She pulled up the hood of her coat to protect herself from the cold. Her lantern swayed in her grip as she walked, intent on exploring the cursed village of Sévérité.

It was nearing midnight when Anna left the Aldens to grieve Susanna's death in private. There was a time when she couldn't imagine the depth of their sorrow. She'd been raised to avoid meaningful relationships, and emotions were like musical instruments she had never learned to play. Her rigorous apprenticeship in the dark arts defined her childhood, leaving no time for friendships. Abigail had taught her that love could be used against her, and empathy, sympathy, and compassion became concepts that eluded her, leaving her hard-hearted and pitiless. The only truly profound human connection Anna had ever known was the blood-drenched thrill of the hunts she shared with her mother.

In a twisted way, Anna had found solace in her detachment from others. Killing monsters silenced the violent impulses Rebecca Hale had whispered into her mind since birth. Freed from the shackles of affection and remorse, Anna threw herself into her grisly work without fear for her own safety or that of others.

All that changed the night she let her mother fall from a cliff.

Now, Anna understood the intensity of human grief, the heart-wrenching pain that gripped Judith and her children as they mourned Susanna. But as the family prepared the young woman's corpse for burial, Anna couldn't help feeling like the intruder that she was. She knew she should try to offer the right words to ease their pain, but she didn't know what those words were. Instead, she had stood there, observing them in the silence while squirming on the inside and wishing she were anywhere else.

Instead of struggling to find her place in their grief-stricken circle, Anna had excused herself and slipped away to explore the village. She was bone-weary from days of travel, but the horrific circumstances of Susanna's death had shaken her to the core. She had never witnessed such malice before, and whatever caused it still lurked, ready to strike again at any time.

Even poor Mercy could be next, Anna thought. She felt a strange connection with the resilient girl, who had already endured so much suffering. They were both outsiders, peering in on a world that would never understand or accept them. But if there was any hope of making good on her promise to protect the surviving Aldens, Anna needed answers only the mysterious village could offer.

As she emerged from the forest, a luminous ocean of stars spilled across the night sky and washed over the giant silhouettes of the distant mountains. Flowing rivers of stardust stretched in every direction, as if reaching out beyond the heavens themselves.

The spectacle halted Anna in her tracks, struck by an overwhelming sense of awe.

I have spent half my life hunting under the cover of darkness, she thought. *But I can't recall ever taking the time to appreciate its wonders…*

It wasn't like Anna to see the beauty in her surroundings. Hers was a life of blood and violence; of screams and dreadful spirits and nightmarish monsters. It had made her far tougher than most men she knew. Abigail taught her to seek out horrors in the shadows, leaving little time for the beauty in the light. She trained Anna to protect against evil, but didn't teach her what made life worth protecting.

Now, the grandeur of the heavens reminded Anna of her own insignificance. Her desperate wish to restore her mother's lost soul was of no consequence to the uncaring universe. The stars shone just as brightly, regardless of her existence.

I am just one of billions whose bones will turn to dust long before these stars ever fade…

The realization was both liberating and unsettling at once.

Further ahead, the decaying village loomed in ominous silence. The moon bathed the crumbling buildings in a pale silver glow. Anna tugged her gaze away from the dazzling sky, her eyes narrowing as she peered into the abandoned lanes.

Again, that unshakable feeling—something was *wrong*

here.

Anna had experienced the same sensation upon arrival in the village that afternoon, but her focus had shifted to the chimney smoke coming from the Alden's cottage beyond the woods. Now, after the evening's deadly events, she couldn't ignore the strange energy in the air, an ancient residue of fear and something far darker that lingered from decades past.

The uncanny sensation grew even more intense as Anna ventured deeper into the village. She felt it tightening its hold on her throat like a noose. The buildings stood frozen in time around her, caught in an everlasting twilight. Their broken windows gaped at her like hollow eyes, and their timeworn doors creaked on rusty hinges, as if protesting her intrusion. Ivy draped over their crumbling walls, the serpentine vines stretching out to ensnare her. The sagging structures and overgrown paths evoked images of forgotten lives, and Anna once again wondered about the people who once called this lonely place home.

Before leaving Boston, she had found few details about the village's troubled history. It was founded in the early 1700s by French settlers escaping the political and religious turmoil of their homeland. Life in this tight-knit community of hardworking settlers must have been simple but content. Anna imagined the villagers carving out a humble existence, tending to their crops, raising livestock, hunting, and embracing the beauty of their secluded corner of the world. But whispers of a curse had soon spread as the settlers tried to make sense of a series of worsening disasters that plagued their village. Fear and superstition took hold, and within a decade, they gathered whatever they could and fled Sévérité, leaving behind a ghost town.

What caused them to flee so suddenly and leave the village for dead? Anna wondered. *And, more importantly, what malevolent force claimed this place as its own?*

Anna's sharp eyes scanned her shadowy surroundings, her senses alert as she delved further into the moonlit ghost town. The flickering lantern illuminated the cobwebs that draped the abandoned structures, creating a mesmerizing dance of light and shadow.

An eerie squeaking crawled from the silence and pricked Anna's ears. It got louder and louder as she crept among the buildings, its source eluding her until she saw a broken sign swaying from a rusty chain. The faded words were no longer visible, as if the village wanted to erase its own past from memory.

Anna steeled her nerves and veered from the overgrown lane. Tall grass and weeds snarled her boots as she waded to the dilapidated structure from which the sign hung. Its wooden facade groaned with age as she pushed on the door. It creaked open on rusted hinges, revealing a pitch-black void that swallowed the light from her lantern.

The old floorboards creaked as Anna crept inside, drawn to the secrets that lay buried beneath the layers of dust and decay.

The air was heavy, stale, and filled with an eerie sense of desolation. Cobwebs brushed against Anna's face, sticky tendrils entangling her in their embrace. With each step, she couldn't shake the feeling that she was walking into a trap, the invisible jaws of an ancient evil ready to snap shut around her. Her heart beat like the wings of a caged bird in her chest, her senses sharpened to a keen point by the oppressive silence. Dust particles danced a spectral ballet in the feeble glow of her lantern as she played it around the room. The light barely penetrated the gloom, and the soft glow only highlighted the unnerving silence.

Everything remained frozen in a forgotten era, just as it had been left a century ago. The hearth lay cold and lifeless, covered in a thick layer of dust. A small wooden table stood in the center of the room, surrounded by rickety chairs with tattered cushions. Pots and crockery remained stacked in the kitchen.

Anna couldn't help but feel an unsettling apprehension, as though she had unwittingly stepped into a realm where time itself came to a standstill. Her eyes darted around, taking in the weathered walls, the dusty furniture, and the cobwebs that clung to every surface. Despite being abandoned for a century, this place felt strangely alive, with lingering spirits from the past watching her every move.

She crept deeper into the cottage. Shadows crowded around the dim radius of her lantern, obscuring whatever lurked just beyond its light. Her footsteps echoed through the empty rooms as she explored one after another. She found nothing but dust—until a telltale sound in the corner of a chamber made her pause.

The floor beneath her boot was hollow.

Anna crouched and let the lantern's glow spill across the floorboard. These cottages all had root cellars, but there was something distinctive about the sound this plank made. She inspected it closer. The wood was worn, and the nailheads were slightly raised. Someone had pried the plank open before, leaving faint gouges around its edges.

Setting the lantern on the floor beside her, Anna worked her fingertips into the gaps between the planks. The wood resisted as she attempted to pry it loose. But with more effort, it relented, exposing the hidden cavity beneath it.

The dim lantern barely illuminated the secret space Anna discovered. Nestled within was a small glass bottle. Its surface was cold in her palm as she retrieved it from its hiding spot and studied it in the lamplight. The aged and dusty bottle was sealed with a cork and contained a murky yellow liquid.

A creeping chill prickled Anna's flesh. She knew what this vial was—a witch bottle.

It was a folk magic used to protect against witchcraft, evil spirits, and malevolent forces. The hazy liquid within was urine from the person seeking protection. But this bottle contained no sharp objects that could harm a witch lured by the bodily fluids, objects like twisted thorns, bone fragments, or pins and needles.

Anna's mind grappled with her questions as she pocketed the vial. After one last glance around the room, she walked out into the night.

She found more witch bottles of various shapes and sizes hidden in the floors, ceilings, and walls of each of the houses she explored—over a half dozen in total. The bottles all contained urine, but they were sealed and devoid of sharp objects.

Anna's blood ran cold when she thought of the pins and nails Susanna had expelled from between her legs. They were exactly like those that were missing from these witch bottles.

But how were they removed without breaking the bottles' seals?

Anna wondered. *And how did they get inside Susanna?*

Anna's gut knotted with unease as she grasped the situation. The sacrificed owl William found in the woods came to mind. Only a powerful hex could explain how those ancient pins and nails found their way into Susanna from these bottles.

But if Susanna was hexed, who could have done it?

Such a curse required the blackest of magics, so ancient and unspeakable it could only be wielded by a powerful witch —one far more experienced than Anna herself. She considered what the Aldens had said about the evil shaman banished to the woods by Kisosen's tribe. Did the hag somehow survive her encounter with Judith? Or did Judith unleash something else that day in the maple grove? An evil spirit who now tormented them from beyond the grave?

In the last house Anna explored, she stumbled upon something unexpected.

It was in the humble rectory next to the chapel. As her gaze scanned the darkened keeping room, her sharp eyes caught the crucifixes first. They hung on the walls among various portraits of saints in unassuming frames, but something was very wrong.

The crucifixes were all inverted.

Dread settled in Anna's stomach like a heavy stone as she stared at the upside-down crosses, each one a blasphemous mockery of the sacred. She wasn't devout by any stretch of the imagination, but even in the world of the occult, crucifixes were no mere decoration. They were warding spells, infused with the power to repel the demonic entities that sought to breach the mortal realm.

Anna stepped closer to one of the inverted crucifixes, her fingers quivering as she reached out to touch it. The wood was cold and rough against her skin. She held her lantern closer, and that's when she noticed the ghostly outline of dust the cross had left on the wall while it had hung upright.

These crucifixes hadn't been left this way a century ago.

Someone did this recently.

Shadows coiled around Anna as she explored the room. She discovered a simple cabinet where the priest stored his chalice and other sacred vessels. A small library of dusty theological tomes lined a set of shelves. A writing desk stood tucked away in a corner, a pewter candlestick standing among the quills, ink-pot, and parchment. The candle's ancient wax was now little more than a melted lump. But that's not what caught Anna's attention.

There was an ancient parchment on the table, held in place by the candlestick's weight. The letter had no envelope, as if its author wanted it to be found, as if it had waited over a century for someone like Anna to discover it.

Anna eyed the letter curiously as she approached the table. The parchment had yellowed with age, its corners curling at the edges. The ink had faded, but it was still legible. With trembling fingers, Anna reached for it and strained her eyes to read the French words illuminated by the lantern.

Chapter 10

March 10, 1708

Our darkest fears have come to pass. Verily, the events that have unfolded in our village have rent my soul asunder. Having delayed only to bury our dead, with a heavy heart and trembling hand do I take up my quill and ink to chronicle the harrowing events that have yet again befallen our isolated mountain settlement. The serenity that once graced our humble sanctuary has come to ruin, and an unspeakable horror has cast our idyllic refuge into the depths of a never-ending nightmare.

It commenced innocently enough, amidst the howling winter winds that whipped through the ancient pines, blanketing our cabins in a shroud of snow. We, sturdy guardians, prided ourselves on our resilience, forged by the harsh conditions we called home. We came to this place for its isolation, for the secret that must remain buried deeper than the graves we have just unearthed. Yet, as daylight waned and the frigid nights lengthened, a sinister darkness seeped into the hearts of our brethren.

Joseph, known to us for many a season, succumbed to madness. His gentle countenance became a mirror reflecting the demons that had laid claim to his very soul. His eyes, once gleaming with mirth, now bore the mark of a deranged mind. Thus, the transformation transpired, striking us with shock and terror, as though confronting the embodiment of pure malice.

Whispers spread among the villagers, carrying tales of Joseph's nocturnal wanderings. They spoke of his meanderings through the forest, guided by an unseen force. Naturally, I admonished against such accounts, dismissing them as superstitious ramblings, the product of an isolated and anxious community. Little did we fathom these whispers foretold a harrowing doom that would soon befall us.

They discovered the lifeless body of the first victim, poor Marguerite, within the clutches of death's icy grip one wintry morn. Her body lay discarded upon the snow, her eyes devoid of vitality, her throat brutally marred by a ghastly slash. The sight was enough to blanch the hardiest of souls, leaving us trembling with fear. Panic swept through our settlement, a tempest of terror and suspicion that choked the air.

We made attempts to capture Joseph, to quell this senseless violence that stained our souls. Alas, he eluded us like a phantom in the night, his movements as agile as the deer that roam our wilderness. It was as if he had been bestowed transcendent abilities, traversing the shadows with an unnatural grace. The mountains themselves appeared to shield him, frustrating our desperate attempts to bring him to justice.

As the weeks wore on, Joseph's madness grew ever more audacious. His insatiable hunger for blood seemed to swell with each passing day. Innocent villagers met their grisly ends at his hands, their violated corpses a ghastly testament to his wickedness. A perverse spectacle, intended to torment our frayed nerves, he left in his wake. We felt the weight of his depravity bearing down upon us, compelling us to huddle together in our meager dwellings, seeking solace and divine intervention, praying for deliverance from his wrath. Some believed Joseph had succumbed to the influence of the dark secret we have buried here. At first, I dismissed these rumors as naught but superstitious fancies, but the events of recent days have shattered my skepticism like fragile glass.

The night was oppressively still, and the village lay shrouded in an eerie silence. I retired to my humble rectory, yearning for respite from the mounting dread that had seized our community. Yet, bloodcurdling screams shattered the tranquility, tearing through the velvety darkness and echoing through the vale. Drawn forth as if by some unseen hand, I ventured outside, my heart beating with trepidation, and what I beheld shall forever haunt my slumbering thoughts.

In the wavering glow of torches, I did bear witness to a scene of unspeakable savagery. Bodies lay strewn about the village square, their lifeless forms twisted in agonizing torment. Our peaceful villagers had metamorphosed into savage beasts, their visages contorted by unhinged lunacy. They spared no one their wrath—men, women, and children all succumbed to this unexplained frenzy that had possessed our harmonious enclave.

I bore witness to the grim carnage firsthand. The air grew heavy with the pungent tang of spilled blood as good men turned upon one another, driven by an insatiable craving for destruction. The echoes of their screams linger still, tormenting my waking hours. Sleep eludes me, for fear that the nightmares *shall return, forcing me to relive the horrors that unfolded. Our once tightly knit community now lies shattered, the remnants of our thriving settlement poisoned by the blood-soaked earth.*

I cannot help but ponder whether our secret has come to haunt us, infecting the hearts and minds of our inhabitants like a pernicious miasma. Perhaps we have trespassed upon some ancient, forgotten ground, arousing ungodly spirits best left undisturbed. Or perchance isolation and hardship have driven us to the precipice of madness, unveiling the darkness that lies dormant within each of our souls.

Now, as I sit here, quill in hand, the distant echoes of agonized screams penetrate the stillness of the night. Each cry reverberates within my very being, a dreadful reminder of the terrors that have penetrated our tranquil sanctuary. The crimson stains that befoul our streets and the haunted countenances etched upon the faces of my fellow settlers bear witness to the horrors we have endured.

I pen these words, not only to document the atrocities that have befallen us, but also as a plea for salvation. I fear that if we do not flee this very night, we will all be condemned to turn on each other in this cursed place, forever haunted by the promise of the murderers we will inevitably become.

May the heavens hear our cries and deliver us from this malevolence that has taken root in our once peaceful village. I implore anyone who may stumble upon this account to heed my warning. Beware this land, for an infernal evil taints it. May this journal act as a warning to future generations of the price we paid to safeguard our secret.

God have mercy on us all.

Monseigneur Jean-Baptiste Renaud

Chapter 11

Anna took a few seconds to realize she had been breathless while reading. She exhaled slowly and let the letter fall back to the table. The priest's grim description of his village's fate lingered in her thoughts. What could have driven the villagers to unleash such murderous fury upon each other?

Anna thought of the witch bottles she had found hidden throughout the village. The settlers had obviously been afraid of being bewitched. Was there a link to the bloody rampage that sent them fleeing? Anna knew of no hex or sorcery dark enough to corrupt so many minds at once. She thought of the evil shaman who killed Judith's husband. These terrible events had predated the hag's existence by a hundred years. She couldn't possibly be responsible for the villagers' madness. So what had poisoned their hearts and compelled them to commit such unspeakable acts? And what was Gideon's purpose for sending her here in the first place?

I should never have come here alone…

Doubt entered Anna's mind for the first time. It was a strange sensation for a young woman who charged headlong into every situation with supreme confidence. Her fingers grazed the iron pendant hanging around her neck, a charmed talisman of protection she had inherited from her mother. It was a small comfort in the face of such a daunting task. The weight of Abigail's legacy was a heavy burden on Anna's shoulders. Memories of her teachings flooded Anna's thoughts —dusty tomes, arcane rites, and the countless hours spent studying ancient grimoires in their secret arcanium deep beneath Boston's streets. The only times Anna truly felt like someone's daughter were during those intimate moments of learning. She knew it was foolish, but she still held onto hope that Abigail's presence still lingered, guiding her from beyond the Veil. She refused to admit it, but right now, she yearned for her mother's company and desperately missed her guidance.

Without her, she had no one.

Footsteps echoed from the floor above her.

Anna froze, her heart leaping into her throat.

She wasn't alone.

Anna's senses sharpened as she held the lantern aloft, straining her ears to catch any hint of what might be hiding in the darkness upstairs.

A subtle sound broke the silence—an almost imperceptible creak. Then, a faint but distinct *thud*.

More footsteps.

Thud... Thud... Thud...

Anna's heart was a war drum in her chest. Her instincts screamed at her to flee, but her discipline rooted her to the spot. With an iron will, she forced herself to stay composed, taking slow, deliberate breaths to steady her nerves.

The timber floorboards groaned beneath her boots as she crept further into the gloom. The faint light from her lantern flickered as it fell upon a staircase, casting a weak glow on the shadowy steps. Worn with age, they beckoned Anna upwards. Each creaking footfall echoed through the silent rooms, announcing her presence to whoever lurked on the floor above her.

Thud... Thud... Thud...

Anna tried to suppress the tremors creeping into her limbs as she crept up the stairs. With each step upward, the oppressive darkness seemed to tighten its grip on her.

Thud... Thud... Thud...

The footsteps stopped abruptly.

Anna froze where she stood. Did the person upstairs sense her presence?

An eerie silence settled over the upper floor as she ascended the final few steps. It was even darker than the floor below, illuminated only by slivers of moonlight seeping through the tattered curtains. The lantern's glow quivered in Anna's hand as she scanned her surroundings, trying to catch a glimpse of what was moving around up here. But the shadows played tricks on her, the dust particles swirling like wayward spirits dancing in the gloom.

A narrow hallway stretched out before her. A door stood half-open, inviting her into the slice of darkness beyond it. Anna hesitated at the threshold, listening for sounds.

Nothing. The eerie footsteps had ceased.

But that didn't mean she was alone.

Anna summoned her courage and gave the door a slow nudge. The rusty hinges creaked like a warning as it swung inward. A waft of cold air hit her like a slap in the face. Anna thought the room's window had been shattered, but the darkness inside was too absolute for her to determine where it was. Her pulse throbbed in her ears as she took a cautious step through the crooked doorframe into the inky blackness. She held her lantern high to illuminate the shadowy corners. A bed stood against one wall, draped in moth-eaten blankets. A dusty mirror with intricate carvings hung opposite the bed, its surface obscured by the passage of time.

But it wasn't the furniture that caught Anna's attention.

It was the dark figure looming in the corner.

Her lantern suddenly flickered violently, casting erratic shadows before abruptly going out, as if extinguished by some unseen hand.

Darkness rushed back through the room and swallowed her.

A gasp escaped Anna's lips. Panic engulfed her as she struggled to find her tinderbox in her pocket. Her other hand shook as she gripped the lantern ring. The darkness was smothering, and she had a terrifying sensation of being stricken blind. Flashes of that silhouette lurking in the shadows flashed through her mind. Was that sinister figure creeping toward her in the darkness at this very moment? Yes, she still felt a presence in the room with her, an oppressive weight in the air that made it hard to breathe. Her ears caught the faintest creak of a floorboard in the darkness and her heart went cold.

But Anna was no stranger to fear. She had faced horrors that would drive lesser souls to madness, and she wasn't about to become prey to whatever malign force had set its sights on her. Abandoning her search for her flint, she reached for the talisman hanging at her throat, praying its power would protect her from the unseen thing stalking her in that pitch-black room.

"Who are you?" she managed to whisper into the dark.

A cold breath brushed against her skin, and she swore she felt icy fingers trace the curve of her spine.

Anna stifled a scream and whirled, thrusting the talisman out before her. The lantern slipped from her grip and crashed to the floor at her feet. Shards of shattered glass skittered across the wide planks and Anna skipped back.

Something strong and icy ripped the talisman from her outstretched hand.

Anna let out a strangled cry and shrank back against the wall. Her chest tightened, her breath growing shallow as her mind spiraled into a frenzy of terror. Her hand shook as she groped blindly along the wall for something solid with which to orient herself. The air in the room pulsed with a malign energy, and a strange scent filled her nostrils, something vaguely sweet and warm like roasted spices.

Anna's fingers grazed a heavy curtain. She yanked hard and the whole curtain rod fell from the wall with a clatter. A bright moonbeam spilled through the shattered window, streaming through the cloud of musty particles that filled the stagnant air.

Anna's gaze darted from one corner of the moonlit room to another, searching for the dark figure, ready to fight to defend herself.

There was no one there. The figure was gone.

Anna released the breath in her lungs and fought to steady

her pounding pulse. Even the air seemed to have lifted its suffocating weight.

A decrepit rocking chair stood at the foot of the bed. It swayed back and forth in the breeze that wafted through the window.

Thud… Thud… Thud…

Were these the footsteps she had heard?

No, Anna knew better. She had felt the dreadful presence in the room. She'd seen the figure skulking in the corner as if it were part of the darkness itself. Some *thing* had drawn its icy fingers across her flesh and yanked the talisman from her grasp. Whatever malevolent force inhabited the room was real, she was certain of it.

Anna tried to recall exactly what she had glimpsed before the lantern went out. All she saw was the silhouette of a tall, willowy woman. The remnants of her once elegant dress hung in scorched shreds, blackened and singed from flames. Wisps of smoke curled and danced around her. And what was that smell Anna had detected in her presence? Licorice? Anise?

Anna searched the room, but her talisman was nowhere to be found. It was gone, taken by the sinister woman who had been there with her in the darkness.

Mourning the loss of her mother's powerful charm, Anna's footsteps reverberated through the empty house as she descended the stairs to the rectory's keeping room. Her hands still tremored with fear and adrenaline, and her breaths were shallow as she stepped out of the dilapidated rectory.

The abandoned village of Sévérité loomed before her. It seemed to breathe with a life of its own now, as if the moonlight awakened its crumbling buildings and cobweb-draped doorways.

Anna's eyes darted around, scanning for any signs of movement, any glimpse of another menacing shape lurking in the darkness. Every creak and rustle of the trees made her nerves jangle like the strings of a violin played by a ghostly hand. But the village remained still, except for the lonesome whistling of the wind.

Despite her young age, Anna's experiences as an occultist led her to face all manner of supernatural terrors. She had spent her life poring over forbidden tomes and delving into the mysteries of the unknown, but even she couldn't shake the feeling that something was profoundly wrong within this village. Alone in that bleak and lonesome place, her mind whirred with questions. Who was that dark woman in the bedroom? A vengeful spirit? One of the unfortunate victims of the massacre that had terrorized the village a century ago? If so, it would be like unlike anything Anna had ever faced. No spirit could overcome the powerful protective magic of that ancient talisman. Anna had never encountered such a dark and powerful presence. It left her shaken in a way she hadn't felt since she was a child.

Anna's breath puffed in small clouds as she navigated the silent labyrinth of decaying buildings, eager to return to the relative safety of the Aldens' homestead where she could collect her thoughts.

It was only after she had put some distance between herself and the rectory that she realized she was being followed.

Chapter 12

Judith sat alone by the fire, her eyes red and raw from her tears as she stared into the crackling embers. Her weathered hands trembled as she clutched a threadbare shawl around her shoulders to ward off the chill. Grief hung heavy in the air, shrouding every corner of the dim room. She longed to cry out, to shake the walls with her screams. But she stifled her sorrow as she had so many times before, as if it were a fleeting ember she could smother with a touch.

Mercy lay asleep in Judith's bed upstairs, having finally succumbed to the exhaustion of her grief and trauma. William and Kisosen kept watch outside while they dug a grave for Susanna on the hill behind the cottage. Judith refused to bury her daughter in the village's Catholic cemetery. She couldn't bear the thought of leaving Susanna alone for eternity in that godforsaken place. She would keep her daughter close, near the warmth of the cottage where Judith could feel her presence.

Left alone with her thoughts and despair, Judith sought solace from the horrific images of Susanna's final moments that still flashed before her eyes. She passed the minutes trying to remember the sound of her daughter's laughter, but she found she couldn't recall the last time she had heard it. Certainly not since they had embarked on their long years in exile. Judith's thoughts had to reach back to a time long ago in Penance Cove, when Susanna's laughter had echoed through the walls like the tinkling of wind chimes on a gentle breeze, filling their cottage with the promise of hope and joy. Susanna was fifteen then. Those were the days when dreams held sway over their lives, when Judith's heart swelled with pride at the sight of her daughter blossoming like the wildflowers that bloomed in their meadows.

But that was before the darkness descended upon their lives. Judith's thoughts lingered on the years that had passed since her daughter's childhood. She couldn't recall any cherished moments they had shared, any milestones of life they celebrated together. Her only memories were of fear and the struggle for survival. Did she do enough for her daughter? Could she have been kinder, more understanding, more patient?

The questions tormented her as she grappled with the awful reality that she could never turn back time, never rectify past mistakes. Ripped from her roots, the wildflower that was Susanna wilted out here in this cold and hostile wilderness, and her laughter withered with her. All that remained now was a silence that deafened Judith with its weight. The threads of those joyous memories were so delicate, fraying at the edges, threatening to unravel completely. Judith clung to them, refusing to let go, unwilling to let the image of her happy daughter fade away into nothing. She found herself reaching out for something to cling to, but all she found was emptiness. A knot formed in her throat, and tears welled in her eyes, threatening to spill over again. She longed to hold her daughter one more time, to tell her how deeply she loved her, and how her death had left a bottomless chasm in her heart.

You speak of being our protector, but who will protect us from you?

Was William right? Was this all her fault?

Judith's memories drifted to her husband and her own misgivings about the people of Penance Cove. She remembered a night not long before they came for Mercy. The children were slumbering peacefully in their beds, and after giving each a kiss on the forehead, Judith had turned to find John filling the frame of the doorway.

John was an imposing man, powerfully-built but with a cool and quiet confidence. Judith motioned for him to follow as she exited the room to the hallway. They spoke in hushed tones outside the closed door to their children's bedroom.

"I heard them speaking of her again at the market today," Judith said.

"Steady, Judith," John replied, his voice a deep baritone. "We must have faith in the forbearance of our neighbors."

"Neighbors? They are hanging dead animals for our children to find."

"What would you have us do?" asked John.

"Leave this place. Find somewhere where no one will look for us."

John fixed her with a stern eye. "Cast ourselves out into the savage wilderness? Our very livelihood is here in Penance

Cove."

"For how long? How long until they come for our daughter? How long until she is accused? Thanks to Ann Walcott, they already whisper that she is a witch. I feel the weight of their stares upon her wherever we go. Do not think she is too young to swing from the gallows, John!"

Realizing her raised voice risked waking the children, Judith caught herself and took a calming breath. A moment passed in silence.

"Have you considered the possibility that we are mistaken, Judith?" John asked.

"Mistaken on what account?"

"That our child *has* been touched by evil?"

Judith's expression darkened. "I'll not hear such talk from my own husband. Our daughter is as innocent as a child unborn."

"God willing, it be so," John said. "And yet, what if we are mistaken? What if there lurks the seed of some dark malice growing within her?"

Judith glowered at him a moment, chewing his words over in his mind. He had hit a nerve, but she could never bring herself to accept what he was suggesting. Her mind recoiled at the very thought.

Now, as she sat by the fireside, mourning the loss of her eldest daughter, guilt washed over Judith. Its relentless waves crashed against the shores of her conscience. *She* was the one who insisted they flee Penance Cove. *She* was the one who followed John into the maple grove that day. *She* was the one who killed that priest. And now she was being punished for it. She was supposed to be her daughter's protector, and yet she was powerless against the dark forces that snatched her away.

How much more can I endure? How long until there is nothing left of my family to protect?

Judith wondered if it was just a matter of time before they all fell victim to whatever baleful presence tormented them. Even if they survived, what was the point of protecting her children if this desolate place was the only life they would ever know?

Do you really expect Mercy to live out the rest of her days here? Do you expect William to do the same?

Even as the answers eluded her, Judith knew she must endure, that she must carry the weight of her sorrow for the sake of her surviving children. It was the price a mother pays for loving so fiercely.

Judith glanced around the room as a lonesome breeze whispered a mournful melody through the cracks in the walls.

But there was something else in the air now.

It was another sound, one so low Judith almost dismissed it as a trick of her imagination, her sorrow playing on her weary mind. She sat up in her chair and pricked her ears.

A faint whisper was coming from upstairs.

The hairs on the back of Judith's neck stood on end. Her pulse quickened.

Someone was in the cottage.

But that was impossible, wasn't it? No one could have slipped past her unnoticed. She strained her ears to listen. *Was* she imagining it?

With William and Kisosen somewhere out in the night, she was all alone, surrounded by the endless darkness of the forest. Over time, she had grown used to the old house's creaks and groans. The isolation never scared her before, but tonight was very different. Tonight, it felt like something dreadful had gotten a taste for their blood and wouldn't relent until it consumed them all.

Judith summoned her remaining courage and stood up from her seat, heading for the staircase. The threadbare rug beneath her slippered feet muted her footsteps. The whispers grew louder with each step she took, and the air seemed to grow colder near the foot of the stairs.

"Mercy?" Judith called out, her voice barely louder than a quivering whisper of her own.

There was no response, just the relentless whispering coming from above.

An icy tingle spread over Judith's flesh. Was Mercy talking in her sleep?

Or was someone up there with her?

The planks creaked beneath each hesitant footfall as Judith ascended the stairs. When she reached the upper landing, the hallway stretched before her in absolute darkness. A pair of bedroom doors stood on either side of the corridor.

Judith glanced down at the firelight on the floor below her and thought about going back downstairs for a candle. But the strange whispering had grown louder here. It came from the last room down the hall.

The room where Mercy lay sleeping.

Judith crept along the floorboards, passing the open door to the bedroom where Susanna's corpse lay wrapped in the linen they used as a winding sheet.

If she had looked into the room, Judith would have seen

her daughter's shrouded corpse sitting upright in the silent darkness.

Judith's footsteps slowed as she moved on. She paused just outside her own bedroom, hesitant to enter. The door was slightly ajar, allowing the eerie whispers to escape and dance along the darkened corridor. The curtains inside were drawn, and the room was cloaked in a murky darkness that concealed the bed where Mercy slept.

Relief flooded Judith when she saw Mercy was alone in the room. She remained perfectly still and listened, not wanting to disturb her slumbering daughter. The poor girl needed her rest; there would be more heartache when they buried Susanna's body in the morning. Still, the pull of her daughter's mysterious whispering was irresistible. What was Mercy saying in her sleep? Even this close, the girl's voice was nothing more than an indistinct murmur, the words indecipherable as they wove together.

Easing the door wider with a soft squeak, Judith tiptoed into the inky gloom and halted just shy of the bed. A faint odor lingered in the air, the same strange fragrance Judith had detected in Susanna's bedroom earlier. She inhaled deeply through her nose. The smell was aromatic, warm, and slightly sweet, with a hint of roasted spices.

The vague outline of Mercy's body nestled beneath the blankets was barely visible in the dark. Judith leaned closer to listen. The whispers were louder now, but still indistinct, as if Mercy intended them only for the shadows that hung over the room. They slipped from the girl's lips like a dark incantation in a language Judith had never heard. But they carried an unmistakable air of something ominous that crawled under her skin.

She leaned closer still, straining to hear but not daring to move for fear of waking her daughter and frightening her in the darkness. Mercy's words had changed to English now. The faint whispers emerging from her lips enveloped Judith like a chilling fog and she felt her blood turn to ice.

"In the dark, the shadows crawl. The night's embrace consumes us all. The weeping trees, they call my name, and in my dreams, I play his game…"

The hair on Judith's arms stood on end. She'd heard her daughter talking in her sleep before, but never like this. These were not the innocent whispers of a child dreaming of fantastical lands. No, this was something else entirely, something dark and frightening.

A chill filled the room, causing Judith's breath to quiver. She fought the urge to pull Mercy close and flee. She needed to understand what was happening to her daughter so that she could protect her at all costs.

As Judith strained to make sense of the girl's words, they shifted and changed, growing darker with each passing moment.

"Voices call from below; ancient power, the seeds I sow. The moon weeps blood, the stars turn black; the Devil's hand guides my track…"

A knot of dread tightened in Judith's chest. She couldn't shake the feeling that there was something in the room with them. She reached out into the darkness, her hand trembling, intent on waking her little girl from this unsettling sleep.

The whispers stopped.

Silence filled the void.

Judith froze, her outstretched hand hanging in the air.

Then, with unexpected clarity, Mercy's voice crawled out of the darkness.

"We're waiting for you, Mama. We're all here, waiting for you."

Fear gripped Judith's heart. She snatched her hand away and stumbled backward in the darkness, her breaths coming in quick gasps.

Mercy's voice went silent, leaving Judith in a suffocating vacuum of dread. Her blood hammered in her ears, and she swallowed hard, trying to push back the fear that was crawling into her chest. She could still feel her daughter's presence there in the room, lying motionless on the bed. Was she awake, or had she spoken in her sleep? No; she had to be awake. How else could she have known Judith was there with her?

"Mercy?" Judith whispered, fearful of what might respond.

Silence.

Frozen there in the pitch-black room, Judith had the dreadful feeling that whoever lay bundled beneath those blankets wasn't her daughter. Something had taken residence inside the young girl, and it inspired a sudden urge for her to turn and flee. Judith didn't want to be alone with her daughter in that black room anymore. Visions of her little girl springing up from the bed and scuttling after her in the darkness danced in her mind. The soft creak of the floorboards beneath her slippered feet echoed through the darkened room as she retreated a step toward the open door, her maternal instincts succumbing to her fear.

But the painful memory of how she failed Susanna kept

her from taking another step. Her instincts screamed at her to leave, but her feet refused to carry her any further. It was as if an invisible force held her in place. She couldn't bear to abandon her youngest child to whatever haunted her dreams.

Steeling her resolve, Judith took a deep breath and reached out to touch Mercy's shoulder.

"Mercy, my angel, wake up." She tried to keep her voice steady despite the mounting dread in her heart.

Mercy lay on her side with her back to her mother, her face turned away in the darkness. Judith still couldn't tell if her daughter's eyes were open or shut, but she felt the soft rise and fall of the girl's chest as she stirred beneath her touch.

"Mama?" Mercy's sleepy voice was a whisper, still caught between the waking world and her dreams. It betrayed no knowledge of the macabre words she had spoken.

Judith hugged her daughter tightly, relief washing over her like a wave. She tried to convince herself that it was just a night terror, the result of the overwhelming emotions her daughter had suffered with the loss of her sister. But deep down, she couldn't shake the feeling that something was terribly wrong.

What Mercy said next sent icy pinpricks deep into Judith's heart.

"Mama," she whispered, her voice faint but haunting. "Mama, she's here."

Judith's hand trembled as she smoothed her daughter's silver tresses from her face. "Who's here, my sweet girl?" she asked, trying to keep her voice from betraying the terror that gripped her.

Mercy left the question unanswered, still lingering in a

dreamy state between waking and slumber. "She wants to play, but her games are dark and cold."

Fear gripped Judith's heart like a vise. "Mercy, you're having a bad dream," she said, her voice quivering despite her best efforts. "It's just a dream, my darling. Nothing more."

But Mercy's voice went on, still soft but laced with an ominous undertone. "She wants me to join them, to dance in the shadows. She promises me secrets, but I'm scared, Mama. I'm scared."

As if sensing her mother's distress, Mercy's whispers grew louder and more urgent, her body trembling beneath the weight of the blankets. "She sees you too, Mama. She wants you."

Judith's blood pounded in her ears, and she felt an icy grip tightening around her chest. She scanned the room, half-expecting to see a dreadful figure lurking in the shadows.

"Who wants me, Mercy?" Judith's voice was barely a whisper, fearful that uttering more words might invite more darkness.

"The Burned Lady. She whispers to me every night," Mercy said, her sleepy voice filled with both innocence and foreboding.

"The Burned Lady?" Judith repeated. Her mind raced, trying to make sense of her daughter's cryptic words. "Where is she now, Mercy?"

Mercy's finger pointed towards the far corner of the room. "There, by the wardrobe. She's waiting for you."

Waves of icy cold shot through Judith's flesh, and a sense of impending doom washed over her. She mustered her courage, her maternal instincts overriding her fear, and turned to look at the wardrobe, half-expecting to see a ghastly figure standing there.

But there was nothing. Just an ordinary wardrobe standing against the wall.

"She's coming for you, Mama," Mercy murmured softly as she slipped back beneath the undertow of sleep.

And though Judith couldn't be certain it wasn't merely the effects of her daughter's drowsiness, she had the chilling impression her little girl's voice hadn't been her own.

It was the voice of the woman that spoke to her every night, too.

The one who drove her to kill.

Chapter 13

The wind carried whispers through the empty lanes of the village, and the darkness seemed to dance and twist, playing tricks on Anna's mind. But as she turned a corner, she glimpsed something. The fleeting movement of a dark shape flitting among the ruins.

She slowed but didn't stop. Her eyes darted from shadow to shadow as she navigated the maze-like paths. Sharpened by years of surviving in a world that demanded toughness and resilience, her instincts told her that whatever followed her was no ordinary menace. It moved with a stealthy silence, its presence felt rather than seen. She was being herded, guided deeper into the heart of this desolate ghost town.

A plan formed in her mind as she weaved through the haunting landscape. Running would only trigger the predator's instinct to chase, and fleeing would only lead it straight back to Judith and her children. Anna couldn't risk endangering them any further. Her only chance was to turn the tables, to stand her ground and face whatever stalked her. She had to become the huntress that she was, not the prey.

She decided to draw her pursuer in by feigning that she was defenseless and easily captured. Moving silently, she slipped into the remains of an old blacksmith's shop. The interior was cavernous and shadowy, illuminated only by moonbeams streaming through the open door and cracked windows. Rust, sodden wood, and the unmistakable musk of damp earth filled the air. Once vibrant with the clamor of ringing hammers and the roar of the forge, the space now lay in eerie stillness, smothered by a century's worth of neglect and decay. A solitary sapling had taken root in a corner, its tender leaves reaching toward a roof that sagged under the moss and ivy that weighed it down.

As her eyes adjusted to the dim beams of moonlight, Anna discovered rusted tongs and discarded tools strewn about a workbench. She quickly rummaged through these forgotten relics of the past and found a timeworn smithing hammer. Despite the cracked handle and pitted iron head, it appeared sturdy enough to still do some damage.

Anna's breath was a misty plume in the cold air as she clutched the hammer and pressed herself against the wall beside the open door. Her eyes scanned every shadow, every nook and cranny, but she was alone. The moments lengthened as she waited, her gaze fixed on the entrance, the silence broken only by the moan of the wind. Just as she was about to doubt her instincts, she heard it—a faint rustle of fabric and the crunch of gravel underfoot.

Whatever was out there was getting closer.

The swelling sound of approaching footsteps echoed in the stillness. Anna's grip tightened on the hammer. Her knuckles turned white as she held her breath and flattened herself against the wall, allowing the darkness to swallow her presence.

The footsteps drew nearer. Unhurried. Deliberate.

There was movement at the edge of Anna's vision. A shadow slithered like a serpent through the night. The silhouette of a man filled the doorframe—a tall figure cloaked in black with a wide-brimmed hat that hid his face. He moved cautiously, a predator stalking its prey, not realizing that the tables were about to turn. He entered the darkness of the shop and halted, his confidence seemingly shaken by the sudden absence of light. Or did he sense Anna waiting in ambush?

She glided like a ghost in the blackness, her steps soundless as she circled behind her would-be assailant. Her heart raced, her senses attuned to every nuance of his posture. The hammer's weight was reassuring in her hand, but she couldn't use it, not yet. If she wanted to know who this mysterious stranger was, and why he was stalking her, she couldn't risk killing him with a misjudged blow.

The man pivoted toward the darkened forge, and Anna saw her moment. In that instant of vulnerability, she sprang from the darkness, delivering a swift and well-aimed kick that sent him sprawling to the ground. He cursed and rolled onto his back. Anna could see his face now, illuminated by the moonlight streaming through the cracked windows. Beneath the brim of his hat, his bearded features were a cold and stony block of raw granite.

Too late, Anna saw the gleam of the pistol in his hand.

The roar of the gunshot rang out like thunder in the confined space.

A searing pain sliced across Anna's upper arm as the lead ball grazed her flesh and whizzed past her, a hair's breadth from amputating her limb below her shoulder. Blood seeped through her scorched sleeve and dripped to the soot-covered floor. She dropped the hammer and stumbled backward, colliding with the workbench and clutching her bleeding wound.

The man rose to his feet, smoke spiraling from the flintlock barrel. His eyes gleamed like shards of obsidian in the gloom.

Anna grit her teeth against the pain. Her fingers groped the surface of the workbench and tightened on the iron handle of a rusty blacksmith's knife. The blade was dull and rough, but it was all she had to defend herself with.

The man lunged, and Anna's instincts kicked in. She sidestepped the attack, her skirts swirling around her as she brought the blade down with all her strength. The man threw up an arm and deflected her blow. Steel met steel with a resounding *clang* as the knife struck the tools on the workbench. The force of the impact jarred Anna's injured arm.

The man's dark eyes bore into hers, his face twisted into a malicious grin. But Anna refused to let fear paralyze her. She no longer cared who he was or why he had pursued her. This was now a struggle for survival, and he was just another nameless adversary that required killing.

She swung the blade again, this time aiming for his chest. The man evaded her strike, his movements fluid and graceful. He countered, swinging the pistol like a club and striking her across the temple. Stars exploded before her eyes, and she staggered sideways before sprawling to the floor. Pain radiated through her body, and her vision blurred as she fought to stay conscious. With her head still spinning, she rolled to her feet, her breath ragged. She could taste the metallic tang of blood on her lips, mingling with the sweat and soot that trickled down her cheeks. The room around her was a spinning whirl of shadows and pain. Her fingers fumbled for the knife at her side, her grip unsteady as she brought it to bear against her foe.

The man circled her, his movements deliberate and methodical, as though savoring every moment of her distress. His cloak flapped behind him like the wings of a night creature as he advanced.

Anna darted to the side, narrowly avoiding another vicious strike. With a surge of determination, she lunged forward, her knife slashing through the air. The man sidestepped her attack with an effortless grace. His hand shot out, his fingers like vipers closing around Anna's wrist. She cried out as her hand spasmed, releasing the blade. It clattered to the ground, just out of reach.

A bright flash of pain blossomed from her wounded shoulder. The world slowed as the man wrenched her wrist around, his fingers like iron vises. His other hand scooped up the knife from where it had fallen. The blade glinted in the moonlight as he pressed it to her throat, the cold steel of the weapon freezing her skin. Her heart shuddered with fright as she braced for the fatal blow. Time hung suspended, a fragile thread between life and death.

The man's smile widened, his gaze locking onto Anna's with a predatory hunger. "It ends here, Anna," he hissed, his voice like the whisper of a serpent.

Anna's mind frantically sought an escape. With a surge of adrenaline, she thrust her free hand up in-between them and straight-armed her palm into his chin with a blow that made his teeth click together. He grunted in pain, his grip loosening enough for Anna to break loose and duck just as the blade sliced through the air where her throat had been.

Fighting through the haze of pain and fear, Anna seized the moment and dove across the floor to the fallen smithing hammer. With a primal roar, she whirled around and swung the blunt weapon with all her strength. The man barely had time to react before the hammer collided with his knee. The joint crumpled sideways at a grotesque angle, and a sickening crack of dislocating bones and snapping tendons shot through the room. His eyes bulged in their sockets, and he let out a bellowing cry of agony as he crashed to the floor.

The blacksmith's shop reverberated with the echoes of their struggle. Anna's face was a grim mask as she staggered over to loom over her assailant. Blood seeped from the gunshot wound in her shoulder, her body a canvas of pain and triumph.

She was alive. She had survived.

For a moment, she remained immobile, her gaze fixed on the figure sprawled before her. His hat had fallen away, and thick strands of black hair hung plastered to his prominent brow. Thin gray streaks shot through his dark beard like bolts of lightning in a night sky. Only now did she realize his black cloak was the long cassock of a priest.

"You're no priest," she said, her voice as cold and sharp as a winter's morning. "Who are you?"

The man's gasps were short and labored as he glared at her

with an maddening mix of arrogance and trepidation. Beads of sweat trickled down his forehead, mingling with the dirt and blood that smeared his face. Still, he stayed silent.

Anna's expression remained fierce as she grabbed a coil of rope from the wall. "Let me be clear," she said. Her voice dripped with menace as she looped the rope around itself into a slipknot. "I have faced terrors that would shatter the souls of lesser men. You're just a riddle waiting to be solved—and you will speak, one way or another."

The man's bravado wavered, replaced by a glimmer of uncertainty that danced within his eyes as he gazed at the noose in Anna's hands. Was she going to hang him with it?

Instead, Anna looped the rope around the ankle of his ruined leg and cinched it tight. He struggled to sit up to fend her off, grimacing in pain at even the slightest jolt to his shattered knee.

Anna tossed the loose end of the rope over a rafter and caught it on the way down. "I will ask you one last time," she warned. "Who are you?"

Laying prone on his back, her captive's face betrayed his fright when he realized what she intended. And yet, his lips still curled in a defiant sneer, his eyes like two black, unreadable pools in the moonlight.

Anna pulled down hard on the rope with her good arm, hoisting his broken leg into the air. The bones of his ruined knee let out an audible crunch as they ground against each other. He released an agonized wail and thrashed in pain until he threw his hands up in submission, pleading for mercy.

"Cotton," he managed through gritted teeth, his resolve crumbling like brittle parchment. "My name is Cotton

Barlow."

Anna released some tension from the rope but kept it firmly in hand. "How do you know who I am?"

"You murdered our brothers in Burlington," he said, his voice a low, gravelly rasp that grated on Anna's nerves. "Our order does not forget such things... or forgive them."

A disquieting understanding took hold of Anna. "Ah... You are part of the Crucible," she said, scowling with contempt. The Crucible of Night was a secret society of powerful and learned men who owed their prominence to arcane pacts with demons. Anna nearly fell prey to one of their initiation rites that terrible night she lost her mother last October.

"If we're being honest, the werewolves did most of the killing that night," Anna said, a grim amusement playing at the corners of her mouth. "Still, I do delight in the memory of the man I castrated and burned alive."

A dangerous fury flashed in the man's dark eyes. Anna got the sense he would wrap his hands around her throat and choke the life from her if he had the chance.

"Why are you here?" she demanded. "Have you been following me?"

Barlow returned her unwavering gaze. "Oh, no. Merely exploring. This place has its secrets, doesn't it?"

Anna gave the rope a sharp jerk, snapping his leg up from the ground. Barlow convulsed with pain, as if shot through with electricity.

"Are you ready to tell me the truth?" Anna growled.

"I am here for the same reason you are," he gasped through clenched teeth. "The Black Testament."

The words struck a chord with Anna. "The Black Testament? The grimoire of Angéle de la Barthe?"

An echo of Abigail's teachings rang in Anna's mind. De la Barthe had a notorious reputation in the history of witchcraft. She was the first woman burned at the stake by the French Inquisition in 1275. But unlike thousands of innocent women who would follow her, she never denied her pact with Satan. She freely confessed to having copulated with her dark lord, to having fed babies to the demonic abomination she had birthed as a result of their unholy union. Under the Devil's guidance, her abilities had grown at an alarming pace. Rumors whispered she possessed the power to summon entities from the depths of Hell, unleash curses that plagued the entire land, and control the minds of men at her will. As her infamy spread, tales of her devilry reached the ears of the Church, setting in motion a relentless pursuit by the Inquisition.

Something about Anna's expression must have given away her mystification. Barlow's thin lips curled into a crooked smile.

"Oh, my…" he sneered, his voice a venomous whisper that slithered across Anna's skin. "Don't tell me you don't know it's here. Why else would you have come? Surely not for that family in the house?"

Anna's stomach tightened into a knot. There was a dangerous glint in Barlow's eyes when he spoke of the Aldens, a spark that set her instincts screaming. What did he want with Judith and her family? Anna had no intention of letting any more harm come to them. Their only wish was to hide from a world that had brought them endless pain.

Anna's eyes were as sharp as flint as they bore into his. "Tell me about the Black Testament."

Barlow's lips pressed into a hard line. "Ah, Anna… There is still so much you don't know. Compared to the men of my order, you are but a faun learning to walk." Despite his battered state, Barlow's eyes gleamed with an unspoken defiance, a glimmer that sparked a fire in Anna's blood.

"She's a murderess, you know," he went on, deliberately changing the subject. "The woman in that house. I didn't come here alone. She murdered my companion in cold blood, even as he begged for his life. She had no reason to suspect he wasn't really a priest, yet she left his body to rot in the woods." The faint smirk crept back into his lips. "I imagine she'll do the same to you when given the chance."

Anna's fingers twitched menacingly on the rope hanging from the rafter. A voice was whispering in the dim recesses of her mind, one that was both hers and yet not hers, urging her to surrender to the primal impulse to kill the man.

Barlow studied her face, as if reading the malice written on her features. "You feel him too, don't you?" he said. "His presence among us in this place."

"Who?" Anna asked.

"Our Master… the Light Bearer."

Anna's eyes narrowed. "Light Bearer? You mean Lucifer?"

Barlow gave a somber nod.

"You're mistaken," Anna scoffed. "I serve no one."

The sound of Barlow's mocking laughter reverberating off the timber walls sounded like shattered glass in Anna's ears. "Is that truly what you believe, Anna? Have you never questioned the source of your dark powers? Witchcraft?

Necromancy? They are *infernal* in nature—and they come at a terrible price."

Barlow's bitter smile faded, replaced by a cold, calculating stare. "Hell grants nothing without sacrifice, Anna. It is why men of my order choose to offer *others* to its demonic princes. But you… you have been a lamb led to slaughter, my dear. You may have fooled yourself into thinking you could use such dark rituals and blasphemous incantations for good, but the burning pit awaits you—just as it awaits your mother."

Anna felt the color drain from her face.

"Oh yes, Anna," Barlow taunted. "We know all about your mother. Her spirit can't remain hidden beyond the Veil forever. Soon, the enchantment preserving her earthly remains will wane, and her flesh will wither and rot. And when it does, the Devil will defile her soul like the whore that she is."

The room seemed to shiver with Anna's rage, the very walls quivering as if they sensed the volatile energy coursing through her veins. Her grip on the rope tightened. With one swift, fluid motion, she hauled on it with all her might.

A guttural cry escaped Barlow's lips as she dragged him across the floor by his ankle. His chest heaved as he tried to suck in air. He opened his mouth to beg for mercy, but only a hoarse whisper came out. His eyes darted around the room, but the walls were like heartless jailers.

This time, Anna didn't relent. She hauled his broken leg higher into the air, not caring about the excruciating damage she was inflicting or the pain lancing from her wounded shoulder. Barlow's gaze became unfocused as his vision blurred, his eyelids weighed down by a heavy darkness. The pain was like a tidal wave, threatening to drag him under. In that moment, Anna saw him slipping, the edges of his consciousness fraying like worn fabric. His pain became a distant echo, his mind retreating into a realm of numbing darkness. The struggle to stay conscious was a losing battle, and with one last feeble attempt to hold on, he finally succumbed to the blissful void.

Anna released the rope and let his leg drop back to the ground, where he lay in a motionless heap. She wiped a bead of sweat from her brow and stared at his limp form. A wave of revulsion swept over her when she felt herself reveling in the power she held, the depraved satisfaction she took in making him pay for his callous words. The room pulsed with an unearthly energy now, as if the walls absorbed the pain and fear, feeding off the cruelty she had unleashed. The sensation lasted only an instant—barely the length of a heartbeat—but it was enough to open an icy hole in the pit of Anna's stomach.

Shaken and repulsed by the extent of her own viciousness, she made a half-hearted attempt to rouse Barlow from the pain-induced stupor she had plunged him into. But his mind had retreated too far into a hazy abyss. Even when he finally recovered, given what he had already endured, she suspected no amount of torture would force him to reveal his secrets.

But there was someone else who might.

Chapter 14

William's knuckles whitened as he gripped the handle of the pickaxe. Kisosen toiled alongside him with a shovel, his tall frame shrouded in the shadows cast by their flickering lantern. The moon spilled a pale light over the small hill behind the cottage as they worked in silence under its watchful eye. The air was thick with the scent of soil and pine sap.

An unspoken heartache hung between the two men as they labored. Words felt inadequate in the face of such sorrow.

They had already marked out the shallow grave, a rectangular patch of stony earth that yawned open like a maw hungry for the dead. The soil, still frozen by the ghost of winter, sent tremors up William's arms with each impact of his pick. The steel blade gleamed in the moonlight as he thrust it into the ground, its piercing sound echoing through the night. William's fingers cramped and his muscles burned, but he kept digging. There was a strange comfort in the task's physicality, a welcome distraction from his overwhelming grief. Bittersweet memories of Susanna replayed in his mind like a flickering candle, casting shadows of the life she could have lived.

William stole a glance at Kisosen, wondering at his young mentor's strength, both physical and emotional. The Indian's smooth face betrayed no emotion. His eyes were deep pools of darkness that belied the deep anguish he must carry in his heart. The light of the lantern flickered over sharp features as he met William's gaze and broke the silence, his voice a low rumble that resonated from his chest.

"The *skadegamutc* will catch her scent and come for her," he said, his words clipped and gruff. "We must bury her deeper."

William paused. "*Skadegamutc?*"

Kisosen remained silent and kept digging.

"Kisosen?" William pressed.

When Kisosen glanced back at him, his face was dark in the lamplight. "What do you know about the witch who killed your father?"

"Only what you and Mother have told me," William replied. "That your tribe cast her out for attempting to bring evil spirits into our world."

"You recall my people's beliefs in the spirit world?"

William nodded. "They believe in a world that exists parallel to our own, a world invisible to the eyes of but a few. These spirits animate and influence the actions of all things—wind, water, fire, animals—everything. Am I correct?"

"Just so. We believe there are those who have the power to abandon their earthly bodies, to move about the invisible world and commune with the spirits which dwell there."

"You are speaking of shaman," William said.

"The Abenaki know them as *medawlinno*. Most interact

with spirits to seek answers in times of trouble. But the woman your father came across that day in the woods was a *pujinkskwes*—a witch who invoked spirits of an evil nature."

"To bring harm and torment to others."

Kisosen gave a grim nod. "The *pujinkskwes* made a pact with the Three Spirits of Darkness—Death, Disease, and Despair. In exchange for her power, she agreed to unleash the ancient spirits upon our world, bringing ruin to untold numbers. But to cross over, the Spirits of Darkness required earthly vessels, the bodies of three innocents who met death at their own hands."

"But life is sacred among your people. Three suicides would be unthinkable."

"So we believed. Such is the way the balance with the spirit world has been forever maintained. And yet, the witch was nearly successful. As a reward for the horrors she committed in their name, the Spirits of Darkness gifted her the ability to change her shape at will, to disguise her true identity from her victims. Using her power, she tricked at least two of my people into taking their own lives. My sister, Katetin, was one of them."

A lone owl's mournful hoot broke through the silence, an eerie lament that made William shudder.

"It happened a year ago, near the time your father was killed," Kisosen said. "Katetin loved a man, but the *pujinkskwes* tricked her into believing he had betrayed her. In her grief, she fled alone into the forest. I was away trading and wasn't there to stop her. Men of my tribe found her days later, dead by her own hand."

Kisosen heaved a sorrowful breath. "When your mother

killed the *pujinkskwes*, she turned the witch into a *skadegamutc*—an undead spirit who feasts on the flesh of corpses."

"And you believe this undead spirit killed Susanna?"

Kisosen frowned. "The Ghost-Witch may yet work her magic even in death. Only three of your family now remain, William. Perhaps the unclean spirit intends to complete the summoning ritual from beyond the grave."

"Nonsense," said William. "You believe the ghost of an evil shaman wants to use our bodies to welcome the Three Spirits of Darkness into our world? What could possibly drive us to kill ourselves?"

"The hauntings that have befallen you since your father's death," Kisosen replied. "They are meant to lead you to madness and despair, to push you to the point where you finally seek release in death."

A shiver crawled down William's spine as he resumed digging. Sweat trickled through the dirt on his brow. The hole grew deeper, the sides jagged like an open wound in the earth. And all the while, the forest seemed to press closer; the trees leaning in like spectators for a secret ceremony.

"This undead witch. How can we stop her?" William asked while he dug

"Fire is the only way to kill the Ghost-Witch," Kisosen replied.

"How do we hunt her?"

"There is no need. We will bring her to us as a hunter traps the wolf."

William caught on. "With bait?"

"The Ghost-Witch feeds on the flesh of the dead."

William couldn't hide his revulsion and outrage. "Never. I'll not have Susanna's remains so defiled."

Kisosen's eyes narrowed to hard points. "No, not Susanna... the woman."

William flinched and looked up, his mind whirling with disbelief. Kisosen was his trusted mentor, his guide now that his father was dead. The young Indian was no murderer, and this suggestion, this monstrous idea that Kisosen had just voiced, shook William to his core.

"Anna? No, you can't be serious, Kisosen. You're asking me to murder an innocent woman?" William's voice quivered with a mix of anger and disbelief.

Kisosen's gaze bore into him, unflinching. "I am asking you to save lives and protect what is left of your family, even if you have to make sacrifices."

These weren't the words of the honorable companion William had known since childhood. Something dark had taken root in Kisosen, something William didn't fully understand. He shook his head. "This isn't right. Father would never want this of us. We can't just take a life to save our own."

Kisosen fixed him with a piercing stare. "Do not be fooled, William. She is a witch, just like the *pujinkskwes* that killed my sister. She will betray you for her own gain—and she'll not be satisfied until Mercy is dead."

Hefting the shovel, Kisosen lowered himself into the grave and got back to digging.

As the hole deepened, so did the silence between them. But Kisosen's warnings had struck a nerve. A troubled look lingered on William's face. The hard soil yielded reluctantly beneath his pick, as though nature itself resisted the intrusion of death. Undeterred, he worked until blisters formed on his hands and the grave was a fitting resting place for the young woman who had been his only confidante.

Once again, William's thoughts drifted back to happier times—laughter around the hearth in their home in Penance Cove; Susanna's infectious smile, and the stories their father told of a world long before their time. Those memories were now tainted by the ache of loss, leaving behind a gaping hole.

William paused. Wiping sweat from his brow, he scanned the surrounding woods.

And then he saw it—or at least he thought he did. Movement in the shadows; a flicker of something not quite human. His heart raced, and he shook his head. It had to be exhaustion. Grief was playing tricks on his mind.

William forced his attention back to the task at hand and continued to dig, the rhythmic scrape of metal against soil punctuated by the occasional thud of a stone. As they worked in silence, the surrounding forest appeared to come alive with more unseen movement. Shadows danced at the corner of William's vision, and he could swear he heard the whispering of voices carried on the wind. Yet, when he turned, nothing was there, only the lantern's dancing light.

He stole a glance at Kisosen. The young Indian was staring back at him.

"Don't look at them," Kisosen whispered from deep in the hole. "Don't speak to them."

"What are they?" William asked.

Kisosen gave no reply as he returned his attention to the digging.

The grave deepened with each shovelful, while the shadows crept closer with every passing moment. William's breath misted in the air as he peered into the night, his blood pounding so loudly he could hear it in his ears. The forest beckoned, its darkness seeming to pulse with a life of its own.

A low, mournful wail echoed in the distance.

William turned pale. Shivers crawled up his spine to the base of his neck. The sound echoed through the trees, filling his heart with a bone-chilling dread. It wasn't the sound of a wolf; William knew the distinct timber of their calls. This was something entirely different, something menacing and haunting.

The thing that had killed his loved ones was out there in the darkness.

He strained his eyes in the noise's direction. The moonlight revealed nothing but dense trees and thick underbrush.

More memories flooded William's thoughts like a surging tide. Susanna's laughter, her bright eyes, and the warmth of her company on countless wintry nights—all were now just ghosts in the recesses of his mind. The pain was a constant companion, a heartache that strangled his soul. He could still hear her anguished screams, wailing for help. He could see her blood, the crimson blossom that had stained the mattress beneath her. He couldn't shake the image of her pale face, once alight with the promise of a future yet unwritten, now rendered blank and lifeless.

William's palms clenched the pick tighter as he replayed the scene in his mind, his guilt gnawing at his insides like a parasite. With his father gone, it was now *his* duty to protect his siblings. And yet, he had stood there, helpless and frozen, as his sister was left ravaged and bloody before his very eyes. There had been a moment in that room when Susanna's terrified gaze had silently begged him for salvation. In her wide eyes, he saw a reflection of himself—a brother who failed to protect his dearest. Father wouldn't have faltered. *He* would have been brave enough to save her.

William wouldn't let it happen again. Not to Mercy. And even not to Mother. He would put an end to the torment.

Now.

He dashed for the forest without warning.

"William, no!" Kisosen cried. But by the time he scrambled up from the deep grave, William was already crashing headlong into the woods with the pickaxe.

The moon cast its silver rays through the dense forest, painting eerie silhouettes of twisted trees and gnarled shrubs that stretched and clawed at the night sky. The moonlight grew fainter, choked by the looming branches as William ventured deeper into the woods. He swallowed hard and clenched the pickaxe, his throat dry. The trees seemed to reach for him, their limbs clawing at his clothes and hair. The ground beneath his feet grew spongy; the air filled with the smell of decomposing leaves.

William knew he should retreat. What was he doing out here alone? He should turn back and flee to the safety of his cottage. But it was too later. Kisosen was shouting his name somewhere in the dark woods behind him, but another voice was calling to him now as well—the same alluring voice that haunted his dreams.

"*Williaaaam…*"

The air grew thick with an unnatural stillness, and the stink of rot clung to his senses. The path became less defined, as if the ground itself was shifting and reshaping. Each step was a whisper of leaves and a crunch of twigs beneath his boots, echoing like ghostly laughter in the dense silence.

"Come, Williaaaam…"

He stumbled, his foot snagging on an exposed root, and he lost his grip on the pickaxe as he fell to his hands and knees. The ground was damp, cold, and he realized he was surrounded by a circle of mushrooms, pale and luminous in the slanting shards of moonlight. The voice echoed from all directions now, a never-ending chorus resonating in his mind.

Struggling to his feet, William looked around, disoriented. He was in a hollow bathed in moonlight. In the center stood a gnarled, ancient tree, its branches stretching toward the moon like twisted limbs. An awful wave of dread washed over William.

He knew this place. This was where he had found the crucified owl.

That was when he realized he was no longer alone.

Figures—shadowy and indistinct—emerged from the darkness beneath the oak tree. Their forms flickered and warped like candle flames. Some were tall and elongated, while others crouched low to the ground, their limbs contorted. Their eyes were empty voids that drew him in. They moved toward him, their movements slow and deliberate, as if they were part of a dream that had slipped into a nightmare.

"William, you've come…"

Fear was a vise around his heart, but something deeper,

something primal, urged him to obey. He fought against it, trying to will his legs to carry him back to safety, but his body refused to respond. It was as if the intoxicating voice had claimed him, woven its roots deep into his heart.

The figures drew closer, their vaporous forms coalescing into a nightmarish dance that encircled him. Their voices were a chorus of torment and desperation. He couldn't tear his eyes away from them, couldn't resist their pull. The voices swelled, and he felt himself slipping, his consciousness unraveling like frayed threads. It dawned on him that escape was impossible. The figures surrounded him now, their forms solidifying, their faces contorted in agony and ecstasy. They whispered to him, their words a maddening jumble. And as their voices grew louder, he felt as if he were walking between worlds, teetering on the precipice of something both awe-inspiring and terrifying. As he reached out to touch one of the figures, his fingers brushed against something cold and insubstantial, like mist. The world around him wavered and shifted, and suddenly he was no longer in the forest. He was somewhere else, somewhere far removed from the world he knew.

"Stop!" a voice boomed through the air, like thunder splitting the sky.

The shout broke the spell that held William in thrall. Startled, he whirled toward the source.

A tall and imposing silhouette charged from the shadows. It was Kisosen, his eyes burning like stars in the night. He grabbed William by the arm and nearly yanked him off his feet as he hauled the young man away from the clearing.

Together, they plunged into the forest, their footsteps

barely audible on the damp earth beneath the towering ancient trees. Terror was their only guide as they sprinted through the darkness. The night pressed in around them like a living entity, smothering and oppressive. The distant and menacing echoes of ghostly moans still haunted them, as if those undead horrors were pursuing them through the dense woods.

Their feet stumbled over gnarled roots, and the underbrush clawed at their ankles as they sprinted through the forest. But they dared not look back. The darkness was alive. The echoes of those tormented moans sent shivers through the night.

William spared a glance over his shoulder and saw only the inky blackness of the woods. He could *feel* something out there, though—a malign presence lurking in the darkness between the trees.

"William, we must not stop!" Kisosen shouted, his voice trembling with alarm.

William's breath came in short, panicked bursts as they fled. The forest seemed to conspire against them, twisting and shifting its pathways. Desperation clawed at his heart. What direction were they headed? Back toward the cottage? Or were they racing deeper into the black woods? The forest stretched on endlessly; the trees closing in around them like bony fingers. William's eyes darted around the darkness, searching for a way out. The path they followed curved and looped in a disorienting labyrinth.

At last, candlelight from the cottage flickered like distant stars through the trees. Hope surged within William, giving strength to his desperate flight. His legs ached, and his throat burned from the exertion, but they had to press on. Drawing upon every ounce of strength they had left, they pushed forward. Branches scraped at their clothes, and unseen eyes peered at them from the shadows.

The cottage loomed in the distance now, its silhouette barely visible through the shroud of darkness. With one last burst of energy, they crashed across the forest's edge and stumbled into the windswept expanse of the pasture. Gasping for air, they collapsed onto the dew-soaked ground.

"What are those things?" William panted, his breath misting in the frosty night air.

Kisosen couldn't find his voice. His face was ashen, and his dark eyes were wide with terror as he stared at the dark maw of the forest.

The wind whispered secrets to the trees, and the rustling leaves vowed to keep them.

Chapter 15

Anna stood before the decrepit well and stared down into the inky water. Her breath formed frosty plumes in the air, and her fingers quivered as they traced the worn grooves of the stones. The well's rim was weathered and crumbling, while the water below mirrored the stars like a fragment of a distant galaxy.

Anna had left Cotton Barlow tied up in the blacksmith's shop while she searched the village for something to use as a scrying pool. She would need to make a decision about him in the morning. She couldn't possibly let him go. Could she simply leave him bound in the smithy? Or should she kill him before he harmed anyone else? It wasn't an easy decision, and there was dark part of her that yearned for the simplicity of the second option. But first, she needed answers to the questions he had planted in her mind like malignant tumors.

The cold air stirred the scent of wet lichen and stagnant water as Anna drew a deep breath. Fear crept through the crevices of her confidence and her heartbeat pounded in her ears. The barriers between the living and the dead were fragile. Meddling with the spirit world was always perilous, especially with the ghost of Rebecca Hale waiting for her on the other side.

Anna's skin crawled at the memory of her ancestor's spirit invading her body, that horrifying sensation of pure darkness seeking to use her as a vessel to live again. Her stomach churned at the terrifying sense of utter violation, of feeling as if her entire being was on the verge of ceasing to exist. A whirlpool of doubts and what-ifs swirled in her mind.

What if Rebecca is there, lurking in the darkness on the other side? What if she is just waiting for me to open the door so that she might reach through the Veil to claim me?

For a fleeting moment, Anna could almost hear the echoed whispers of Rebecca's wicked spirit, a siren's call that promised unimaginable power while nurturing Anna's most violent instincts. What if Anna was unable to resist her again?

But she had no other choice. Time was running out, and Gideon was her only hope.

Anna closed her eyes. There was a faint tremor in her voice as she began the incantation. The words flowing from her lips were a river of shadows, wrapping around her like a cloak.

Drawing the blacksmith's knife from her belt, Anna drew the blade across her palm. The bright flash of pain grounded her in the moment. She extended her bleeding hand over the well's edge, allowing the crimson drops of her offering to fall into the blackness.

Anna took another breath. She stood at the boundary between the living and the dead now. This was her last chance to turn away and let the words of the incantation slip into silence. Instead, she chanted in a serpentine language long forgotten by the living.

As her invocation grew in strength, the surface of the black pool grew unnaturally still, like a mirror awaiting its reflection. A shiver ran through the night, growing into a low rumble that seemed to rise from the depths of the earth. The wind intensified, tugging at Anna's coat as if to pull her back from the precipice upon which she'd ventured. A chill seeped into her bones, and her heart pounded against her ribs. But she didn't relent. She gripped the well's edges, fixating her unwavering gaze into the dark water.

Her words echoed into the night, charging the air with an energy that crackled with a life of its own. The water rippled and churned until it suddenly burst forth in a swirling mass of inky tentacles. They spiraled upward like a cyclone before merging into a single entity.

Anna's blood pounded with anticipation as a figure appeared in front of her, its ghostly presence forming in the swirling darkness. A young man hovered in the air above the well, his appearance a haunting echo of life. His clothes were tattered and reminiscent of a bygone era, and his translucent face might have once been handsome but for the broken holes of his eyes.

"Gideon," Anna breathed, her voice barely audible in the charged air. Her heart swelled with awe and trepidation. Her guardian's presence was both comforting and unnerving, a paradox mirroring the world of the occult into which she was born.

Gideon's gaze bore into hers, his empty eyes digging into her soul. His lips parted, and his voice was hollow and resonant as it echoed across the void. "You risk everything in summoning me, Mistress."

"What do you know about the Black Testament?" Anna asked.

Gideon's form wavered, suspended between the realms of the living and the dead. "In the dead of night, beneath the cloak of a blood moon, Angéle de la Barthe ventured to a desolate crossroads between realms both mortal and diabolical. There, she invoked the very essence of evil itself—Lucifer, the Morning Star. In exchange for her loyalty, he bestowed upon her the accursed Black Testament, a grimoire bound in human skin and inked with the blood of traitors to the Divine. It was rumored to be the gospel of Satan himself, entrusted only to his most faithful servants. It contained spells that could scorch the gates of Heaven and unleash untold horrors that defied the laws of creation itself. Its pages dripped with forbidden incantations, curses, and rituals that could grant power beyond human imagination—but at a grievous cost. Each spell, each verse, demanded a piece of the caster's soul, a toll that only fueled de la Barthe's insatiable hunger for supremacy.

De la Barthe's Black Testament was presumed lost forever when she met her fiery demise. But somehow the dark grimoire survived. It remained hidden away in the shadowy corners of history until three centuries later when it found its way into the hands of Countess Elizabeth Bathory."

"Bathory?" Anna interjected. "The woman who bathed in the blood of virgins to remain eternally youthful?"

Gideon's hollow eyes narrowed in the moonlight. "Where do you think she might have gotten such a notion?"

Anna pursed her lips in understanding but remained silent.

"Bathory was a woman of extraordinary cruelty," Gideon said. "She and four of her servants tortured, mutilated, and killed hundreds of girls before her bloody reign finally came to an end. Bathory herself was imprisoned in her castle, but three of her servants suffered torture and execution for their crimes. Fearing for her life, a fourth servant named Katarina Szentes fled Europe, presumably with the Black Testament. Once again, the grimoire was believed lost or destroyed during her journey across the Atlantic to New France. But tales of its influence persisted, its cursed pages passing through the hands of those corrupted by its promises. Many came to believe the tome held the key to resurrecting Angéle de la Barthe herself. Whispers of cults and covens seeking the book's infernal knowledge endured, but its location remained a mystery—until something awakened its dark power here."

Anna said nothing while Gideon spoke. The memories of the dreadful woman she had encountered in the rectory consumed her thoughts. Only now did she recognize the strange odor that had accompanied the sinister figure. It was fennel—the same herb burned by villagers in the Middle Ages to mask the stench of human flesh being roasted at the stake.

Was that dark woman Angéle de la Barthe herself? Anna wondered. *Is that why she had been powerful enough to overcome my protective talisman and snatch it away? Was her undying spirit intertwined with her evil grimoire here in this cursed village?*

A chill ran through Anna's flesh when she thought of the bloody massacre that took place here a century ago. Had the Black Testament's malign power somehow corrupted the villagers? She remembered her own appalling urge to kill

William. Had she, too, fallen prey to the evil book's poisonous influence?

"Is this why you sent me here?" she asked. "To find the Black Testament?"

Gideon nodded. "Find it, and you may find the key to your mother's salvation."

The revelation sent Anna's mind into a tornado of emotions.

The sacrifice her mother had made wounded her heart, but Anna had sought solace in the belief that she could make the impossible real and bring her back. She spent months poring over the most ancient and esoteric of texts in the arcanium. They spoke of the fragility of existence, the delicate balance between life and death that held the world together. Anna believed that her grief-fueled determination could defy those boundaries, that her love for her mother could rewrite the rules.

Yet, she soon realized that her quest might be futile. Abigail herself had devoted her life to returning her own parents from beyond the Veil. It was what drew her to the occult as an adolescent. For years, she had immersed herself in the dark arts, driven by an unquenchable longing to reunite with the family she lost as a child. The pain of that absence forged her into a woman with an unbreakable will.

But the more Abigail had delved, the more she realized all of her efforts had been in vain. Spirits could be conjured from beyond the Veil, and on rare occasions—such as All Hallows Eve—they could sometimes slip through on their own. But once a soul crossed over, there was no way of restoring their mortality without dire consequences.

Now, a tremor of hope stirred within Anna's chest. What if the Black Testament contained such a powerful spell? Could it be? Could the impossible become possible? The revelations before her seemed to hold the key to defying death itself, to rescuing her mother back from the abyss that had claimed her.

There is a way…

These were the last words Rebecca Hale had whispered into Anna's mind before Anna had banished her into silence. Is this what she had meant? Was Anna's hope of seeing her mother alive again more than just a dream?

Hell grants nothing without sacrifice…

Anna felt the weight of Cotton Barlow's words press down on her like a tombstone. The promise of the Black Testament's power was both enticing and terrifying, like a knife cutting through darkness to expose hidden horrors. If she had any hope of rescuing her mother, she would have to delve deeper into Hell's infernal magic than she ever imagined.

"Is it true what that man said?" Anna asked. "Will my mother burn in Hell?"

Gideon hesitated, and in that moment, the weight of his silence shattered all of Anna's hopes. "We haven't much time, Mistress," he intoned. "Find the Black Testament, but remember this: for every step you take into the realm of the damned, a piece of your own humanity may be left behind. The forces you invoke are ancient and unforgiving."

A sudden chill swept through the air and made the well's surface shiver.

Anna's skin prickled with an awareness of something

unseen, something that lingered on the periphery of her senses. She could almost feel a presence, one that wasn't hers, stirring in the darkness of her consciousness. Something dark was uncoiling inside her mind. Her chest tightened, her breath growing shallow as her thoughts spiraled into a frenzy of terror. Images flashed in her mind—Rebecca Hale's face draped in her terrifying black mourning veil; her baleful eyes burning with malice; her voice a bewitching whisper, offering insidious promises of power.

In a panic, the words to dispel Gideon's spirit and close the window into the Veil spilled from Anna's mouth. His spectral figure convulsed, his features twisting in a pantomime of agony and release. With a shudder that sent tremors through the core of the earth, his ethereal tendrils dissolved into the black water.

Anna watched in silence as the shadows swallowed Gideon's form, drawing him back into the well. The surface smoothed over; the water returning to its calm stillness.

Anna tried to steady her breath, to quell the rising terror that threatened to engulf her, but her heart pounded as if trying to escape its bony cage. Dawn was approaching, and the stars had vanished from the indigo sky. The moonlight was all but gone now, leaving behind a desolate, eternal solitude. Anna's exhausted eyes burned, but she had work to do and no time to wait.

A corpse awaited her in the village cemetery.

Chapter 16

Cotton Barlow shifted uncomfortably on the cold, hard floor as the first hints of daylight bled through the cracked windows. Anna had used a leather strap to tie his wrists behind his back, and his ankle remained tightly cinched to the rope strung from the ceiling beam. A dull pain radiated from his broken knee. Dirt and blood still lingered in his mouth. His mind seethed with hatred and vengeance, a swirling storm of bloody thoughts.

Anna Jacobs...

Her name echoed in his head like a curse, a bitter reminder of the humiliation she had inflicted on him. Trapped in the blacksmith's shop, the embers of his fury smoldered deep within him.

But as he lay hobbled and bound, a sudden wind rattled the windows.

A strange chill flowed through the room and the temperature dropped. Cotton's breath materialized in the frigid air. He sensed a sudden presence that froze the blood in his veins.

He was no longer alone.

A disembodied voice echoed through the air, an enchanting whisper that seeped from the very walls.

"Cotton Barlow…"

Barlow's eyes darted around the room, searching the darkness for the haunting voice. The air grew heavy with the scent of smoke and fennel. Something moved in the corner, just beyond the limits of his perception. The shadows seemed to coalesce, drawing together as if they had a life of their own.

Barlow strained against his bindings, peering deep into the inky void that surrounded him. He couldn't be sure, but he thought he caught a glimpse of a woman, her long, scorched gown floating in the air around her vaporous figure.

"Show yourself! Who are you?" he demanded, his voice hoarse and raw.

"One who can grant thy heart's desires. I can see through the wounds in your soul, Cotton Barlow. Wouldst thou have thy revenge on the Crucible of Night?"

All at once, Barlow's memories came rushing back. His mind was dragged across the years to his past as a revered member of the Crucible, the secret society that had once welcomed him as a brother.

That was before they had cast him out.

The son of a wealthy Connecticut surgeon, Barlow had emerged as a prodigy in the arcane arts because of his father's membership in the order. Steeped in clandestine rituals and demonic pacts, the Crucible thrived on secrecy, its members bound by unholy oaths. Their relentless pursuit of forbidden knowledge fueled their every action. And Barlow, hungry for power, embraced it with a zeal that unnerved even the most seasoned among them. The Crucible was his sanctuary, where like-minded souls danced on the edge of the earthly and the profane.

But once Barlow tasted the allure of power, he became insatiable, and his pursuit of ascendance resulted in a trail of bloodshed. As he delved deeper into the dark arts of demonology, his experiments became increasingly more perverse, his rituals more sadistic. Whispers of his terrifying actions spread, and as his thirst for cruelty grew, his fellow acolytes recoiled in horror at the extent of his depravity. It wasn't long before his name became synonymous with unspeakable savagery.

Blinded by their obsession with the arcane, the order's elders eventually had no choice but to recognize the monster Barlow had become. The Crucible thrived in the shadows, and above all else, their laws forbade any act that might expose them to the light. When the mutilated bodies of Barlow's victims began surfacing around New Haven, the elders couldn't turn a blind eye to the truth—Cotton Barlow was a maniac. The blackest ink stained his soul, and he reveled in shedding innocent blood for no other purpose than it brought him pleasure.

The order, bound by its own perverse code, could no longer abide Barlow's defiance of their sacred rites. The night he was banished was carved in his memory like a scar that refused to fade. Barlow stood before them, his gaze devoid of remorse, as they laid bare the accusations—the mutilated corpses, the forbidden rites, the sacrilege that defiled the society's sacred halls. The evidence against him was damning, and even Barlow's silver tongue couldn't weave a convincing defense.

The air was thick with tension as they pronounced his sentence.

When it was done, the hooded figures turned their backs on Barlow, severing all ties with the man who had become a monster and forever striking his name from their unholy annals. Barlow knew expulsion meant more than the loss of his coveted position within the Crucible; it meant exile from the dark secrets and forbidden knowledge he so craved.

But Barlow was not one to swallow defeat. The society, in its misguided attempt to purge itself of his wickedness, had unwittingly unleashed a far greater evil upon the world. Now unbound by the society's restraints, Barlow indulged his bloodiest fantasies. The months that followed were a blur of black magic and unholy rituals. But even as he reveled in his newfound freedom, a darkness within him yearned for the recognition and power he had once wielded within the Crucible. The secret brotherhood that had cast him out became the object of his deranged obsession, and he swore to exact a vengeance that would shake the very foundations of their arcane order.

"Wouldst thou claim my infernal grimoire, Cotton Barlow? Wouldst thou wield its dark power to bring the Crucible to their knees?"

That enchanting voice whispered into Barlow's ear as he lay captive in the blacksmith's shop. His blood froze in his veins. He knew with terrifying certainty who that voice belonged to.

"Angéle de la Barthe…" he whispered into the darkness. His voice trembled with fear and awe in the presence of the infamous heretic burned alive for witchcraft. Here was her spirit risen before him, as if the flames that had consumed her still couldn't illuminate the darkness of her soul.

It was with Barlow's desire to find Angéle's fabled Black Testament simmering in his gut that he had set out in disguise with his young apprentice, the only person in this world who hadn't abandoned him—his son.

And Judith Alden had shot him dead.

Barlow's memories stirred, and the pain of his recent loss surged through him. A week had now passed since that fateful day. He remembered the events vividly. Aaron, with his youthful face and chestnut curls, had stood cowering before Judith's rifle in his muddy black cassock. His hands trembled as he held them high in surrender, and his dark eyes were wide and fearful. As Barlow watched, concealed behind the thick trunk of a maple, he could actually *feel* his boy's fear, the palpable terror that spread out among the trees like a fog.

"Please, spare me…" Aaron pleaded.

Judith's hard expression didn't change. Neither did her finger's pressure on the trigger. Her eyes were chips of ice.

"You do not have to kill me. No one will come looking for you," Aaron vowed. "You have my word on it as a man of God. I promise you!"

Trembling, he slipped his rosary from around his neck and clasped it between his palms as he sank to his knees, pleading for his life.

From where Barlow stood, his son looked small and pathetic; too young to die. A surge of paternal instinct swept through his insides, an unfamiliar sensation he had long suppressed in his pursuit of power. But there was nothing he could do. If he revealed himself now, this mysterious woman might only kill them both. His only option was to stay concealed and hope Aaron could talk his way out of it. This strange woman wouldn't dare harm a man she believed to be a man of God.

"I beg you!" Aaron pleaded. "Let me continue on my way. I swear to you I will put my back to this place and never return. I will tell no one that you are here. On my life and soul, I promise I will not reveal what I saw!"

A frantic cry echoed through the forest. "Mother!"

Barlow had inched around the tree trunk far enough to see William racing along the path.

"Mother! Stop!"

With her son rapidly closing the distance, Judith swung back to Aaron. "Are you alone?"

Barlow saw Aaron hesitate for just a fraction of a second— but long enough to reveal everything.

"Yes!" he exclaimed. There is no one—"

The rifle roared.

Barlow watched in silent horror as his son's head exploded with a spray of blood, brains, and bone. Aaron's lifeless body toppled over into the muddy leaves and snow.

The thundering echo of the gun-blast resounded endlessly among the trees.

"*No!*" cried William.

Even from a distance, Barlow could smell the smoke curling from the muzzle of Judith's rifle. She paused a moment, letting the pent-up air out of her lungs before advancing to peer down at Aaron's headless corpse. Blood gushed out into a patch of snow, staining it crimson. Judith stooped and plucked Aaron's rosary from the spreading pool. Her expression betrayed no remorse; neither did it hold any satisfaction—there was nothing personal about this killing.

William skidded to a halt and gasped with revulsion. He recoiled and stared at Judith in horror.

"Harden your resolve, William," she said. "We always knew this day might surely come. You know my mind on it: Let them live if possible; kill them if necessary. 'Tis the only manner by which we shall remain safe."

William glanced back at Aaron's corpse and looked away, too appalled to speak.

"Drag him deeper and leave him for the wolves," Judith instructed. "Be quick about it and be vigilant upon your return. 'Tis doubtful he travelled alone. "

Shouldering her rifle, she had left William with Aaron's corpse and went after the young white-haired girl who had run off at the first sight of Aaron.

The Alden boy did as he was told and abandoned Aaron's corpse in the woods. Barlow could still remember the taste of copper on his tongue as he cradled his son's headless body in his arms. The earth was too hard to dig a grave. All he had were stones with which to protect his boy's corpse from the scavengers.

In the days that Barlow had since spent skulking around the village, each heartbeat carried the weight of his grievous loss. It was the kind of grief that seeps into the marrow and festers, spawning a vengeful determination that burned within him like a raging inferno.

Aaron's desperate pleas echoed through Barlow's memories, a haunting refrain that echoed ceaselessly in his thoughts. His heart was now consumed by a grief so profound it threatened to devour him whole. The murder of his son, the only heir to the infamous Barlow lineage, left him with an emptiness that no potions or forbidden rites could fill. When darkness fell and he took refuge in the rotting buildings of the village, Aaron's face plagued his nightmares. His boy's terrified gaze pierced Barlow's heart, blaming him for not safeguarding the bloodline. And in the dead of night, when he stood studying the Aldens' cottage from the cover of the forest, Barlow's thoughts danced with macabre fantasies, each more depraved than the last.

Now, trapped in the smithy, Barlow's pulse raced as Angéle's seductive whispers sent tendrils of darkness slithering through his mind.

"I can help you, Cotton Barlow. Together, let us tear through the Veil and reclaim thy stolen son."

Barlow hesitated, the weight of her offer pressing down upon him like a fallen star. His eyes narrowed, suspicion intertwining with desperation. Yet, the pain of his son's death and the lust for vengeance overcame any sense of caution.

"Anything," he said, his gaze locked on the shadowy figure in the corner. "I would give anything to see my son again. Tell me, what must I do?"

A cruel smile ghosted across Barlow's lips as he listened to the spirit's response. He envisioned the suffering he would inflict upon Judith Alden. Vengeance seethed like a storm within him, ensnaring every thought with its violence. The hatred and bloodlust eclipsed his fading rationality. Judith had robbed him of everything, and soon it would be his turn to take everything from her—starting with her daughter.

As the first rays of dawn crept across the floorboards, a newfound sense of purpose stirred within Barlow. Angéle vowed to be his avenging angel, if only he would do her sinister bidding. The pages of her unholy book held the means for him to exact his revenge. All he had to do was obey. It was a small price to pay for such unfathomable power. He would raise Angéle's spirit up from perdition… and Mercy Alden would be the vessel for her return.

Chapter 17

Mercy couldn't bring herself to look at the motionless figure shrouded in moth-eaten linen just a few paces away. With her sister's freshly dug grave yawning open before her, she clutched an embroidered handkerchief she had found while exploring the village. Despite her best efforts, silent tears stained her bone-white cheeks and fell onto the dewy grass.

Dense gray clouds burdened the dreary morning sky, threatening an impending downpour. The early light of dawn struggled to seep through, casting a gloomy pallor over the land. Down the hill, a shroud of mist wrapped around the cottage like a mourning veil. The mountains loomed in the distance, cloaked in a thick fog that clung to their forested shoulders. The biting cold and dampness tingled Mercy's skin.

William, Judith, and Kisosen joined her in a semi-circle around Susanna's body. Their faces were dark with sorrow, their breaths shallow. Only the haunting cawing of crows in the encroaching forest broke the early morning stillness.

Mercy sniffled and wiped her nose with the handkerchief.

Had those crows come for her sister? Did they smell her flesh already beginning to rot as she lay dead at Mercy's feet?

"'Tis time," Judith murmured, her voice trembling with a grief too profound for words.

William's hands shook as he knelt beside his sister's shrouded corpse. His throat tightened against the swell of emotion. Kisosen placed a reassuring hand on his shoulder and William took a deep breath, inhaling the pine and earth, trying to steady himself. Together, they raised Susanna's body and lowered it gently into the open grave. The linen of the makeshift shroud rustled like a sigh beneath their hands.

William's vision blurred with tears and he whispered a last goodbye, his voice barely audible even in the stillness. Kisosen murmured a prayer in his native tongue, a melodic chant that rose and fell like the wind.

Mercy's chest clenched as she realized that this was truly the end—the last farewell to her sister. Her guilt-ridden eyes were heavy with grief as she stared into the pit, knowing it would soon be Susanna's final resting place. Struggling to hold back her sobs, her tender heart grappled with the enormity of the tragedy. She felt her curse crawling through her veins, an invisible noose that tightened with every misfortune her family faced. Her father murdered by an evil witch; her sister brutalized by some unseen tormentor; her mother's slow descent into madness—the afflictions hung like a shroud over Mercy's life. It was as if she had already lived a lifetime of despair in these godforsaken mountains. In this place, she was nothing but a trembling bud in a garden of tragedy.

As she stood over her sister's corpse, surrounded by the remnants of her shattered family, Mercy felt as though there was no escape from the darkness that clung to her. She was a pawn in a game she didn't understand, a sacrifice to forces beyond her control. And though she had no choice but to endure the weight of her despair, she couldn't rid herself of the idea that she was somehow fated to destroy her loved ones. All the sorrows they experienced had come to pass because of her presence among them. She was a cursed child, doomed to see her family fall apart one by one until only she remained.

In the quiet recesses of her troubled thoughts, Mercy replayed the events that brought about this unending series of misfortunes. Each tragedy was connected to her own actions, as if she had unwittingly orchestrated this tragic dance. It was *her* footsteps that had led her family to this fateful place, her presence that tempted the heavens to rain down calamity upon them.

Mercy's chest tightened with guilt as she recalled that horrific night when the villagers had come for her. Their whispers and suspicions had followed her ever since Abraham Brinley's barn collapsed while she was on her way to the market. That bitter twist of fate still haunted her to this day. She replayed the moment endlessly in her mind: the panicked neighing of the horse, the splintering wood, and the thundering crash that resonated throughout the village. Was it her appearance that had spooked the beast? Had her wicked eye set off that tragic chain of events?

Memories of that fateful night seeped into Mercy's thoughts like a venomous stream. She remembered huddling on her bed in the corner of her small, candlelit room. Fear tightened its grip on her as darkness fell, and she clutched her shawl around her shoulders. The fabric was soft, but it failed to calm her as a distant clamor announced the gathering of the mob. The howling wind carried the voices of the angry villagers, their rage fueling the flames of terror within her.

"Unclean! Wicked!" Their shouts grew louder. Mercy's pulse raced in time with the thunderous beat of the villagers' footsteps approaching her home. A sickening realization gripped her trembling form: they were really coming for her. She whispered desperate prayers, begging for deliverance and salvation as tears cascaded down her pale cheeks.

The image of their torches flickering through her bedroom window remained vivid in Mercy's mind. When she closed her eyes, she still saw their fiery glow like dancing spirits in the night. The mob had gathered outside, their faces twisted with hatred and ignorance. Mercy's heartbeat raced in her chest, her breaths quick and trembling. She had never knowingly harmed anyone, never dealt in dark arts or made pacts with demonic forces. But her peculiar eyes and translucent skin were a blank canvas for their prejudice and superstitions.

And tonight they hungered for blood.

"Bring her out!" they shouted, their voices rising in a frenzied chorus. "She's a witch! She's cursed us all!" The entire house shuddered under the relentless pounding of their fists on the front door. "Witch! Show yourself, foul creature of darkness!"

From below, there came a tremendous crash and commotion. She heard her father's angry shouts, and then the door to her bedroom splintered open, revealing the hostile faces of her neighbors. Their eyes blazed with the fervor of hysteria as they poured into the room like a swarm of angry hornets, spewing accusations.

"Witch! Sorceress! Spawn of darkness!"

Mercy's heart felt like it would explode from her tiny chest. She shrieked as they bound her hands and dragged her into the cold, unforgiving night. The torrent of their rage drowned her terrified pleas. The last thing she remembered before they stripped her naked was her mother's shrill screams. Mercy had never heard Mother's voice so *loud* before. Where did that sound come from? How had Mother ever kept something so powerful hidden inside her without it bursting free?

And as their pins and needles had pricked her flesh, Mercy's mind again sought refuge in her mother. She imagined the soft touch of her mother's hand and the reassuring lilt of her voice, memories that were a lifeline in that maelstrom of terror.

Now, with Susanna's body laying there in her grave, Mercy knew she was responsible for the devastating pain that had torn her family apart. She longed for redemption, a path to purify her soul from the sins that haunted her. But amid these desolate mountains, Mercy found no salvation, only a lonely journey with guilt as her only companion.

Judith looked at her, and it seemed to Mercy that the sorrow of countless lifetimes filled her mother's tired eyes.

"Speak your goodbyes, little angel," Judith said. "Let your sister hear your voice."

More tears sprang up in Mercy's eyes, and her throat felt as if she had swallowed a handful of stones. She wanted to speak, to whisper words of love, of memories shared and dreams shattered. But her voice couldn't make it past the lump clogging her windpipe.

"I can't, Mother," she choked with a wretched sob. "This is my doing."

Judith stepped closer and cupped Mercy's cheek with a weathered hand. Her weary eyes searched her daughter's forlorn face. "Don't say such things, my sweet."

"No, Mother. I *wished* this upon her," Mercy sobbed. "I envied her beauty and I coveted her charm. I have seen the way Kisosen sets his eyes upon her. No man will ever look upon me in such a manner. I know in my hidden heart that I wished Susanna malice and now look what has come of it." Mercy's voice cracked. Swollen with tears, her eyes gazed at the open grave in front of her. Heaps of rocky soil stood piled high on either side of the pit, waiting to swallow her sister forever. "'Tis the Devil in me."

Judith's heart shattered as she drew Mercy close and held her tight, offering the only comfort she could. Tears carved salty trails down her face while her daughter pressed against her and trembled like a fragile leaf in the wind.

After a moment, Judith gently pulled back to wipe Mercy's cheeks. "We will lay her to rest now, with love and reverence," she whispered. "It is not the darkness of the grave that should haunt your heart, but the beauty of the life she knew because of you."

The crows cawed again, indifferent to their suffering.

A distant rumble of thunder echoed through the valley as Kisosen began to fill the grave. Mercy flinched, and her heart broke anew with each soft thud of earth. William joined him, working mechanically.

Susanna's face, now forever frozen in death, plagued

Mercy's thoughts. Her older sister had been her closest confidante, her playmate in this desolate place. Mercy averted her eyes before the dirt covered Susanna's shrouded head. Her gaze fell upon a solitary tree, its bare branches reaching out like bony fingers, and she shivered.

"Mother," she whispered as she clung to Judith. "I feel so lost."

Judith tightened her grip, folding Mercy into a tender embrace. "You mustn't carry this burden alone, my sweet. We will find our way through this darkness together. We'll carry Susanna's memory in our hearts and find the strength to—"

A bone-rattling scream shattered the silence.

Judith spun around in time to see Kisosen and William dropping their shovels as they scrambled away from the grave, their faces contorted with sheer terror. She felt the blood drain from her cheeks an instant before her own horrified shriek tore free from her throat.

Susanna's corpse was rising into the air from her grave.

Slowly and with a macabre grace, her shrouded body emerged from the earth upside down, as if drawn upward by an invisible string tied around her ankles. She rose higher and higher, inch by painful inch, until her shoulders and head came into view from the deep pit and she remained hanging suspended in the air above it. Dirt and mud clung to her shroud like a second skin as the fabric came loose and unraveled, revealing the corpse underneath it.

With the crown of her head pointed toward the earth, Susanna's eyes were hollow and devoid of life, her skin a ghastly pale hue. Her hideous mouth seemed to smirk with rictus, her auburn hair cascading downward toward the pit. More of the shroud fell away the higher she rose, freeing her arms from its confines. Her lifeless limbs dropped from her sides but froze in mid-air, where they remained outstretched like an inverted crucifix.

William had slipped on the wet grass as he retreated, and Kisosen was now dragging him away from the blasphemous figure hanging suspended like a grotesque mockery of Christ.

Judith couldn't resist the uncontrollable need to scream as she clutched Mercy and fell back from the nightmarish spectacle of her daughter's unholy resurrection. In the years since they had fled Penance Cove, she had known her share of terror. But this was something far different. This was a new depth of horror, one that drowned her in despair. Panic spread through her like wildfire. She knew she should flee, that she should get her youngest daughter to safety. But her limbs were heavy and unresponsive, as though bound by invisible chains. The anguished wails bursting from her mouth made her light-headed and her knees wobbled beneath her. Her vision swam in and out of focus as she collapsed to the wet grass.

Mercy tore loose from her grasp and ran, fleeing toward the refuge of the cottage. Judith lunged for her and cried out, but her warbling screams had left her hoarse and breathless. Mercy was halfway down the hill when a shadowy figure came rushing out of the mist and intercepted her.

It was the stranger, the young Jacobs woman. She looked battered and bloody as she swept Mercy up into a tight embrace, as if she had survived some fearsome struggle.

In a final act of desecration, Susanna's corpse convulsed

violently in the air, contorting in ways no human body should. The sickening sounds of cracking bones shooting through the stillness drowned out Judith's horrified cries. Some unseen *thing* was doing this to her. Invisible fingers pried her dead eyes wide open so that she stared back at Judith with milky white orbs. Her lips split open in a hideous grin, and blood seeped from between her teeth as she hung upside down. It streamed in crimson rivulets down her cheeks and forehead before dripping into the dirt. Then, with a sudden and nauseating crack, Susanna's neck snapped, her head jerking unnaturally to the side.

Judith couldn't look away, even as she quaked with anguished sobs. Terror chained her gaze to the abomination levitating before her. She hovered on the edge of shock as her daughter's broken corpse plummeted back into the open grave and landed in a heap of tangled limbs.

Judith's legs buckled. The ground tilted beneath her and her vision blurred. She hunched over, vomiting bile onto the grass. The last thing she heard before consciousness slipped away was the haunting cries of the distant crows, as if beckoning her to join her daughter in the cold grave.

Chapter 18

Anna tore blank pages from William's journal and spread them over the rickety table in the Aldens' dining room.

"I need a map," she said. "The entire village. Every road and landmark you can remember."

William's fingers trembled as he took the charcoal stick she thrust at him. Still shaken by the harrowing spectacle at his sister's grave, he gave Anna a blank stare for a moment, blinking as if his ears were ringing from cannon fire. Then he hunched over the table and set himself to rendering a map.

Sickly bands of cold daylight cut through the windows as Anna laid a leather satchel on the table next to the parchments. After summoning Gideon at the well, she had ransacked a dilapidated storage shed for supplies. There, she found the rusty shovel she had needed for her grim task in the cemetery.

Standing alone in the burial ground, her breath had escaped like spectral wisps in the pre-dawn air. She surveyed the crumbling tombstones, their mossy epitaphs barely discernible in the dim light. A gnarled oak tree loomed over the graves, its branches crooked and skeletal, as though reaching out to deter her from the sacrilege she was about to commit.

Anna had waited for a moment, clearing her mind and allowing herself to be drawn to a grave. She ran her fingers over the cold, damp earth and sensed a powerful, dark energy rising from below the soil. Yes, this is what she needed—a victim of the brutal massacre that took place a century ago was buried here.

Anna's pulse quickened as she excavated the grave, one shovel-full at a time. The earth had compacted over the decades and resisted her efforts, but she was relentless. If she had any hope of finding the Black Testament and saving her mother from Hell, she needed what lay buried deep beneath the rocky soil. Her breathing grew heavy and her fingers went numb while she dug into the dirt. She didn't sense any restless spirits haunting this hallowed ground, but she couldn't shake the feeling that the eyes of the dead were upon her, their ghostly stares penetrating her soul.

With one last powerful thrust, her shovel connected with wood, producing a hollow echo that pierced the silence. She hadn't been digging long. This grave was shallow, the deceased buried quickly. Anna's palms were slick as she pried open the crumbling coffin lid, exposing the remains of the long-forgotten soul within. The skeleton lay bare and desiccated, its jaw hanging open in an eternal scream. Anna's hand stayed steady as she reached for the skull, her fingers curling through the hollow eye sockets. As a child, the feeling would make her flesh crawl. These days, she didn't even flinch.

Now, while William focused on his sketch of the village, Anna could feel the uneasy energy in the Aldens' cottage, like static electricity prickling her skin. Judith and Mercy huddled together in Judith's bedroom upstairs, trying to recover from the shocking desecration of Susanna's corpse. Anna and the two men had caught up on all that had happened since they last saw each other. Anna disclosed what she had learned about the Black Testament, but omitted her clash with Cotton Barlow. Instead, she blamed her injuries on her encounter with Angéle de la Barthe's dark spirit in the rectory. She also chose not to reveal what Barlow had said about Judith being a murderer. Iit was a secret best kept to herself, especially since Judith had already tried to shoot her once. How far would the woman go to keep the truth hidden?

Kisosen studied Anna's scorched cloak with suspicion. She wasn't fooling him; he recognized a gunshot wound when he saw one. But despite any doubts he had about her story, he remained silent. Anna paid no attention to his scrutinizing gaze as she sorted through her stolen satchel, unpacking the macabre artifacts she had taken from the graveyard. William glanced up from his sketch as she crafted a makeshift pendulum using twine and the pointed tip of a finger bone.

"How is that going to help us?" Kisosen asked. He stared at her skeptically, his arms crossed over his broad chest. The strain he'd endured since Susanna's death was clear on his smooth features.

"Trust me," Anna replied. Her cold blue eyes met his, daring him to challenge her further. She didn't need their approval; she needed to focus on the task at hand as she suspended the bone pendulum above William's detailed map of Sévérité. With a deep breath, she cleared her thoughts and started reciting incantations in the serpentine language of magic. When the pendulum began to sway on its own, guided by the unseen hand of a familiar serving her from beyond the Veil, she followed the tiny movements with her eyes, noting the spots where the supernatural energy was most concentrated.

"Something's wrong," she murmured, furrowing her brow. The pendulum's oscillations became more aggressive, fighting against her control. "It's resisting."

"Resisting?" William asked. Exhaustion and fear dulled his gray eyes as he gazed at her.

"Sometimes dark forces are strong enough to push back against my attempts to locate them," Anna explained. She grit her teeth as she continued to wrestle with the pendulum. "Damn it," she cursed under her breath. She felt the frustration boiling within her, but she refused to let it show. She needed to remain calm and collected. "Whatever we're dealing with here isn't afraid to challenge me directly. It's powerful, and it doesn't want me here. Let me try something else." Abandoning the pendulum, she reached back into the satchel.

William's eyes widened at what she produced. "Are those —"

"Teeth, yes. Now please remain silent unless I speak to you again."

Anna closed her eyes and whispered a few words over the yellowed teeth she had extracted from the skull in the cemetery. She then cast them skittering across the map as if she were a gambler playing dice. A heavy, oppressive silence hung in the air as Anna began another chant in a long-forgotten tongue. Her eyes blazed with the ecstasy of power as she became enthralled in the rapture of witchcraft.

A cold gust of wind swept through the room. The teeth on the map began to vibrate, and the map itself seemed to come to life, its lines and symbols glowing with an otherworldly light. Anna sensed an unseen force in the room with them, a presence not of this world.

The teeth shifted, their movements erratic and frenzied. Anna's heart raced, beads of sweat forming on her brow. Suddenly, the teeth snapped together from all corners of the table, shooting across the parchments and converging in a tight mound on one specific spot.

"The chapel," Anna breathed, her chest heaving from the mental exertion of the ritual. "The Black Testament is in the chapel."

She leaned over the table, scrutinizing the crude map. Her fingers traced the cobweb-like lines that outlined the abandoned streets. Each lane appeared to be an artery, pumping lifeblood into the center of the town. There, beneath the labyrinth of charcoal lines, the truth became clear. The two main roads formed an unmistakable cross, intersecting at the village chapel, which loomed in the heart of the forsaken settlement.

A chill slithered over Anna's flesh as she recognized the symbolism. The crossroads: a place of convergence where the realms of the living and the dead intertwined. It was an ancient symbol, potent with meaning and power. In the occult texts she had studied, tales of unholy rituals and dark pacts centered around such intersections. But crossroads were also places of protection, of powerful warding against evil.

Anna's pulse pounded in her ears as she realized the magnitude of the discovery. The entire village was one big cross. Sévérité was no ordinary ghost town; it was a nexus of energies, a place where the lines between the worlds were thin. The chapel's purpose became even clearer.

"It's a vault," she murmured as it all came together in her mind. "The French settlers didn't come here to escape persecution. They came here because they were hiding something, something so evil that they had to guard it out here in these desolate mountains where no one would ever come looking for it. They brought the Black Testament here and built the chapel as a vault to keep it hidden away forever."

And then another realization. She remembered the warning the village priest had left in the rectory:

I fear that if we do not flee this very night, we all shall be condemned to turn on each other in this cursed place, forever haunted by the promise of the murderers we will become…

"The villagers never fled," Anna said. "They turned against each other and died here, all of them—their minds poisoned by the Black Testament's evil influence. It was their spirits you came across in the forest."

"If I hadn't seen them with my own eyes, I never would have believed it," Kisosen vowed.

"Belief isn't the issue," Anna said. "The issue is finding the source of this evil spirit's power before it destroys this family." *And using it to save my mother from Hell,* she thought. "Let's not waste time."

Gathering her coat from where it hung draped across a

chair, she turned to leave.

Mercy stood at the foot of the stairs.

"Mercy," said William. "What are you doing down here? Is Mother still resting?"

But Mercy didn't answer. Instead, she ran across the room and flung her thin arms around Anna's waist.

"Are we safe here?" she whispered. Desperation filled her milk-white face. "We have nowhere else to turn."

Anna's chest tightened, a familiar ache arising as memories of her mother's death scratched at her. As a child, how many times had she turned to Abigail for the same comfort and reassurance that Mercy now so desperately craved?

And how many times had she been turned away? Told it was foolish to be afraid?

"Of course," Anna replied, though her voice was distant, put off by the girl's unexpected display of affection.

After a moment, Mercy released her embrace and offered Anna a torn scrap of paper. In the dim light of the room, Anna scrutinized the parchment—ancient symbols and cryptic markings filled every inch. Her brow furrowed as she tried to decipher their meaning. Mercy watched her, her mismatched eyes wide with fearful curiosity.

"Where did you find this?" Anna asked, shooting Mercy a questioning glance.

"Under my bed," the girl whispered, her voice trembling. "I never put it there, I swear."

"Of course not," Anna murmured, her gaze returning to the parchment. The symbols seemed to dance before her eyes and she could feel a hum of dark energy emanating from the page. It made her skin crawl.

"Anna," William said. "What does it mean?"

"Summoning," Anna replied, her mind racing. "And binding. This is powerful magic, far beyond anything an uninitiated could handle. Someone's been dabbling in forces they don't understand—and they've targeted your sister."

"It is the Ghost-Witch," Kisosen said, his voice laced with contempt.

"Perhaps," Anna conceded, her thoughts turning darker. "Or something worse, far worse—the spirit of Angéle de la Barthe." Anna's eyes never left the parchment. "Mercy, can you recall anyone who might have had access to your room? Anyone besides your family or Kisosen?"

Mercy pondered briefly before shaking her head. "None but us."

An icy dread wormed its way into Anna's gut. Either Cotton Barlow had somehow slipped into the Aldens' cottage unnoticed, or one of *them* had left the scrap of paper under Mercy's bed.

It seemed unthinkable, but Anna couldn't arrive at any other conclusion.

"We must act quickly," she said, her voice cold and determined. "Before these threats escalate further."

Without another word, she rolled up the parchment and tucked it into her satchel.

"I will come with you," Kisosen said.

Anna turned, her eyes narrowing with suspicion. But it was William who objected before she got a chance.

"I don't think that would be wise."

He doesn't trust Kisosen around me, Anna realized. It was a useful piece of knowledge. She would have to be careful around the Indian.

"I agree," she said, her tone leaving no room for argument. She leveled her eyes at Kisosen. "Stay here and keep watch over the others."

"Thank you, Anna," William breathed, relief etched on his face. "We're in your debt."

"Save your gratitude until this is over," Anna replied, striding toward the door. As she went, she couldn't help but notice that the shape of the scrap Mercy gave her matched a missing corner from one of the parchment sheets laying on the table—the sheets that had come from William's journal.

Chapter 19

The paths twisted like veins toward the heart of the forsaken village. A fine, gray drizzle shrouded the desolate mountain pass in a ghostly embrace. Anna's wet coat clung to her figure, her raven-black hair plastered to her pale neck as she and William trudged toward the chapel. Their boots left muddy prints on the path as they went. The smell of damp earth, decomposing leaves, and rotting wood filled their lungs as the air hung heavy with moisture.

Anna's breaths came quick from the anticipation coursing through her veins. Once again, she felt that terrible dark energy in the air. Electric and tingling. As if the Devil's infernal grimoire beckoned her closer. She felt her spine stiffen with every step she took, a sense of unease that refused to be ignored. She tried to rationalize it, to convince herself that it was merely her imagination playing tricks on her. But deep down, she knew the truth—she was falling under the Black Testament's dark influence. Even amidst the turmoil of her thoughts, there was a perverse thrill that coursed through her veins, a forbidden ecstasy that she couldn't deny. The darkness called to her, promising power beyond imagining—if only she would surrender herself completely.

"Mercy comes to play here," William said. He wore a stony expression to hide his apprehension as he glanced at the hollow buildings. A glistening veil of misty rain covered the dilapidated ruins. "She always said she wasn't afraid of the ghosts."

"I imagine she has since had a change of heart," Anna remarked.

William went silent for a moment. The drizzle's soft pitter-patter resonated through the silent lanes, punctuated by the occasional drip from leaky rooftops. "You believe this book, this Black Testament, is responsible for the horrors that happened here?" he asked.

"I believe it is not just a book," Anna replied. "It is a *phylactery* for Angéle de la Barthe's malevolent spirit."

"I beg your pardon?"

"A phylactery is like a soul cage, binding a necromancer to the mortal realm," Anna explained. "The Black Testament is a vessel containing Angéle's undying spirit. The Devil himself bestowed his gospel upon her. She wielded its infernal power, and when the Inquisitors condemned her to burn, she transmuted her soul to live eternally within its cursed pages. But like all arcane items, the grimoire requires sacrifice to sustain its power. Over the centuries, Angéle's ghost has reached out for victims, whispering into their minds, driving them to unspeakable acts and feeding on their souls. She drove the villagers to massacre each other here a century ago —and she very nearly compelled me to kill you last night. Even now, I can feel her power, like icy fingers probing my defenses, searching for weaknesses she can exploit."

Anna noticed a peculiar expression on William's face. He was keeping something from her.

"You've felt her too, haven't you?" she prodded.

He hesitated, unsure about how much he wanted to reveal. "There is a voice that calls to me when I am alone in the dark, tempting me with sinful promises."

Anna's lips pressed into a grim frown. "It is the book calling to you. If we are to save your family, we must find the Black Testament and banish the witch once and for all."

"But how do you intend to destroy it? If it were possible, wouldn't the settlers have already done so?"

Anna nodded but remained silent, keeping her true motive a secret. She had no intention of destroying the Black Testament; her sole interest in finding it was to use it to redeem her mother's soul before it was too late.

As they walked together in silence, a more troubling question crept into Anna's thoughts: Why hadn't Angéle de la Barthe's spirit killed her last night in the rectory? It was a mystery that had been stalking the edges of her mind all day. Stripped of her protective talisman, Anna was defenseless and at the witch's mercy. Why did de la Barthe spare her after tormenting Susanna so mercilessly? This question scratched at Anna's mind like a persistent, unsettling whisper. Was there a hidden purpose that she was supposed to unravel? She recalled what she knew of vengeful spirits and their cunning ways, tales passed down through generations of witches who had possessed her mother's Book of Shadows before her. What if de la Barthe's apparent act of mercy was but a ploy to ensnare her? To use her for some nefarious purpose beyond her understanding? The unanswered possibilities weighed heavily on Anna, and a growing sense of foreboding gnawed at her gut the more she thought about them.

Anna's pulse quickened as they approached the looming silhouette of the old chapel. Its spire reached for the clouds like a skeletal finger. The soft, rhythmic sound of their footsteps broke the eerie silence as they splashed through the shallow puddles of the town square. Even the earth seemed to absorb the anguish and torment of this place.

Together, they ascended the chapel's steps, their boot heels echoing through the empty air. Anna hesitated a moment, her resolve tested by the creeping dread that seeped into her bones. Was de la Barthe's spirit in there? Waiting for them?

"This place reeks of darkness," William muttered, as if reading her thoughts.

Pushing aside her apprehensions, Anna steeled her nerves and hauled on the chapel's massive oak door. The heavy iron hinges emitted a slow creaking groan as they cracked open.

The interior was an ominous cavern of darkness, the pale daylight barely penetrating the oppressive gloom. A musty smell of old wood and dust drifted out to greet them. They paused at the threshold to spark their lanterns before moving deeper into the sanctuary.

Dead candles lined the aisles, their waxen remains twisted like pale corpses. Benches lay overturned, hymnals scattered, and dust coated every surface. The air was stale, cold, and thick with age-old incense and decay. Rays of light filtered through the stained glass, casting macabre patterns on the crumbling altar. Cobwebs hung like veils, their delicate threads swaying in the breeze wafting through the door. The chapel seemed alive and aware of their presence, as if it breathed.

"Anna," William whispered. "The voice, I can hear it calling to me."

"What does it say?"

"That you are not to be trusted." There was a fearful tremor in his whisper now. "That I should kill you before you destroy us all."

His words sent an icy tingle racing down Anna's backbone. "It is the book preying upon your fears," she replied evenly. "Stay close."

Their lantern flames danced as they combed through the decaying remnants of the chapel, searching the debris-strewn floor and dilapidated pews.

Something awful happened here, Anna thought. *Only a terrible struggle could have left the sanctuary in such disarray. Is this where the villagers turned on each other? Is this where they died?*

Anna brushed her fingers over the worn wood of the confessional booth, seeking out hidden compartments. Only the constant patter of the rain on the roof broke the oppressive silence. Time seemed to slow down with each minute that passed during their futile search, and nagging sense of doubt eroded Anna's confidence. What if she was wrong? What if the Black Testament wasn't here?

No, it *had* to be here somewhere. Anna sensed its presence, its dark energy calling to her. Just as she began losing hope, her attention drifted up to the radiant stained glass window at the end of the chapel.

William stopped what he was doing and followed her gaze

upward. "What is it?"

"That window shouldn't be here," Anna murmured, her eyes fixed on the multicolored glass. "This chapel is over a hundred years old. This sort of stained glass would have been unimaginable out here in the wild. Most meeting houses of this age were simple and humble out of necessity. And yet, the settlers somehow saw fit to devote the time and resources necessary to craft this image."

Anna approached the window, peering up to study it closer. Its once magnificent fragments had dimmed with age and neglect, their vibrant colors now muted by the passage of time. But its depiction of an angelic warrior was still unmistakable. Anna noted the blue and gold hues of the angel's armor; the flaming sword he held aloft with one hand, and the spear he wielded with the other. His features were stern and determined, the wings spread wide in a display of power and authority.

"It's Michael, the archangel who fought against Satan and his legions," Anna said. She marveled at the craftsmanship, so out-of-place in this remote wilderness. The archangel appeared almost alive, poised for battle. Yet, as her gaze lingered on the glass, she noticed something peculiar. She had seen countless depictions of Michael in her studies, but this one was different. Curiosity scratched at her thoughts as she approached the window, her footsteps echoing through the emptiness of the chapel.

"Something isn't right," she said. "Most representations of angels depict their eyes looking skyward in the veneration of Heaven. But in this one, Michael is looking down, with his spear aimed toward the floor."

"As if he is standing watch over something," William murmured.

Anna nodded and let her gaze roam over the wide floorboards. They were worn and darkened with age, but what struck her was an irregularity in the direction of the planks. They weren't laid in straight, uniform lines across the room. Instead, long strips of iron were inlaid among the timber, cutting across the room in various angles and directions—a design that felt intentionally hidden.

"Help me clear these away," Anna said, shoving the pine benches aside to get a better look at what lay obscured beneath them. Within minutes, they had cleared enough of the floor to expose the full image inlaid into the wood under their feet.

A giant five-pointed pentacle.

"What blasphemy is this?" William said, inching backward toward the circle's periphery. "Devil worship in the house of God?"

"Nothing of the sort," Anna said, her gaze still riveted to the floor. The pentacle occupied most of the sanctuary with its massive size. "Five-pointed stars have been found scratched into the walls of churches all over the Old World. They were believed to be a protective symbol as far back as the Middle Ages. It is supposed to symbolize the five wounds of Christ. Their protective powers were based on the folk belief that a demon couldn't resist following a line to its end. These stars, forming just one interlocking line with *no* end, could forever trap the evil spirit as it pursued its endless task." She glanced up at the stained glass window looming over them. The archangel Michael stared directly at the center of the pentacle.

"It's under the chapel," Anna whispered, her breath trembling. "They buried the Black Testament underground and built the church over it to seal it away forever on sanctified ground." Her gaze wandered around the floor. She knelt and traced her fingers along the cold, hard iron, feeling the energy radiating from the symbol. She had delved deep into the forbidden arts and battled creatures from beyond the grave, but this was unlike anything she had ever encountered. It thrummed with power.

"There must be some way down there," William said. "Perhaps this chapel has a crypt."

Anna gave a doubtful shake of her head. "These mountains are solid granite; excavating anything deeper than a root cellar beneath the chapel would have been impossible, let alone a whole crypt." Intermittent water droplets fell from the sodden roof as she rounded the altar at the heart of the chapel. Rotten from decades of water damage, the floorboards were soft and spongy beneath her feet as she looked around.

Without warning, the planks beneath her gave way with a sickening crack.

A horrified gasp escaped Anna's lips as she plummeted into the darkness. She had time to suck in a ragged breath as she fell, and then she plunged into water.

Freezing liquid filled Anna's mouth, and panic surged within her. She thrashed and sputtered in whatever subterranean pool she had fallen into, her feet scrabbling beneath her until they brushed against solid rock. The frigid water seeped into her very bones, numbing her limbs. She had to get back onto dry land—fast.

In the inky darkness, Anna dragged herself from the water onto a slab of rock and strained her eyes to see. Her lantern had hissed and died when she hit the water, leaving her in near-total blackness. From what she could tell, she had fallen perhaps twenty feet from the hole in the chapel's floor. As her eyes adjusted to the darkness, she marveled at her surroundings.

The church was built over a giant cavern carved by the relentless force of an underground river. Monstrous, teeth-like stalactites hung from the ceiling. The black river flowed through the bedrock of the mountain, stretching into darkness in both directions as it travelled down toward the Connecticut River in the south.

Soaked and shivering, Anna fumbled with her lantern until she spotted something in the water—a pale skull, eyes wide and empty, teeth exposed in a grim rictus.

"Anna!" William's alarmed face appeared over the jagged edges of the broken planks overhead. The flickering light of his lantern cast an eerie glow across the underground cavern.

"I'm alright!" Anna called back. "Stay where you are with the light!"

She inched closer to the water, peering into its depths. The surface shimmered as William's lamplight revealed a chilling scene—bones scattered across the underground riverbed. Over a dozen skulls swirled just below the water's surface, distorted by the river's current. Hollow-eyed corpses, preserved by the icy waters for more than a century, stared up at her. Some were shackled with rusty chains, others wrapped in tattered shrouds, all bearing the cruel marks of time's relentless march.

Anna's heart started pounding as she came to a realization. This hidden catacomb was a mass grave. This is where they had condemned the cursed villagers who had succumbed to the sinister power of the Black Testament.

And there, perched atop a mossy rock jutting like a tombstone in the middle of the rushing torrent, was a massive chest.

Anna charged back into the water, her veins pulsing with hope. As she waded across to the glistening stone slab, the subterranean river churned around her, swollen by the spring thaw and carved over eons of erosion.

Intricate pentacles were engraved on the surface of the old, weathered chest. The wood appeared blackened, as if scorched by something smoldering within. The surrounding air seemed to pulse with a dark and malevolent energy that throbbed against Anna's frozen flesh. Her trembling hand reached out to touch it, her fingers tracing the patterns etched into the wood. The chest's iron strappings were rusted and cold to the touch. As she brushed her hand across the latch, it squeaked slightly.

Anna hesitated, an icy tingle of dread creeping over her. Why was the latch hanging open? And where was the lock? Why wasn't this chest sealed tight?

With trembling hands, she gripped the lid. The chest cracked open, its hinges protesting with a shrill wail.

There was nothing inside.

The Black Testament was gone.

"No," Anna whispered. "No, this can't be." Her voice carried through the sepulchral catacomb as a bitter taste filled her mouth. Someone, or something, had emptied the chest before her. Any hope of saving her mother from Hell vanished as quickly as the current rushing around her. An overwhelming sense of despair crashed over her.

Without the Black Testament, Abigail was lost forever.

Anna stood back, still staring at the empty spot in the chest where the grimoire should have been, as if she could somehow will it to return. She thought of the owl William had discovered crucified in the woods; of the scrap of parchment Mercy had found hidden beneath her bed. Not only had someone already claimed the Black Testament; they were *using* it. But who? Who would have cast such a gruesome hex on Susanna?

Anna's mind raced through the only suspects she could think of. With Judith's husband now dead, her life would be much easier if she had fewer children to care for. Then again, were it not for William's obligations to his mother and siblings, the young man could leave the farmstead and start a family of his own. And considering the circumstances under which her family fled Penance Cove, it was possible that Mercy always *had* been a witch. Anna shuddered as William's words came back to haunt her.

Mercy comes here to play...

A bone-numbing apprehension gripped Anna as she considered the possibility. Had the girl come across de la Barthe's infernal book during one of her wanderings around the village? Had the Black Testament called to her the same way it beckoned Anna herself?

Anna suddenly sensed a presence in the cavern with her. She wasn't alone. William must have found a way down to join her. She turned around, determined to track down the one who had stolen the grimoire and stop them before it was too late.

Kisosen was in the water behind her.

Anna had but an instant to see the malice burning in his dark eyes. Then the butt of his pistol grip came crashing into her temple and her world went a deeper shade of black.

Chapter 20

The Burned Lady told Mercy where to find the man, her whispers guiding Mercy's footsteps as she crept through the silent village. She moved with the grace of a phantom, drawn forward by an otherworldly pull she couldn't ignore. Her alabaster skin was nearly translucent in the dreary afternoon drizzle. Dew made her white hair shine like a silken web, and her heart raced with a restless energy, driven by a longing that had led her away from the cottage while her mother slept.

Mercy had seen him in her dreams again. The mysterious stranger she had encountered in the chapel days ago. The Burned Lady whispered his name as she led Mercy onward—Cotton.

Mercy couldn't resist. She had to see him again, to know him, to understand the strange connection that bound them together. Her pulse quickened as she scanned the crumbling buildings, searching for any sign of the priest, the only outsider she had spoken to in years. He'd been so kind to her that day when she'd encountered him in the chapel. Though he still feared for his life, he had forgiven Mother for murdering his companion. Among all the men Mercy had met, he was the only one who didn't find her repulsive. He spoke of salvation and redemption, of a life away from the suffocating shackles of her confinement.

And he had spoken of a cure.

It was the hope of seeing him once more that drew Mercy back to the chapel again and again, not her concern for her mother's everlasting soul.

As she wandered through the desolation, she tried to find solace in the lonesome silence. The ghost town had become her sanctuary over the years, a place where she could escape the endless boredom of her existence. But today, something was different. The guilt of Susanna's death followed Mercy everywhere she went.

A soft and familiar voice sliced through the eerie silence of the empty village. "Mercy."

Mercy's heart skipped a beat. She turned around slowly.

It was him. Calling to her from inside the old blacksmith's shop.

The wooden sign above the entrance had faded, and Mercy could barely make out the engravings as she approached the darkened entrance. The heavy wooden door creaked open as she pushed it aside. Her breath was rapid and shallow as she paused at the threshold, a thrilling sense of anticipation rushing through her.

The air inside was heavy with the smell of iron and rust. Abandoned tools littered the floor. The dim light struggled to penetrate the gloom through the cracked and dirty windows. It cast fractured rays across the floor and left the corners of the room shrouded in shadow.

As Mercy's eyes adjusted, she made out the shape of the room. To her right stood the ancient forge, long extinguished, its heavy anvil covered in a layer of dust. Rusted chains and hooks hung from the walls, relics from when this place had been a thriving smithy.

And there, in the center of the room, she saw him.

Cotton Barlow lay propped on his elbows on the filthy floor, a shadowy figure draped in his dark robes. His hands were tied behind him, and one ankle was tethered to a rope strung from a sturdy beam. There was something sickening about the grotesque angle of his knee, and blood streaked his bearded chin. His presence was like a void, sucking all the light and warmth from the room.

Mercy's heart thudded in her chest at the sight of him.

"Mercy." His soft and raspy voice, like silk slipping through Mercy's fingers, broke the stillness. "You came. I've been waiting for you, child."

Mercy approached cautiously. "How did you know I would come?" she whispered, her voice quivering with fear and curiosity. She took a hesitant step closer, her footsteps crunching across the cracked and uneven floorboards.

"Because she speaks to me, too," Barlow replied. His words were a low, hypnotic murmur, drawing her nearer with each syllable. "That voice that you hear, the one that guided you here to me—the angel's voice. She has chosen you, Mercy."

Mercy stared at him, stunned. The Burned Lady was an angel? How could that be? It felt wrong. She remembered the awful fear she felt whenever the Burned Lady came to her. How could she possibly be an angel? But this man was a priest. Surely he wouldn't lie to her about such things.

Mercy recalled Reverend Finneran's sermons back in Penance Cove. Finneran was a slight and reedy man, but his voice spewed fire and brimstone whenever he described the seven angels in the Book of Revelations. Far from being benevolent protectors, they were merciless and ferocious as they executed God's wrath, turning the sea to blood and unleashing darkness and destruction during the End Times.

Perhaps the Burned Lady was an angel just like them?

Angel…

The word resonated in Mercy's mind. With her snowy hair and moonlight skin, Mother always called her an angel. But Mercy knew better.

"Why me?" she asked. "Why did the angel choose me? There is nothing heavenly about me."

Barlow struggled to sit, his dark eyes pleading as he leaned forward to show her his bound wrists. "Please…"

Mercy knelt beside him. Her fingers trembled as she fumbled with the leather strap that bound him. "Who did this to you?"

Barlow winced in pain as Mercy's clumsy fingers worked to free him. "It was the Jacobs woman. She is not what she seems. She worships something… something dark and ancient. She tied me up here as a sacrifice."

With one last pull, Mercy released him from his restraints. Barlow groaned in relief as his hands sprung free. He massaged his aching limbs before gently loosening the noose from around his wounded leg.

"Thank you, my child," he said. "I thought I would die here, alone. You've shown me a kindness I didn't expect to find in this forsaken place." His eyes twinkled as he fixed them on Mercy's crimson one. "Perhaps this is why the angel brought us together. She wants me to save you."

"Save me? From what?"

"From the Devil's grasp," he replied. "From the curse that marks you as one of his favored. I can help you, Mercy. I can cleanse you, free you from this affliction."

Mercy furrowed her brow, looking at him with a mix of confusion and suspicion. "How?"

"Have you ever wondered why the Lord cursed you with your appearance, Mercy? It is not His will, but the work of Satan himself. *You* are to blame for the calamities that have befallen your family, just as you suspect. The bleeding trees, the birds, your father's ghastly death—they can all be attributed to *you*. You may not even be aware of your actions, but you are the cause, nonetheless."

The priest's words filled Mercy with a sense of dread. "How may I be both innocent and guilty at once?"

"An evil hand was laid upon you as a babe. You have been forever cursed for it, your blood poisoned and your flesh corrupted. You have become an unwitting portal, a gateway through which the Devil may exert his infernal influence. The abomination that killed your father that day in the woods was nothing less than a succubus sent by Satan himself."

"A succubus?"

"A demon intent on defiling the souls of the righteous. Its presence among you was made possible by the dark forces that gather around you. You are a beacon for Hell—and wherever you go, its demons will follow."

A wave of disbelief washed over Mercy, but an insidious doubt still crept into her mind. She glanced at her hands, the pale skin that set her apart from everyone she had ever met. Could it be true? Was she truly touched by the Devil?

Barlow sensed her inner turmoil and seized the opportunity. "I fear your father's death was just the beginning, Mercy. Do you know how the Devil wages war for souls? He preys upon your most secret of fears. He does it with infinite patience, tormenting you with one affliction after another, shaking your faith little by little until you would rather die than endure it any longer. And then, when you are at your weakest, he comes to you offering salvation. This is what has been happening to your family. Through you, Satan has been testing you and your loved ones, throwing horror after horror at you, breaking you down until you all can take no more. Soon, you will yield the first blood of your womanhood. When that day comes, at long last, you will fulfill the curse that was laid upon you years ago."

"What will happen then?" Mercy asked, though she dreaded the answer.

"You will bring about the deaths of your entire family. Unless you are purified, you can expect the Evil One will not stop until he has seen each of you destroyed."

Mercy stared at him. "Even if you are being truthful, you have yet to explain how you intend to release me from this curse."

"The Puritans believed there is no cure for witchcraft; death is the only remedy for sorcery. But men of my faith share a much different perception of witchcraft. There is an ancient ritual, one known only to a select few of my order. If performed correctly, it may deliver you from the clutches of the Adversary and return you to the light."

Mercy's pulse raced. What if it were possible? What if what he was saying was true? "And you can perform this ritual?"

Cotton nodded. "The Roman Church does not recognize the rite. Even among my brotherhood, it remains a forbidden secret. That I speak of it now might well see me branded a heretic. But I am certain I can cleanse you and free you of this affliction."

Mercy's face darkened, her instincts immediately on the defensive. Could she trust him?

Cotton read her suspicion. "I know what I am asking of you. You must entrust yourself to a man you have known for but days, a priest who may very well see you hanged for witchcraft. Truthfully, I fear there is nothing I can say that will convince you to trust me. I can only tell you that if you wish to cleanse yourself and save your family from Satan's malice, it will require a leap of faith. You can prevent the unthinkable, Mercy. You have the power to save what remains of your family."

Having made his case, Barlow fell silent to let Mercy think it over.

Mercy was trembling now, her fingers clutching the edges of her threadbare dress. "This ritual that you claim will cure me. How does it work?"

Barlow paused, his expression going dark and solemn. "It is an ancient rite of exsanguination, a sacred sacrament passed down through the ages."

A chill rolled down Mercy's backbone. "Exsanguination? You mean bloodletting?"

"The Devil's unclean hand defiled your blood with his touch. The only way to cure you before you give yourself over to him is to drain you of your poisoned blood and replace it with that of another."

"What do you mean, drain me?"

"The ritual is not without its risks. It will take you to the brink of death, but it is the only way to save your soul from eternal damnation."

Mercy shook her head. "Mother will never allow it. And Kisosen—"

"Ah, Kisosen… your Indian friend. Would it surprise you to learn that I am no stranger to his tribe?"

Mercy gave him a stunned look.

"I spent years ministering to the Abenaki. Tell me, Mercy… how exactly do you think I came to learn about your family's whereabouts?"

Mercy's expression darkened as she caught on. "Impossible. Kisosen would never betray us."

"Can you be so sure? Has he told you about his sister?"

"Only that she fell victim to the same evil sorceress that killed my father."

Barlow threw his head back and let out a derisive chuckle. "Is that what he told you?"

His laughter made Mercy cringe. She went quiet, afraid that he was mocking her, that she had somehow disappointed him.

Sensing her discomfort, Barlow's voice dropped to a low, soothing murmur. "Have you ever longed for a life beyond this solitude, Mercy? Perhaps a husband and family of your own? You may yet have them… once I set you free from your curse. Allow me to remove the Devil's mark and make you whole again, born anew like any other child of God. It is not too late."

Tears welled in Mercy's strange eyes as she contemplated the gravity of his offer. What if he was telling the truth? Could this man of God truly rid her of her curse? The hope of being accepted, of no longer being an outcast, was a tantalizing promise. The unbearable weight of her isolation pressed down upon her, a festering wound in her heart that begged for healing. She yearned for a future that no longer involved hiding in the shadows.

Without realizing it, Mercy nodded. "What must I do?"

Barlow's gaze never left hers. "You must trust in me, for I am the vessel of the angel's will. We will perform the ceremony tonight, under the full moon, when the power of the divine is at its strongest. But first, you must prove your commitment."

Mercy's stomach knotted in fear. But she couldn't turn back now. She had lost too much to resist the spell woven by the priest's words. "How?"

A strange smile tugged at the corners of Barlow's lips. For one brief moment, his eyes glinted with something predatory and unsettling that might have scared Mercy if she wasn't so blinded by the hope he had instilled in her.

"The steps for the purification rite can only be found in a very special book," he said. "And I believe the angel wants you to have it. She will lead you to it, if you but call upon her."

Chapter 21

Anna's eyes fluttered open, and the first sensation that crawled into her consciousness was the cold, wet earth beneath her. The pungent scent of mulched leaves filled her nose. Her head throbbed with a dull ache that echoed through her skull like distant thunder. She tried to move, but her limbs felt heavy. Her vision blurred, and a metallic taste lingered on her tongue. Thick strands of her wet hair lay plastered over her eyes and face. Her clothes were soaked, and the cold seeped deep into her bones. Through the foggy haze that clung to her mind, she struggled to make sense of her surroundings.

The drizzle had grown stronger and was now a steady rain. Anna blinked as plump drops fell through the gnarled limbs of a tree above her, and she realized she was no longer in the underground cavern beneath the chapel. She lay flat on her back on the ground with mud squelching beneath her. Panic gripped her as she discovered her wrists and ankles were bound with a coarse rope that cut into her skin. She struggled to sit up and craned her neck enough to take in the desolate cemetery surrounding her. Cracked tombstones jutted from the earth like severed fingers, and the twisting limbs of the giant oak reached toward the darkening heavens above her.

Anna's pulse quickened and ice trickled through her veins when her eyes fell upon the open grave just a few paces away. It was the same muddy pit she had unearthed only hours earlier. The yellowed bones of the desecrated skeleton now lay exposed to the rain. The rusty shovel she had used still lay discarded beside the misshapen hole where she abandoned it. How long had she been unconscious?

Anna strained against her restraints. The rope bit into her flesh and chafed her skin. Her thoughts raced, her mind struggling to pierce through the fog of confusion that clouded her memories. Her last recollection was of Kisosen in the water with her below the chapel. And then, darkness.

Fear knotted Anna's stomach as she strained to see beyond her limited visibility. That's when she noticed him—a shadowy figure pacing in the periphery of her vision. The dark silhouette was barely visible against the gloom gathering among the trees, but it soon came into focus.

Kisosen stood before her. His eyes gleamed with an icy intensity, and the corners of his lips curled downward into a grim frown. He clutched his hunting knife in one hand as he peered at her, its sharp blade gleaming in the fading light of day.

A groan escaped Anna's lips as she attempted to speak, but her voice was feeble. The awful realization of her helpless situation hit her like a punch as she struggled against the tight rope around her wrists.

Another figure took shape several feet behind Kisosen. Anna cleared more of the cobwebs from her mind and saw

William there. His face was ashen and filled with fear, like a man losing a struggle to keep his head above water.

Anna's eyes narrowed with fury. "What are you doing? Let me go!" She tried to shout, but the words came out slurred as they left her lips.

Kisosen ignored her pleas, his eyes drifting to the open grave. He approached her with deliberate slowness, the cold light casting hard shadows over his stony features. He reached out for her with dirt-stained hands, and she recoiled. But there was no escape, nowhere to go. He grabbed her by the hair and dragged her up from the mud with an ease that belied his wiry frame.

Teetering on her knees on the edge of the open grave, Anna tried her best to fight him off. Fear tightened its grip on her heart as the earth's open mouth awaited her. Fire shot through her scalp as Kisosen yanked her head back to expose her throat. He pressed the gleaming knife to her neck, the blade flashing in the rain. Murmuring something in his own language, he closed his eyes and prepared for the kill.

Horror filled Anna's eyes. She was going to be sacrificed. But for what purpose? And why had Kisosen chosen her? She thrashed against her bonds, her muscles protesting the effort. But the futile struggle only sent her scattered thoughts whirling around in her head again. Vertigo churned her stomach, and she had the distinct sensation that she was going to vomit. Swallowing hard, she scanned the cemetery, searching for any means of escape. But the knots around her wrists and ankles were too tight. Her unfocused gaze fixed on William. He was her only hope of getting out of this alive.

"You must stop him, William," she croaked as she tested

the strength of her bonds again.

Kisosen's eyes flared open. "Do not listen to her. She comes to you with promises of salvation, but evil is what she brings and blood is what she craves, just like the witch that killed Susanna and my sister."

William's wide eyes darted back and forth between them, his face screwed tight with tension. "Kisosen, what if she is telling the truth? She doesn't deserve—"

Kisosen's harsh laughter echoed through the graveyard. "Deserve? The Ghost-Witch cares not for such trivial matters, William. Deserve has no place here, but survival does. This is the only way to bait and kill the monster that haunts us. I have been a brother to you. Who are you to believe? Me? Or this accursed sorceress?"

"Your family is lost if he kills me, William," Anna insisted, her voice finding some strength. She spat the words out, her defiance a feeble attempt to assert control over the impending horror. She twisted and writhed, fighting against her restraints with all her might. "You must stop him. Do it. Do it now!"

"Enough!" cried Kisosen. "The time for words is over. The Ghost-Witch craves blood and we must give it to her!"

Kisosen dug the knife into Anna's throat and nicked her flesh. She felt the warmth of her own breath against the blade as scarlet rivulets mingled with the rain trickling down her skin. Kisosen resumed his chant and the world froze, the moment stretching into eternity as the knife hovered against her windpipe.

Anna's mind raced, searching for any way out. Her eyes darted around, desperate for a glimmer of hope. The cold mud beneath her clung to her like a second skin, and the rope that held her felt like an iron chain. In her struggle, her hand brushed against a sharp shard of broken tombstone partially buried in the mud. An idea sparked in her mind.

As Kisosen's chant intensified, the blade poised to open her throat, Anna gripped the rock and swung it with all her might. The blow landed squarely on Kisosen's temple and tore away a flap of skin. He staggered back, his grip on her hair loosening. Summoning all her strength, Anna gathered her energy and whipped her bound legs around. The element of surprise worked in her favor. Kisosen stumbled backward and windmilled his arms before pitching over into the open grave.

Anna seized the opportunity and rolled through the mud toward the half-buried shovel. The ropes cut into her flesh, but she fought through the pain. With a burst of strength, she ran the rope over the edge of the shovel's blade, trying desperately to saw through it. The old and rusty blade failed to cut more than a few fibers.

Kisosen lurched up from the muddy hole and caught Anna struggling to free herself. She scurried backward through the mud as he came at her, her body aching but fueled by adrenaline. Her bound hands grasped the shovel clumsily as she swung it like a club with all her might. Kisosen dodged and let out a feral growl. His fist collided with Anna's jaw and the impact reverberated through her skull like a cannon blast. Darkness encroached on the edges of her vision, threatening to pull her into a black abyss. The metallic taste of fresh blood flooded her mouth as she sprawled backward on the uneven ground, fighting to keep her grip on consciousness.

Kisosen caught her by another fistful of hair. His knife

flashed up into the air, ready to be plunged deep into her heart. This time, he wouldn't hesitate.

"Stop!" A woman's voice shot through the rain. "Release her, Kisosen!"

Anna's heart leaped. She glimpsed a figure emerging through the downpour—Judith was there with her rifle aimed at Kisosen's head.

"Lower the knife, Kisosen," Judith growled through clenched teeth. "Sacrificing this woman will not put an end to the hauntings."

Kisosen glared at her balefully and kept the blade pressed to Anna's throat. "It was *you* who gave rise to the Ghost-Witch. Now summon the courage to kill it."

"There is no Ghost-Witch, Kisosen," Judith stated wearily.

"You mistake yourself."

"No, I am certain of it. There is no Ghost-Witch because the woman I put to death in the woods was no witch." Judith closed her eyes and took a shuddering breath, as if gathering the strength for a gut-wrenching confession. "The woman was your sister... and I killed her on the same day I killed my husband."

Chapter 22

That fateful day, Judith carries a stack of tin sugaring pails. Spring has yet to banish the wintry grasp on the mountains, and the cold sinks into her bones as she follows the crude trail through the forest. With her skirts hiked up to her ankles, and her coarse brown cloak tightly fastened, she trudges through the pockets of snow and rotting leaves. The morning sun struggles to break through the gloomy tangle of gnarled branches overhead, casting mottled shadows that dance across the forest floor.

Suddenly, she stumbles upon it—John's hatchet, partially hidden in the underbrush at her feet.

Something about the way it lies there, discarded and forgotten, fills her with an inexplicable foreboding. It's not like her husband to be so careless. First, he ventured out for sugaring without the pails, and now here lies one of his most indispensable tools, buried in the mess of sticks and dirt.

Judith reaches down, her fingers quivering as they grasp the worn handle. She doesn't know why, but she senses there is more to her husband's uncharacteristic absentmindedness.

She can't deny the unease scratching at her. Something has been amiss for weeks. John's been absent more often these days, finding excuses to venture off to the abandoned village or to make the five-mile trek to visit Kisosen's tribe. His once gentle demeanor has grown harsh and volatile, leaving Judith frightened in the company of the man she has loved for so many years.

What is he doing out here alone in the woods?

She continues on, slower and warier now, gripping the hatchet tightly. A nagging apprehension clings to her like a second skin. She isn't alone out here, she can feel it. She casts a glance over her shoulder. There is nothing to see—just the trees, their gnarled branches now resembling sinister, outstretched fingers.

She hears the sounds first.

Rustling. Sighs. Moans.

A rapturous cry, aching with ecstatic pleasure, carries through the misty air. It's a sound that sows a seed of dread in Judith's gut.

It came from a woman.

Judith peers deep into the woods ahead, her breath forming puffs of mist in the cool air. That's when she notices it—a dark silhouette swaying among the trees. Her footsteps slow as she approaches, her resolve now weakening. She knows she should turn back and abandon this pursuit. Nothing good can come from this. Yet an inexorable curiosity draws her further, like a moth lured to immolation.

The woman's breathless, sensual voice weaves through the trees, entangling Judith's heart like a thorny vine. Her calloused hand grips the handle of the hatchet.

The forest opens to a large maple grove.

Two figures writhe in a tangled embrace on a bed of leaves and moss at the foot of a massive maple tree. Their clothes lie strewn about the underbrush. Judith can't see their faces; the naked back of the young black-haired woman obscures her view as she straddles the man, grinding her hips into him, riding him vigorously. The man's hands wander over her body, eliciting wanton moans of pleasure.

Judith's breath catches in her throat, her hand flying to her mouth to stifle any noise. She feels her face flush with crimson and she knows she should retreat. But that gnawing dread in her gut has overtaken her now. Her instinctive urge to flee collides with something more profound, more elemental. An odd compulsion roots her to her spot in the shadows. She *needs* to know.

Caught in their own world of lust and ecstasy, the couple remains unaware of Judith's presence as she draws closer…

Closer…

Their forms undulate and writhe like serpents, their moans and gasps punctuating the silence of the forest.

Closer…

Finally, Judith peeks over the woman's shoulder. Glimpses the man on the ground.

There lies John, his half-lidded eyes gazing up at the young woman's exposed breasts as he caresses them with his powerful hands.

A gasp claws its way from Judith's throat, tearing through her as she stands there, paralyzed by the depth of her husband's betrayal. The tin pails hit the ground with a clatter.

Startled, the woman's head whips around. She's barely a

teenager.

It's Katetin—Kisosen's sister.

The revelation tears through Judith like lightning on a stormy night. It's enough to make her stomach spurt bile into her throat. The strain and deception that have festered beneath the veneer of her marriage for years are finally laid bare. A guttural cry wells up from the depths of her soul, a cry of anguish, of rage, of violence. But a crippling powerlessness strangles her scream in her throat. Her chest constricts when she thinks of the history she has shared with John. Their children. Their home. It's all crumbling around her. After all they have sacrificed and endured together, she can't believe this is how it ends.

This moment is irreversible.

And suddenly, Judith has the strangest sensation that there is a presence there beside her, an unseen entity lending her its strength. The air comes alive with its palpable malevolence, a force that consumes her like a ravenous fire burning her from the inside out. A mysterious scent overwhelms her as a whispering voice slithers into her consciousness, fanning the flames of her anger and despair.

"Unleash thy wrath, Judith. Make them suffer as thou art suffering…"

Judith has never known such violence in her heart, nor such a darkness that beckons her toward it. She has been a good and loyal wife, obedient and pious, but the voice in her head presses her onward down a blood-cursed path. A path she can't avoid.

Judith's jaw clenches. Her knuckles turn white around the handle of the hatchet.

WHACK!

The blade slices through the air and bites deep into Katetin's neck—but it doesn't hack through all the way. Blood sprays in spurts, drenching John's naked chest. Droplets splatter in an arc across the snow, sowing a field of crimson blossoms.

Katetin slumps over, convulsing and gurgling as her life drains away into the earth. Bewitched by the voice raging in her head, Judith yanks the hatchet from the girl's neck and brings it swinging down again, finishing the job. Katetin's head rolls across the forest floor, her sightless eyes staring up at the tangled canopy of tree limbs.

John staggers to his feet, his naked body slick with blood. There's something about him that cuts through the red fog that has descended on Judith. Rage distorts his features into the grotesque mask of a monstrous stranger. His eyes blaze with murderous fury, betraying no trace of the man Judith loved.

Alarmed by his ferocity, Judith backpedals. But a gnarled root reaches up from the ground like an undead hand, tripping her and sending her sprawling to the forest floor. Her breath escapes her lungs as John towers over her, his hands outstretched like the talons of some predatory beast. He grabs her by the shoulders and shakes her violently.

"What have you done?" he shrieks into her face. "You bring ruin to everything, damn you!"

His hands find her throat and begin to squeeze.

Judith's hands claw at his fingers, her nails digging shallow, angry trails into his flesh. But his grip is unyielding. Her fingers scrabble over the ground, groping at roots and stones.

There's a dim part of her that can't help but wonder if her husband is hearing that same seductive whisper in his head, too. Blood beads on his nose and chin, his teeth clenched in a rictus of fury. His hot breath washes over her as he presses his fingers deeper into her throat. The weight of his body bears down on her, crushing her into the mossy forest floor.

Judith's struggles grow feeble as her vision darkens, and the world loses its form. It's as if the forest itself is closing in around her, shrinking in size. John will not stop. She knows it now. He's going to kill her. As her consciousness wanes, her groping fingertips graze cold metal. John's pistol rests among his pile of clothes. She strains to reach it.

BOOM!

John's brains explode from his head with a mighty blast of sparks and smoke.

The dead weight of her husband's body collapses upon Judith, bleeding out in gushing torrents. She wrestles her way out from under him and struggles to her feet.

The forest seems to tremble with a malevolent energy as Judith stands there, her hands and face drenched in gore. In that moment, she feels a profound satisfaction, a dark vindication that drowns out her grief and heartache. She remains there a moment, swaying in an unsteady daze.

The voice in her head has fallen silent now, abandoning her just as the full horror of what has just happened crashes over her. Her mind races, and she feels her memory becoming fragmented, as if someone has snatched away pieces of a terrible puzzle.

What has she done?

Her legs give out from under her and she stumbles

sideways, colliding into a giant maple. She clings to the trunk, giving herself over to sobs and moans. Mortified by what she has done, she staggers to John's body and collapses at his side, cradling his mutilated head in her lap. Tears well up in her eyes. Her fingers, slick with her husband's blood, shake as she touches his bloody face.

Across the hollow, an enormous crow swoops low and lands on Katetin's headless corpse. It's soon joined by another. And another.

Their shrill cries punctuate Judith's sobs as they feed, ripping through skin and stripping flesh from bone with their sharp beaks…

Chapter 23

Judith fell silent and a moment of thunderstruck stillness followed as the others stared at her in shock.

William couldn't breathe as he listened, his mind grappling to reconcile the image he had of his father with the sordid details of his infidelity. He stared at Judith in wide-eyed disbelief.

"Mother," he said, his voice barely above a whisper. "*You* killed Father?"

Judith's hands trembled on the rifle as she drew a shaky breath. "I shouldn't have been surprised that he sought solace in another woman's arms. They thought themselves hidden, but I knew. Once I found them, I couldn't look away. The betrayal, William. Betrayal so profound it seared my soul."

William couldn't stop staring at her. Judith's expression remained haunted and distant, as if still reliving the horrors of that afternoon. His voice quivered as he spoke, searching his mother's pale and haggard face for a sign that this was some morbid joke. "What have you done, Mother?"

Judith's eyes brimmed with unshed tears as she met her

son's gaze. "I did it to protect you, to protect Mercy. Their secret was a flame that threatened to consume everything in its path—including our family. And so I did the unthinkable. I was blind with fury, and there was a… a voice in my head urging me on—the same voice that drove me to kill that young priest. I couldn't control myself. I couldn't stop. That voice held me in its grip until there was nothing left but silence. I struck them down; I killed them both. And when I was done, I couldn't bear the shame. I couldn't bring myself to admit what I had done—what *John* had done in betraying us. So I blamed his death on a figure from Kisosen's folklore. For a time, I might have even believed it to be true…"

Judith turned to Kisosen. "The guilt has tormented me every day since. I buried them in that grove, their secret buried with them. I thought I could bury the truth along with their bodies, but their ghosts will not cease haunting me. I cannot endure it any longer. The weight of what I've done… it's been unbearable." Her voice cracked with sorrow. "No one tricked your sister into taking her own life, Kisosen. I murdered her and let you believe she had fallen victim to the banished witch of your tribe. There is no Ghost-Witch; I am the monster that killed your sister, and if any ghost haunts us, it is Katetin's."

The emotions of her confession seemed to exhaust Judith. Her shoulders slumped as she lowered the rifle, reversed her grip, and offered it to Kisosen. Her legs lost all their strength, and she sank to her knees in the mud, surrendering herself to his mercy.

Kisosen remained silent, glaring at her as he took the gun from her hands. Judith looked up and met his gaze, silently pleading for forgiveness. But his expression was unreadable. She expected to see sorrow and grief and rage as years of misplaced loyalty collided with a betrayal too ugly to bear. But there was nothing in his face at all—no shock and no surprise, as if he had somehow been expecting this all along.

And then it hit her.

"You knew, didn't you?" Judith whispered. "You knew I killed her. You knew this whole time…"

More revelations crashed into her head, slamming into each other one after another. "It was *you*, wasn't it? You are the one who has been cursing us." She motioned to Anna. "Using this woman as bait was never your intention; you intended to *sacrifice* her."

Anna swayed unsteadily where she stood listening, the hazy image in her mind becoming clearer as the last pieces of the puzzle fell into place. The Black Testament had called to Kisosen, preying upon his silent rage. It had revealed itself to him, and with Angéle de la Barthe's help, he had unlocked its power to have his revenge on the family that betrayed him.

At last, Kisosen's face betrayed some emotion, a black and scorching hatred that seared Judith where she knelt. "She was just a girl," he said. "Just a child."

William took a step toward him. "Kisosen—"

Kisosen pulled the trigger.

The rifle roared unexpectedly. Blood spurted from Judith's back as the bullet tore through her heart. Her body jolted backward and crumpled in the mud.

"*No!*" William cried.

In a flash, he grabbed the shovel and struck Kisosen in the face with the solid steel head. The blow knocked teeth from the young Indian's mouth and sent him to his knees. The rifle flew from his hand, still smoking from the shot that had blown a fist-sized hole in Judith's chest.

William lunged at him, but Kisosen quickly regained his wits and stepped aside. The mud made each movement treacherous. William's momentum carried him forward, but he recovered just in time to see Kisosen raise his flintlock pistol. The shot rang out, a concussive explosion in the otherwise silent graveyard. The pain hit William like a lightning bolt. He stumbled backward, clutching his shoulder where the bullet had grazed him.

Blood gushed from the wicked smile playing on Kisosen's lips as his voice cut through the rain. "You're even more pitiful than I thought, William. A wounded dog, trying to avenge its master."

William gritted his teeth against the pain and charged again, his shovel slicing through the air. This time, he felt a satisfying resistance as the blade pierced Kisosen's side. A gasp escaped the Indian's lips, and for a moment, the sinister facade of his face wavered.

But Kisosen recovered quickly, retaliating with a vicious kick that sent William sprawling into the mud. The taste of copper filled William's mouth. He wiped the blood from his split lip, his eyes never leaving Kisosen.

"You've always been resilient," Kisosen said, circling like a vulture closing in on its prey. "But resilience won't bring your mother back… or your sister."

A surge of anger fueled William. He pushed himself upright, his rain-soaked hair plastered to his forehead. In a desperate move, he lunged forward once more. But with a sudden burst of strength, Kisosen drove his elbow into William's wounded shoulder, causing him to release the shovel.

The two men locked together in a frenzied struggle as they grappled in the mud. Each punch, each kick, reverberated through the whispering raindrops that danced across the tombstones. William's grief-fueled strength surged as he fought to overpower the man he once considered his friend and mentor. But Kisosen fought with a cruel efficiency, his movements calculated and precise. He flipped William to the ground and pinned him down, hammering him with relentless blows to the face and head.

Bruised and bloodied by Kisosen's overwhelming assault, William's hand managed to close around the fallen flintlock pistol. With a desperate twist, he broke free from Kisosen's grasp and aimed the pistol directly into his face. The raindrops danced in slow motion as he pulled the trigger.

The wet powder failed to ignite.

Kisosen knocked the pistol aside with a vicious snarl. His hand flashed out and seized his knife from the mud.

"Your father defiled my sister's innocence," he hissed, raising the blade high over his head. "So I slaughtered yours —along with the child I planted inside her."

An ear-splitting scream tore through the cemetery before he could strike the fatal blow.

Kisosen's attention flicked sideways. Mercy was sprinting past the chapel toward them. In the same instant, a powerful gust of wind swept through the cemetery along with her. It whirled through the maze of tombstones, whipping the rain into a frenzied dance as it went. Too strong to be natural, the wind slammed into Kisosen and William with the force of an invisible battering ram, lifting them up from the earth as if they were weightless leaves caught in a gale. The young men spiraled through the air in opposite directions, limbs flailing like discarded playthings.

William's descent was abrupt and violent. His head slammed against a moss-covered tombstone with a sickening crunch of bone meeting stone as he crashed back down to the ground.

As quickly as it arose, the supernatural wind dissipated into the air, leaving behind an eerie calm.

William's body lay crumpled and dreadfully motionless in the mud. Blood streamed from a gash on his forehead and mingled with the rain running down his face.

Further away, Kisosen looked broken where he lay. It took a moment before he stirred. Disoriented and dazed, he dragged himself to his knees. A searing pain tore through his abdomen. He coughed and blood bubbled from his mouth. He looked down and discovered the blade buried in his gut.

A horrified gasp escaped Kisosen's lips when he realized he had impaled himself on his own knife when he hit the ground. He clutched the hilt, but found it too slick with rain and blood to remove. Blood-soaked soil clung to his clothes as he struggled to stand, but the damage to his insides was too great. The pain was both visceral and numbing, and his breaths came in wheezing gasps as he collapsed back into the mud.

Still stunned by Kisosen's vicious blow to her head, Anna scanned the surroundings for any sign of the spectral forces that had intervened. Draped in rain and shadows, the cemetery exuded an unsettling aura of emptiness. But Anna knew they weren't alone. The air carried an odd scent, one that felt out of place in the rain—the distinctive aroma of fennel and scorched flesh.

Mercy ran to where William lay motionless and shook him, her tears mixing with the rain like tributaries flowing into a river. "William! William, speak to me!"

There was no response.

Over her shoulder, Mercy glimpsed Anna staring at her. She rose, retrieved the rifle from where Kisosen had dropped it, and aimed it at Anna's chest.

"I am responsible for this." Mercy's voice was low and sullen as she swept her hand over the motionless bodies strewn about the cemetery. Judith's corpse lay just a few paces away, the rain washing away the blood that seeped from the gruesome hole in her chest. "I can no longer deny I am corrupted. I cannot control the evils I commit, but I am certain they will continue unless I am stopped. I must be purified. Now. Tonight."

Purified? Anna tried to make sense of Mercy's words, but her thoughts were too rattled and she found it hard to focus. But then, a disturbing understanding crystalized in her mind.

"Have you spoken to the man in the village, Mercy?"

Mercy ignored the question and motioned with the barrel of the rifle, flicking it away from the cemetery. "Away. Now."

Anna considered making a move to disarm the girl, but her wrists were still bound and she didn't fully trust her dull reflexes. Mercy was too frightened and distraught to think clearly; there was a very good chance she could get a shot off before Anna could react. She had no choice but to let Mercy march her through the narrow lanes of the village.

Raindrops pattered in the muddy puddles as they walked. Mercy's white hair clung to her face, and her crimson eye glinted with a feverish intensity. She kept the muzzle of the rifle against the small of Anna's back, guiding her with an insistent force that left no room for resistance.

The winding lane opened to a small clearing, revealing an old stable with a sagging roof. Mercy's boots squelched in the mud as she forced Anna toward the dilapidated structure.

"Inside." Mercy's command cut through the rain.

Anna hesitated at the threshold, her eyes scanning the gloom. Unused lengths of timber cluttered the space. Broken beams for a roof that had never been finished crisscrossed like cracked ribs hanging from a spine. Cobwebs hung like tattered banners from the rafters, and the stink of damp hay mingled with the musty odor of decay.

Anna shuffled forward and Mercy followed, the rifle still trained on her captive. When she felt she had gone far enough, Anna halted and turned around. "Mercy—"

"Stay where you are." Mercy leveled the rifle, her expression filled with deadly menace.

"You won't kill me," said Anna. "And you won't kill your brother. This isn't your fault."

"Yes, I will. Perhaps not tonight, but someday soon I will be his undoing as surely as I was Susanna's. It is why Father Barlow must perform the ritual now, before it is too late. And it is why you mustn't interfere."

"*Father* Barlow?" Anna cursed herself as it all became clear in her mind. She had committed a fatal mistake—she should have killed Barlow when she had the chance. "No, don't do this, Mercy. That man is a liar. He is not even a priest. He has been deceiving you since his arrival and now he has turned you against each other. He is using you to fulfill his own bloodthirsty appetites."

Mercy's face remained a mask of grim resolve.

Anna tried another approach. "With your mother dead, you and William are finally free to leave this dreadful place. Come with me to Boston. Let us flee together and never look back."

Anna heard the words leave her mouth and came to a stunning realization—the same could be said of her. With Abigail gone, she was finally free to live a life of her own choosing. No more secrets and double-lives. No more nights of blood and violence. No more isolation and loneliness. Why, then, was she so determined to bring her mother back? What prevented her from walking away, as she had always fantasized? Was it guilt? Anna knew she could never live with herself, knowing that she'd left her own mother to burn in Hell. There had been a time when Anna had convinced herself that she hated Abigail for what she had done, for initiating her into this cursed and lonesome life when she only just a child. But now that Abigail was gone, Anna found it harder to hold on to her resentment. Perhaps, despite Abigail's failings as a mother, there was still a part of Anna that genuinely loved her.

Mercy shook her head resolutely. "No more running, Anna. The whole of my life has seemed like a nightmare within a nightmare. I can endure it no longer. Tonight I wake of it." With the gun still aimed at Anna, she backed toward the open door. "Whatever becomes of me, know that I never chose to let the Devil in."

The rusted hinges groaned as she slammed the stable door shut. An instant later, there was the telltale scraping of wood-on-wood as Mercy slid the heavy timber bolt into place on the other side.

Left alone, Anna hurled herself against the door. "Mercy! Mercy, open this door!" Her voice rose above the drumming of the rain, desperation lending strength to her plea.

"You can't escape," Mercy's voice rang out from the other side, chilling in its certainty. "She won't let you leave. The angel has a plan for you too… she has a plan for all of us."

Chapter 24

The narrow lanes became a slippery maze, but Mercy pressed on through the rain. Her alabaster skin was almost translucent in the fading light, and the chill of the muddy earth numbed her feet. The village crowded around her, the shadows of twilight swallowing the leaning buildings.

But Mercy wasn't alone. She felt a pull, an unearthly force guiding her forward with an irresistible gravity. The angel's ghostly whispers echoed in her mind, leading her inexorably toward the rectory. Somewhere within its decrepit walls lay the key to her salvation. The angel promised her she would find it there.

A biting gust of wind shook the gnarled branches of the oaks that lined the village square. Mercy's heart hammered against her ribs as she approached the hulking silhouette of the old priest's house. The walls were crawling with ivy, and darkness shrouded the windows, as if they were absorbing what little daylight remained.

Icy tendrils of fear coiled through Mercy's stomach as she reached out and pressed her fingers against the weathered door. In her secret explorations of the village, this building was one of the very few she always avoided. There was something dreadfully wrong about this place. She could feel it, like something rotten festering in her gut.

But she couldn't turn back now.

The wood was rough under her fingertips as she pushed on the door. It swung open with a reluctant moan and Mercy hesitated at the threshold, wary of the unnerving stillness that hung in the foyer. The only sounds were the rain on the roof and water trickling down the eaves. Ravenous shadows devoured the few dying rays of light that dared to enter.

The angel's voice whispered in Mercy's ear, urging her forward, leading her deeper into the gloom. Mercy felt the damp air wrapping around her like unseen fingers. The creak of the floorboards beneath her feet echoed through the silent halls. Rain drummed against the windows like a ghostly horde demanding entrance. She traced her fingers along the walls of the keeping room, her red eye darting nervously from side to side.

With a trembling hand, Mercy found the pewter candlestick where Anna had left it on the writing desk. She sparked a flint, and the pallid glow revealed the remains of furniture draped in cobwebs. Faded portraits of saints stared back at her from the walls. Crucifixes filled the empty spaces. Mercy had no way of knowing that those same crucifixes had hung inverted less than a day ago. She moved through the corridor, the candle's feeble flame casting shadows that crawled across the walls. The rain outside intensified, hammering the roof like the gnashing teeth of an unseen beast.

A long, slow creak crept from the darkness behind her.

Mercy jumped at the sound, her stomach lurching into her throat. She whirled around, the candle sputtering and nearly going out with the sudden movement.

A trapdoor lay open in the corner of the kitchen.

It wasn't open a moment ago.

Mercy's fearful eyes fixed on the black hole that opened to the rectory's root cellar. A spine-tingling realization made her porcelain skin ripple with gooseflesh.

The angel was showing her the way.

She hesitated before creeping toward the gaping hole in the floor. Dust motes danced in the flickering candlelight, revealing a narrow staircase that descended into absolute darkness. A stale odor, like the breath of a corpse, wafted up to greet her. Mercy's courage failed her as she stared down into that black pit. She couldn't go down there. She was too afraid of what she would find, of what might be lurking in the darkness. Waiting for her.

Then she felt a shift in the air. An unseen presence pressed upon her like an invisible hand. The angel was there to protect her.

Mercy trembled with fright as she descended one step. Then another. The wooden risers were barely visible in the dim light. She clutched the flickering candle in her slender fingers, its pale glow struggling to fend off the oppressive darkness that enveloped her. It was only when she protected the delicate flame with her hand that she finally realized the wax was nearly gone. There were just barely two fingers' worth left. The old tallow candle would burn itself out at any moment.

Dread coiled in Mercy's stomach, and the wooden steps groaned under her weight as she descended further into the inky darkness. The air grew colder with each step, and the faint sound of dripping water echoed through the cavernous chamber as she neared the bottom. Mercy's pulse quickened, her nerves frayed by the ominous silence that clung to the air.

When her feet touched the earthen floor, she found herself in a low-ceilinged cellar. Its shape was indistinguishable in the complete darkness. Mercy played the candlelight around the chamber. Its feeble light struggled to pierce the shadows, and its shallow radius revealed only flickering hints of the damp stone walls.

Shelves lined one side of the room, filled with canning jars of various shapes and sizes, their contents hidden by layers of dust. Mercy approached one shelf and brushed the grime from a jar, revealing something floating inside a murky liquid. From what she could make out, the dark corners of the cellar were cluttered with rusty tools, empty casks, cracked pottery, and religious paraphernalia. Cobwebs hung from the ceiling like funeral shrouds, fluttering and dancing in and out of the light in time with each of Mercy's shallow breaths. She shivered involuntarily, her breath visible in the cold air. Her fingers traced the dusty jars as she moved cautiously among the shelves.

And then the light danced over something that made Mercy gasp and stumble backward.

Piles of bones lay scattered on the floor.

They looked too small to be human, but in the dim light, Mercy couldn't be sure. She leaned closer to get a better look, and that's when her gaze landed on a makeshift bed nestled nearby.

A tattered quilt lay shrouded in darkness over a crude straw palette. The quilt wasn't dusty or moth-eaten, and it appeared reasonably new—far too new for someone to have left it here a century ago. Someone had arranged a collection of tools and utensils beside it—an oil lamp, a tin cup, frayed rope, and bits of bone. Mercy's pulse quickened when she saw the remnants of a recent fire pit, the embers still smoldering.

Someone had been living here, hidden beneath the rectory.

Mercy's skin crawled, and a sharp bolt of panic shot up her spine. What if she wasn't alone? What if someone else was down there in the darkness with her?

With her heart slamming against her ribs, she retreated a step and knocked into another shelf of jars. The clatter of glass echoed through the cellar and Mercy froze, her breath caught in her throat. In the sudden silence that followed, she strained her ears for any movement, any sign that she wasn't alone. All she could hear was the sound of her own heartbeat pounding in her ears.

Long moments went by until Mercy felt she could move again. The candlelight drifted over the quilt, and it occurred to her it looked familiar. She had seen that distinctive diamond pattern before, that same quilt spread out over her cottage's keeping room floor whenever Kisosen spent the night.

Kisosen...

Was he living here all this time?

Mercy stared at the quilt, searching for any other explanation. She remembered the knowing look in Father Barlow's eyes when he'd questioned Kisosen's loyalty. She heard the echoes of the priest's derisive laughter, and an uneasy knot tightened in her stomach.

He had known. The priest tried to warn her about Kisosen.

Something glinted in the candlelight.

Mercy bent down to rummage through the objects left near Kisosen's makeshift bed—dried herbs, melted candles, and cryptic symbols drawn with a dark substance that might have been blood. Mercy's fingers trembled as she uncovered a woman's hair comb. The sight of it punched the air from her lungs.

The wooden comb belonged to Susanna.

Father had carved it himself from a solid piece of maple. He had spent hours polishing the wood to bring out its warmth. Mercy felt as if spiders were crawling all over her skin as she held it up to the candlelight to inspect its intricate floral carvings. She must not have been the only one sneaking away to the village. Did Susanna and Kisosen come here to be alone? The thought of her beautiful sister down here in this dark and squalid pit made Mercy feel sick.

And then an image flew into her mind. She remembered Kisosen murmuring strange words over Susanna's body just minutes before its violent desecration. What if it wasn't a blessing?

What if it was a curse?

Still shuddering, Mercy slipped the comb into the pocket of her cloak and forced herself to continue exploring. As she reached the far end of the cellar, the candlelight illuminated an ancient trunk. She had the strangest sensation that it pulsed with a dark heartbeat, emanating an unearthly energy that made the hair stand up on the back of her neck. Despite the knot in her stomach, she ran her fingers over its cracked surface and lifted the lid.

There it was.

The black book was larger than Mercy expected. It seemed to draw her in as she reached for it, her fingertips brushing over the pentagram embossed on the worn leather cover. An uncanny sensation surged through her the moment she grazed its surface, a jolt of electricity that sent tingling sparks up her arm. Her blood raced with fear and fascination as she gingerly lifted the book from the trunk.

It felt strangely warm to the touch, despite the cool, damp air of the cellar. The pentagram's lines pulsed with power, tempting Mercy to answer their call. Against her better judgment, she carefully pried the book open, the pages crackling with age.

An acrid smell instantly filled the air, and the room seemed to vibrate with an unseen force. The stiff and brittle parchment yielded to her touch like the flesh of a corpse. Illustrations of eldritch symbols and arcane words filled the pages, their spidery script seeming to dance across the parchment. The angel's whispering voice, hollow and ancient, seeped into her consciousness as she leafed through the text. Her surroundings suddenly blurred as an unearthly presence coalesced in the cellar, a formless darkness that drew strength from her fear. Unfamiliar memories invaded her mind, visions of a time long-forgotten—a village consumed by darkness; a woman bound to a stake, writhing and wailing in agony as flames devoured her flesh. Mercy glimpsed the faces of those who had gathered to watch the woman burn, their eyes filled with cruelty.

The candle went out with a sudden hiss, plunging the cellar into complete darkness.

Panic constricted Mercy's chest. She stumbled backward, her foot catching on something on the ground. She fell hard; the book slipping from her grasp and skidding across the floor. Terror seized her as she scrambled to her hands and knees and fumbled blindly for it.

But before she could find the book in the darkness, she heard it—the faint sound of something slowly scraping across the floor toward her. Her heart hammered as she scurried backward across the dirt, only to find herself cornered against the shelves of jars.

The eerie scraping sound crept closer, closer.

"Who's there?" Mercy tried to sound strong and brave, but her voice trembled and barely exceeded a child's whimper.

No answer came. Only that unnerving scraping approaching her in the endless silence.

Whatever lurked in the darkness was drawing nearer.

Something warm brushed against her fingertips.

A bloodcurdling scream tore from Mercy's throat an instant before she recognized what she was touching.

It was the book.

Someone—or something—had slid it back across the floor to her.

A woman whispered directly into Mercy's ear, so close Mercy could feel her icy breath.

"Take it, child of flesh…"

Terror shot through Mercy's veins.

It was her. The Burned Lady. Mercy's angel.

Mercy felt her presence by her side in the darkness, the air around her charged with the angel's otherworldly electricity.

"Who are you?" Mercy's whisper was barely audible over the wild pounding of her heart. As her eyes adjusted to the darkness, she perceived a figure looming in the gloom like a black silhouette among the shadows.

And then it was gone, the angel's unearthly energy vanishing along with her.

Mercy gasped for breath and clutched the book to her chest as she staggered backward, fumbling for the stairs with her free hand. The darkness coiled around her like a living entity, resisting her attempts to escape. With a surge of adrenaline, she stumbled up the steps and bolted into the keeping room. There, she found a worn leather satchel still stuffed with the pages of the village priest's last sermon. The brittle parchments crumbled in her fingers as she dumped the contents on the floor and tucked the black book safely inside. She slung the satchel around her neck; she would need both hands for her next task.

The rectory door groaned on its hinges as Mercy pushed through and spilled out into the twilight. She cast a final, terrified glance at the accursed building looming behind her and clutched her thin cloak tightly around her slender frame. Was she shivering because of the dampness in the air or the ominous power emanating from the book in her satchel? The rain was slowing now, and the village square lay in ghostly silence. Soon the moon would rise, and the dead awaited her in the churchyard.

Chapter 25

Moonlight filtered through cracks in the walls of the smithy, casting jagged shadows across the dusty tools and rusted anvils. Barlow used a stiff broom as a walking stick to cross the room, the sound of the broomstick hitting the floor echoing in the large space. He swept the tools aside on the cluttered worktable and set down the fabled Black Testament.

The old forge was now ablaze with a fire, illuminating the pentagram embossed on the book's cover. Bound in human skin flayed from the damned in the depths of Hell, the binding was black as midnight and pulsed with a life of its own. Even the edges of the pages were singed and blackened, worn from the grimoire's journey through the centuries.

Barlow could feel the dark power radiating from the tome in waves as he hovered over it.

This is it, he thought. *The Black Testament of Angéle de le Barthe. The gospel of Lucifer himself.*

Barlow's hand trembled as he opened the book with cautious reverence. The words on the parchment came alive, dancing before his eyes with an unholy energy. The language was ancient and foreign, yet he intuited their meaning as if the knowledge had been dormant within him. As his fingers traced the intricate symbols, the wondrous secrets they held captivated his imagination.

During the forbidden experiments that had led to his banishment from the Crucible of Night, Barlow had aspired to the godlike mastery of the secrets of life and death themselves. And yet, his efforts to pierce the mysteries of the Veil had failed time and again with ghastly consequences. His attempts at resurrection never resulted in reversals of death. They were mere bridges to a realm where the living were never meant to tread. Those poor souls that he'd attempted to reanimate never returned as whole people, the same as they had been before their spirits had crossed over. Instead, he was forced to dismember and bury the monstrous abominations all over New Haven.

Now, Barlow's obsidian eyes flicked from side to side over the pages of the Black Testament with an unsettling fervor, his heart quickening with excitement—Angéle *wanted* him to understand. She wanted him to be reunited with his son, and she would help him decipher her cryptic grimoire to unlock its mysteries, if only he raised her up from perdition.

And for all of his gruesome failures, Barlow did know how to prepare a vessel for possession.

He shifted his gaze toward Mercy, who stood near the forge. An iron cauldron hung above the flames. Two chairs faced each other in the room's center. Tin pails sat on the floor on either side of one chair.

Kisosen's body lay on the floor between the chairs and the forge.

"Is he dead?" Mercy asked as Barlow hobbled over and searched the Indian for a heartbeat.

Barlow shook his head. "Not yet, but our time is short. Already he grows cold." He crossed the room to the door and slid the bolt into place. "Are you ready, Mercy?"

Mercy glimpsed an unsettling intensity in his gaze that sent a cold prickle up the back of her neck, despite the blazing heat of the forge. But she couldn't back out now. She had come this far, and the hope of being purged of her affliction was too powerful to resist.

She nodded, her pulse racing. "What must I do?"

"First, you must remove your outer garments." Barlow's voice dripped with honeyed poison.

Mercy hesitated, her mind filled with apprehension. She didn't know what drove her to follow this enigmatic stranger, but the promise of redemption had clouded her judgment. She slowly disrobed, shedding her clothing one piece at a time until she stood in the sweltering, fire-lit room, exposed and vulnerable in nothing but her cotton shift.

Barlow stepped closer and motioned to the chair stationed between the pails. "Be seated, Mercy."

He waited for her to sit before drawing a shovelful of ashes from the forge. Hobbling gingerly around where she sat, he poured the ashes in the shape of a sigil on the floor and marked the cardinal points with the remnants of old candles, invoking the elemental forces that bound the physical and spiritual planes.

Satisfied that all was in order, Barlow then eased himself into the chair opposite Mercy and produced Kisosen's hunting knife from the folds of his robe. Kisosen's blood

234

stained the blade, but it still reflected a fiery glint.

"You have done well gathering all that we require," Barlow said. "You understand the risks that the ritual entails?"

Mercy clenched her jaw and gave a timid nod, her body trembling.

"The ritual will be painful, but it is a pain that will cleanse you. It is the price you must pay for your salvation. You must be drained entirely of your cursed blood. I will collect it to be purified on the fire. When it is done, I will use Kisosen's blood to replenish your flesh and resurrect you from the brink of death."

Barlow looked her in the eyes. She was breathing heavier now. Fear was setting in. Doubt clawed at her mind, but she pushed it aside. Barlow's persuasive words and the weight of her own faith in him held her in place.

He laid a hand on her shoulder, his touch reassuring. "Trust in me, Mercy. The pain will be fleeting, but the salvation everlasting. The Devil will have no hold on you once the ritual is complete."

Mercy nodded hesitantly and her voice quivered when she spoke. "I understand what must be done, Father."

Barlow reversed the knife and offered it by the handle. "The purging must be of your own free will. *You* must be the one to do it."

Mercy took the knife from him and stared at the blood-stained blade. She looked at Barlow, just a scared little girl now. "I'm afraid, Father."

He gave her a sympathetic nod. "It is a brave thing you do, to fight the Devil so." Barlow watched as Mercy studied the sharp blade gleaming in the firelight. "You must do it soon,

Mercy. While Kisosen's heart still beats. This is the only path to redemption."

Fear filled Mercy's eyes as she looked at him, then shifted her gaze to the knife. She felt the weight of it in her hand, the coldness of the steel. Closing her eyes, she steadied her shaking hand and pressed the blade against her pale wrist. Her chest heaved with her breaths as she murmured a soft prayer.

And then she ran the blade through her skin.

Mercy bit her lip to stifle a scream as the knife sliced a cruel path through her flesh. The pain shot through her and a gasp escaped her lips. Blood welled from the deep wound and spilled across her bare legs as she quickly switched hands to slash her other wrist.

The knife clattered to the floor.

Mercy let her arms drop to either side of the chair. The blood flowed, crimson against her white skin, running in rivers into the tin pails.

It was done.

Barlow began to chant, his voice resonating in a language Mercy didn't understand. The words flowed from his lips like a dark river. The air crackled with a strange energy and the room seemed to close in around her. Her vision blurred with pain and shock. Barlow's chant filled her ears, a dark and eerie incantation that hung weightless in the hot air. She could feel her blood dripping from her fingertips to the pails, and a strange sense of serenity came over her. The room was darkening around her, and the words of the priest became a distant echo. She swayed in her seat, barely conscious of what was happening. She closed her eyes, laid her head back, and resumed her prayer, repeating it over and over until her strength waned to nothing and her voice was but a faint murmur.

Barlow droned on with feverish rapture. As the pails filled with Mercy's blood, the next task was to establish a protective barrier against forces that might seek to interfere with the ritual before Angéle took possession of Mercy's empty vessel.

Barlow limped around the perimeter of the room, chanting ancient words gleaned from his unspeakable pacts with demons. His free hand traced intricate sigils in the air, weaving invisible threads of magic. His fingers moved with precision, each gesture charged with a potent energy that shielded the room.

A sudden gust of wind rattled the cracked windows, extinguishing several candles. Barlow's chant wavered for an instant, but he pressed on. Beads of sweat formed on his brow from the heat of the forge. He could feel the Veil between the realms thinning with each passing moment, a sensation both exhilarating and terrifying.

A distant rumble reverberated, like the wrathful growl of a creature from the depths of the underworld. The floor trembled, sending tiny particles of ash dancing across the planks. Barlow's heart raced, his breaths shallow as he brought his incantation to a sudden halt. He opened his eyes.

Mercy was dreadfully pale now. Her arms dangled limply at her sides, and the blood flowing from her wrists had slowed to mere drips.

It was time.

Barlow took the bloody pails to the fireplace and emptied them into the cauldron hanging over the flames. Steam twirled from within the vessel.

The iron tip of the fire poker glowed red-hot as he grabbed it from the forge and turned back to Mercy.

Chapter 26

Anna felt time slipping away as she assessed her confines. The creaking timber of the old stable sounded like ghostly whispers around her. She tugged at the hemp rope binding her wrists, feeling the coarse fibers digging into her skin. Her eyes darted around, searching the gloom for something she could use to free herself. She found very little—rotting hay, rusted tools, unused roof beams, and the skeletons of long-dead horses left to wither and die a century ago.

Anna's frantic breaths and the rhythmic tap of the raindrops on the rotting wood filled the haunting stillness. Her hands trembled as she strained against the constraints of the rope, her skin chafing, the flesh reddening and raw. But the knots held fast. Despair set in with each passing moment. What had Mercy meant about an angel having a plan for her? Was she talking about Angéle de la Barthe? And what horrors did Cotton Barlow intend for the girl?

That's when she saw it. As Anna's eyes adjusted to the darkness, she spotted a heavy workbench tucked away in a dim corner. A variety of dusty tools and an old lantern, partially hidden by a tattered cloth, were spread out on it.

Anna's determination surged as she snatched the lantern and hurled it to the ground. Shards of glass shattered and scattered around her boots. She gripped a large shard in her bound hands and struggled to saw through the rope. The glass bit into her skin and beads of blood smeared with the dirt on her fingers and wrists. Anna winced but kept cutting, gritting her teeth against the stinging pain. The rope resisted at first, its fibers stubbornly holding on. But the frayed strands eventually snapped and her hands sprang free. Relief and triumph coursed through her veins as she rubbed her raw and bleeding wrists.

But her escape was anything but certain.

The stable's double doors swayed and creaked in the wind, but the heavy beam outside still prevented her from escaping. Anna spun around, desperately searching for something to help her break through. Her gaze landed on a rusted pitchfork resting against a wall. An idea ignited within her. She grabbed it from its resting place and hustled to the entrance. With a deep breath, she wedged the tines through the gap between the doors and slid them upward until they contacted the beam. Bracing herself, she gathered her strength and strained to lift the beam with the tines. It resisted, but a creak of protesting wood soon echoed through the barn as it inched upward. Anna took heart. The muscles in her hands cramped with the exertion until a screech of sheering metal suddenly shot out. One by one, the rusted tines of the pitchfork bent and snapped under the beam's heavy weight. It slid back into place with a dull thud.

Anna's heart sank. Her breaths were quick and ragged as

she cursed with dismay and tossed the broken pitchfork aside. She launched herself at the doors in frustration, putting her weight into it, but she only bounced off.

Her gaze went skyward and found the gaping hole in the unfinished roof. Could she somehow climb up through it? She rushed to a wall and leapt into the air, straining to reach the upper edge. It was too high, just out of reach. She whirled and tried stacking some of the heavy lengths of timber against the wall, but they were too unwieldy; she would exhaust herself before the pile of lumber was tall enough to climb.

And then it hit her. The beam outside reinforced the doors —but not the rotting walls.

Anna wasted no time grabbing a heavy piece of timber and smashing it into the closest wall. The planks splintered and cracked. Dust filled the air as the wood shuddered under the impact of her makeshift battering ram. Over and over, she struck the weakened wall, driven by her desperate need to break through. Finally, the planks fractured and gave way with a screech of rusty nails.

A rush of frosty night air greeted Anna as she went crashing through the jagged opening. Propelled by her momentum, she tumbled from the stable and cast the length of timber aside.

The rain had subsided, and the wind now swept through the desolate lanes. It whipped Anna's wet skirts around her legs as she raced deeper into the village, desperate to find Mercy before it was too late. The way ahead was a maze of shadows, twisting and turning in every direction as she dashed between the dilapidated buildings. Her senses were alert, every rustle of leaves and creak of wood magnified in the silence. The edges of her sodden cloak billowed in the cold night air and her boots stomped through the mud as she skidded around a corner. Her wide eyes caught sight of the blacksmith's shop standing ominously against the night. Warm firelight spilled from the windows and the acrid smell of smoke drifted on the wind.

The air trembled with an unearthly energy as Anna approached, a staggering malevolence that clawed at her senses. Fear gripped her with its icy fingers. What if she was too late? What if Mercy had already fallen prey to Cotton Barlow's evil designs? Anna swallowed hard, steeling her nerves against the dread creeping into her stomach. She pushed on, accelerating her stride. When she found the door to the smithy bolted from the inside, she pounded on it and rammed it with her shoulder.

It was no use. It wouldn't budge.

"Mercy!" she cried. "Mercy, answer me!"

No response.

Anna dashed to a window and smashed it with her elbow. The glass shattered inward, but the window frame was too small for her to squeeze through.

Inside, Cotton Barlow stood bathed in firelight. He towered over Mercy, who sat unconscious and bleeding from her wrists. Her chest was dreadfully still, and the piercing blue and red hues of her eyes were glazed over as they stared into nothingness.

The molten tip of a fireplace poker glowed red in Barlow's hand.

"Stop!" Anna shouted.

Barlow paused and swiveled his head toward her. A

frightful silence enveloped the room as his black eyes drilled into her.

"Ah, Anna." He grinned wickedly, his eyes glinting in the firelight. "I wondered when you would come. You cannot save her. She rests now in the shadow of death, and there is but one hope for her resurrection…"

Raising one of Mercy's severed wrists up with one hand, he pressed the glowing tip of the poker to her open wound.

Mercy's flesh sizzled and steamed under the searing heat until Barlow finally relented and removed the tip, leaving behind a ghastly burn in place of the wound.

Anna hammered the window frame with her fists. Helpless, she could only watch as Barlow reached for Mercy's other wrist and cauterized the second wound. He then hauled the dying girl from her chair and laid her on the floor beside Kisosen.

And then, illuminated in the firelight, Anna glimpsed the black book resting on the workbench. There it was, the Black Testament—the key to her mother's salvation.

Suddenly, an idea came to her.

She spun from the window and dashed around the building to the root cellar door. Her fingers trembled as she crouched and fumbled with the latch. Throwing open the bolt, she whipped the door wide, revealing a yawning black abyss. She plunged into the inky darkness, guided only by the flickering slivers of firelight slicing through the gaps in the ceiling planks from the floor above. The cellar smelled of earth and rot, the feeble light barely illuminating the damp, earthen walls that enclosed her.

Anna scrambled blindly until she found the ladder to the

ground floor and scurried up the rungs. Panic gnawed at her insides as she traced the edges of the wooden trapdoor with her fingers, searching for any sign of weakness. The rhythmic drone of Barlow's haunting chant resonated from the floor above her head. Anna recognized the serpentine language of black magic, but not the incantation. She pressed her shoulders into the trapdoor and pushed it upward.

The hinges groaned in protest as it cracked open an inch or two. Then stopped.

Something heavy weighed it down.

"No," Anna whispered, her voice quivering with despair. She strained against the trapdoor with her shoulders, glimpsing the room above through the crack, her eyes level with the floor.

Barlow's figure stood silhouetted by the blazing light of the forge. Mercy's pale form lay on the floor before him. Still hobbling, Barlow struggled to drag Kisosen's limp body to his knees, positioning the Indian's throat over Mercy's face. Holding him in place with one hand, Barlow pressed the knife to Kisosen's throat and slit it wide open. Blood gushed in a crimson torrent and filled Mercy's mouth.

With a primal cry and a burst of adrenaline, Anna used all the strength in her legs to propel herself upward, ramming herself into the trapdoor. There was a loud crash as the cabinet pinning it shut teetered and toppled over on its side. The trapdoor flew open and Anna surged into the room. She charged straight at Barlow, intent on putting an end to his unholy ritual.

She was too late.

With a blinding flash, the pentagram on the Black

Testament ignited, bathing the room in a hellish light. The force of it sent Anna sprawling to the floor, shielding her eyes from the brilliance.

When she dared to open them again, the blacksmith's shop lay in eerie silence. The wind ceased its mournful wail. Even the shadows seemed to retreat into the corners, as if cowering before an unseen force. Tendrils of black smoke writhed and twirled around the Black Testament as a spectral figure materialized in the air above it—a woman shrouded in darkness.

Angéle de la Barthe.

The shadowy wisps of her scorched dress floated in the air, and her eyes burned with an unholy fire. Her form was ethereal and translucent, yet it radiated a sinister energy that made Anna's blood run cold. A surge of terror and fascination overwhelmed her as she shrank back. De la Barthe had remained bound to her phylactery for centuries. She fed on the blood and despair of lost souls, waiting with undying patience for a vessel strong enough to sustain her evil spirit.

Mercy was that vessel. And Barlow was about to set the witch free.

The atmosphere crackled with dark energy as de la Barthe's spirit, given new life by Barlow's bloody ritual, slithered through the air toward Mercy's still form. Barlow's eyes gleamed with a fanatic fervor as he let Kisosen's bloodless corpse slump to the side and quickened the pace of his incantations. Sweat glistened on his pallid forehead even as the temperature dropped even further, a bone-numbing cold that penetrated to the very marrow of Anna's bones. Frost formed on the walls despite the blazing heat of the forge, creeping towards the center of the room where Barlow chanted. Anna shivered involuntarily, her breath forming icy clouds in the frigid air. Barlow's voice rose, infused with an urgency bordering on desperation. He reached the crescendo of the incantation, his words laced with exultation.

Suddenly, a blinding light erupted from the center of the room, engulfing Mercy's body. Anna shielded her eyes as the force of the unearthly energy surged through the chamber, a tempest of raw power threatening to consume everything in its wake.

A deathly silence fell.

Anna blinked the starbursts from her eyes. De la Barthe's spectral form was gone. Mercy's corpse still lay spread on the floor where Barlow had laid her. The room was still around her.

Anna's breath hung in the air as Mercy's pale fingers suddenly twitched, a ghostly echo of life returning to her cold, still limbs. Her form stirred, a faint quiver passing through her body. It started as another subtle twitch of her fingers. Then a slow rise and fall of her chest, as if she were breathing life for the first time in an eternity.

And then her hand curled into a claw.

Mercy's eyes snapped open, revealing the milky white orbs of a dead woman.

Barlow's heart thudded in his chest as he took a cautious step back. The Black Testament slipped from his trembling hands and fell to the floor with a loud thud.

There was a moment of stillness, a precarious calm that belied the charged energy in the room. Barlow approached Mercy, his steps tentative.

"Mercy?" he called out, his voice barely a whisper.

The girl's lips parted, but the sound that came out was not of this world. It was an otherworldly echo, a haunting growl that crawled up from Hell itself.

Mercy rose from the floor with her terrible gaze fixed on Barlow. Her once lifeless eyes now held a baleful spark, a malice that made his bones shudder. He retreated, knocking over a stack of long-forgotten tools that clattered and echoed through the chamber. Mercy's gaze followed him, unblinking and relentless.

Slowly, slowly, the thing that was Mercy dragged herself across the room toward the man who had reanimated her. Her movements were faltering and unsteady, as if she was not fully in control of her own body. The candles flickered as she shambled past, casting ominous shadows that seemed to elongate and reach out toward Barlow. In that eerie half-light, his elation spiraled into terror. His ritual had worked. Angéle de la Barthe stood before him, a living specter between the realms.

A voice that wasn't Mercy's tore loose from her mouth, a horrible rasping screech like iron prongs being raked over steel.

Barlow recoiled, realizing too late the gravity of his folly. Now that de la Barthe possessed Mercy's body, she had no intention of rewarding his loyalty. He stumbled backward as the possessed girl advanced, his eyes widening with fright. He had enough time to raise his hands up in a futile gesture of defense before Mercy grabbed the sides of his head with her claw-like hands. A tortured wail burst from his lips as she pressed her thumbs into his eyes and gouged them in their sockets until rivulets of blood oozed down his cheeks.

Chapter 27

Barlow's blood-curdling screams filled the smithy and echoed through the empty village. Breathless and shaken, Anna staggered to her feet and grabbed the Black Testament from where it had fallen. She felt it vibrating with unholy power, the book seeming to coil around her, enveloping her in a dark embrace.

Mercy let out a bone-chilling shriek as she dropped Barlow's lifeless body and whirled. Long strings of his blood dripped from her fingertips. A low growl rumbled from her throat as she glowered at Anna, and the room trembled with the rage of the spirit inside her. She lunged, reaching out for the Black Testament with claw-like fingers. Panic surged through Anna's veins as she stumbled backward, narrowly evading the possessed girl's freezing grasp. Desperation shot through her, and she spun and bolted for the exit. With the grimoire clutched against her chest, she burst through the creaking door into the frosty night.

The full moon peeked through the dissipating clouds, casting a pale glow on the deserted lanes. Anna's breath came in heaving gasps as she raced over the muddy ruts, her skirts fluttering like the wings of a night creature. Shards of wood exploded behind her with a crashing sound that broke the silence. But she kept her gaze fixed on the winding paths ahead, unwilling to look back. She knew she was being pursued; she felt Mercy's presence getting closer, poisoning the air like an insidious fog.

Anna's mind raced as she contemplated her next move. She couldn't outrun her pursuer for long—Mercy was possessed by Angéle de la Barthe, an undead witch with untold power. The girl was now a vessel who moved with preternatural speed. Fear constricted Anna's chest as she darted past crumbling walls and broken fences, her wild eyes scanning for any sign of refuge. She skidded around a corner and froze, her stomach leaping into her throat.

There was a figure lurking in the gloom ahead.

It moved.

Relief washed over Anna when she recognized the pallid face of the young man approaching her in the darkness.

"William!" she gasped.

"Anna! Where's Mercy?" William's voice trembled. Dirt and blood coated one side of his head, and his eyes were wide with fright.

"Run! We must run!" Anna grabbed his hand and dragged him with her, fleeing together through the winding paths.

A sudden, spine-rattling scream echoed through the deserted streets. Anna stumbled in a panic. The Black Testament seemed to throb with an ungodly power in her grip, its cover hot to the touch. Whispers slithered into her ears, unintelligible yet laden with ancient malice.

Determined to put as much distance between herself and Mercy as she could manage, Anna's feet carried her instinctively toward the village outskirts. The dense forest awaited them, black and sprawling. With the uneven ground threatening to betray her with every step, she glanced over her shoulder, half-expecting to see Mercy's ghostly figure materialize from the shadows. But the only company they had was the uneasy rustle of leaves and the far-off hoot of an owl.

Anna heard the distant murmur of a river as they neared the edge of the village. A glimmer of hope ignited within her. Spirits were bound to the earth that held their human remains. If they could reach the river, Mercy might not be able to follow them. Perhaps she and William could flee the village on foot, or at least make it as far as the nearest road.

But just as hope flickered in Anna's heart, an inescapable fact extinguished it: Angéle de la Barthe was never buried. They burned her alive, and her evil spirit wasn't bound to anything but the book Anna carried pressed to her chest.

The book…

De la Barthe had signed her name to it in her own blood. It was why she never crossed over the Veil—her phylactery kept her spirit eternally tethered to this world. Anna knew she no longer had any choice. She couldn't let de la Barthe walk the earth, resurrected in Mercy's body. If she had any hope of freeing the innocent girl from the witch's clutches, she had to destroy the Black Testament. But how? How could she possibly destroy a grimoire that had survived centuries? That the Devil himself had crafted in the fires of Hell?

The sound of rushing water grew louder. Ahead, moonlight

glimmered off a swift stream that burst forth from a rocky mouth where the underground river flowing beneath the village surfaced. Further downstream, the village's old watermill stood in eerie silence, surrounded by the dense shadows of the ancient forest. It was a weather-beaten monolith of rugged stone and timber, standing stoically against the relentless passage of time. Moss and ivy smothered its framework. Its oaken beams had aged to a deep, weathered gray and bore the scars of countless seasons. The thatched roof sagged like a tired traveler, the straw and reeds matted with moss. The wheel hung askew in the rushing current, its spokes encrusted with rust as it still slowly turned, creaking with each tortured revolution. Remnants of an intricate network of wooden channels and sluices were now clogged with debris and decay. The relentless flow of the river had long ago overtaken the derelict mill dam, but a deep pool of placid water still remained, choked with reeds and lily pads.

With nowhere else to go, Anna and William darted toward the looming structure. The thud of their footsteps reverberated through the stillness of the forest. Anna cast a wary glance over her shoulder, her senses still on high alert. The village lay in darkness behind them, but she knew de la Barthe would never let them escape. Their only hope was to find some way of severing the dead witch's link to this mortal realm.

They found the mill's wooden door hanging from rusted hinges as they approached. It sagged open at a crooked angle, creaking in the wind while inviting them into the mill's shadowy depths. They hustled inside, their steps muffled by the thick layer of dust that had settled over the years. The pale glow of the moon cast ghostly rays through the broken windows, revealing the hulking remains of the machinery.

The wooden beams overhead groaned with the weight of the slumping roof, and the rhythmic pulsing of the waterwheel outside echoed like a distant heartbeat. A rickety staircase near a corner led up into the darkness of the upper level. The massive millstones at the center of the space had worn smooth from decades of ceaseless turning. Moss and ferns sprouted between the cogs, reclaiming their territory with undying persistence. Cobwebs clung to the rafters, and the slow and steady cadence of dripping water echoed through the musty air.

"Stay quiet," Anna whispered. Her eyes darted around the gloom, hoping to find a way to destroy the Black Testament. Forgotten tools lay strewn about like discarded relics— wooden shovels with worn handles, rusted saws, and broken millstones. It was hopeless. Anna was certain that de la Barthe had taken precautions to charm her phylactery, ensuring that it would seal her soul within it forever. Anna knew she wasn't powerful enough to dispel such wards, even if it were possible. William was right: if the villagers could have destroyed the Black Testament, they would have done so instead of sealing it beneath a chapel. Anna felt sick with despair.

And then it came to her. She might not be able to destroy the Black Testament, but she could send it somewhere from which even Angéle de la Barthe could not return—beyond the Veil.

"William," she whispered. "I know how to save your sister. We must—"

Footsteps echoed through the blackness. Slow and deliberate.

Mercy was outside.

The oppressive weight of her supernatural presence bore down on them, threatening to suffocate every ounce of courage they possessed.

"We can't let her find us." Anna's gaze darted toward the entrance where the moonlit night spilled through the shattered doorway. "We must find still water, a reflective surface to—"

"*Anna…*"

The voice that called to her from Mercy's lips was an unholy rasp devoid of humanity.

"*Oh, how I long to devour thine eyes, to pluck them from thy skull and roll them over my tongue like candied cherries. But thou hast nothing to fear, for the Master hath marked thee as one of his chosen…*"

One of his chosen.

De la Barthe's words turned Anna's insides to ice as a paralyzing horror surged through her. Was this why the witch hadn't killed her when she had the chance in the rectory? Because the Devil had claimed Anna for himself?

"*Would thou resurrect thy mother, Anna? Would thou save her from the fiery pit? Come unto me, child. Sign thy name to his black book and such great and terrible power will he reveal unto thee.*"

Anna and William pressed themselves against the cold, damp wall, their bodies tense with fear. They kept their eyes fixed on the entrance as if expecting the shadows to take shape at any moment. The footsteps outside drew nearer, each haunting echo rattling their nerves with the promise of impending doom.

"Stand with him, Anna, and thou will never walk alone again..."

Anna bit her lip, her nerves strained to the point of agony. She motioned for William to follow, and they moved deeper into the bowels of the mill, their footsteps muffled by the dust-covered floor. The massive wooden gears churned above them now, creaking and shuddering with each slow revolution of the wheel. Anna's eyes darted around. There was no escape. Mercy lurked just outside the only exit, and they couldn't possibly hope to defeat the ancient spirit inside her. The only other way out was the narrow staircase ascending to the upper level. But Anna knew that would be a mistake—fleeing upward almost always resulted in being trapped. Her gaze fell upon a length of thick rope coiled among some rotten barrels. It gave her an idea.

She always did have a talent for breaking things.

"Take this and wrap it around the millstone spindle!" she instructed, tossing one end of the rope to William.

He caught it and did as she asked while she stood on her tip-toes and stretched to loop the other end around the cogs of the massive gear turning overhead.

"Anna, what are you doing?" he asked.

"Flooding the mill."

"What? But—"

An ominous creaking filled the silence as the rope stretched tight between the revolving gear and the thick post of the spindle. The millstone jammed with a jolt, and for the first time in over a century, the machinery ground to a shuddering halt, their grinding rhythm now replaced by a tense silence.

A low groan shook the mill as the giant waterwheel outside ceased its turning. The outer wall instantly began to tremble as the rushing water that had once flowed under the wheel was now diverted by the unyielding dam it had become. Leaks sprouted and sprayed from between the cracks, a hesitant admission of defeat as the planks strained and flexed under the pressure of the powerful current that battered them. Anna and William stood back, eyeing the wall warily as a low rumble filled the cavernous space.

Suddenly, a faint glimmer of moonlight seeped through a crack in the front door, casting a feeble glow across the floor. In that dim illumination, Mercy's silhouette emerged, her white hair billowing like a specter in the night. The very foundation of the mill trembled under the weight of her supernatural presence, its frame straining against a force that should never walk the earth.

The rumbling beyond the wall grew louder, a roar now accompanied by an ominous gurgling sound. The floorboards quivered beneath their feet as the waterwheel, still jammed, held back the fury of the ancient river. It no longer felt like they were in the bowels of the old mill; they were now in the wooden hull of a great ship taking on water.

A guttural growl emanated from Mercy's throat. She flew at them in the same instant the wall burst.

The pent-up river surged through the splintered breach, and a deafening roar filled the air. Water rushed into the mill with frightening speed, a frothing, unstoppable force. The room transformed into a nightmarish aquatic realm as the cold, murky waters flooded in, swallowing everything in their path. Shattered wood, dislodged stones, and broken machinery were swept away in the relentless torrent.

The churning flood slammed into Mercy and sent her crashing across the room, where she disappeared beneath the rising water. Anna and William were both swept off their feet, but not before Anna managed to make a desperate grab for the flimsy railing of the stairs. William was nearly carried away until he flung out a hand and seized the hem of her coat, clinging to it desperately. Gasping for breath, they fought against the powerful current, their hands clawing at anything that might anchor them. Panic seized Anna as she struggled, frantically seeking higher ground within the rapidly flooding mill. She strained with all she had, her muscles screaming with the exertion, as she slowly, slowly pulled them both to the stairs.

"Upstairs, now!" Anna shouted over the chaos, shoving William up the steps. She was right behind him as they scrambled upward, the wooden risers creaking beneath their hurried ascent. The cold and merciless water was already lapping hungrily at their heels. The mill shivered around them, the ancient timber structure groaning under the strain.

Reaching the top, they found themselves in a dusty loft filled with forgotten relics of a bygone era. Barrels and sacks lay scattered, and the air hung heavy with the acrid reek of decay and bat droppings. The windows were too high and too small to offer any escape. Moonlight knifed through the broken glass, illuminating dust motes dancing in the air.

Below, the mill's remaining walls strained and groaned under the power of the rushing waters, their protests echoing up through the storage loft. Anna and William huddled in the shadows, staring at the staircase. The water was rising rapidly, filling the lower level of the mill and threatening to reach them even here. The supporting beams shook under the furious torrent. With any luck, the powerful current would wash away the steps, leaving them stranded but safe.

Without warning, Mercy's snowy head slowly rose into view from the stairs. Her eyes smoldered with hellish intensity as she withered the duo with her gaze.

"Mercy," William whispered, his voice a tremulous plea.

The possessed girl's presence seemed to suck the air from the room, leaving only an icy chill in its wake. Gone was the innocent child they had once known—replaced by a vessel of pure malice, consumed by the darkness that had claimed her. The soaked remains of her tattered white shift clung to her frame. As if eager to be reunited with its baleful owner, the Black Testament pulsed in Anna's hands. She fought against the paralyzing fear, her mind racing for a way to escape. There was only one door, a crooked portal beyond which nothing was visible.

Without thinking, she grabbed William and yanked him through it.

A blast of icy wind rocked them on their heels as they stumbled outside onto a narrow walkway overlooking the waterwheel. The roar of the river slamming into the frozen wheel resonated beneath their feet, drowning out the sound of Mercy's pursuit.

Anna reached the edge of the walkway and stared down into the darkness. The river churned and roared below, a black abyss swallowing the moon's reflection. Her chest clenched as she glanced back, glimpsing Mercy's ghostly figure emerging from the shadows.

"Jump, William!" Anna shouted to be heard over the noise of the river. "We have to jump!"

William's eyes widened in terror, his gaze darting between the swirling waters and his possessed sister. Mercy was closing in on them now. A cruel smile crept across her lips, and the cackling laughter that escaped them was not her own.

Anna didn't wait. With her heart lodged in her throat, she leaped into the void. Plummeting downward, everything around her turned into a blurry haze, drowned out by the whooshing of air.

Chapter 28

The impact with the water hit Anna like a cannonball; the river swallowing her whole and dragging her down into its icy embrace. She tumbled beneath the surface, the current pulling and tossing her as if it had a will of its own. Panic strangled her heart. Her lungs screamed for air as darkness threatened to claim her. She fought against the rushing water, struggling to keep her grip on the Black Testament while straining desperately for the surface.

Cold air hit her face as she broke through. The moonlight revealed the watermill drifting further away, an ominous silhouette against the night sky, as the current carried her downstream. She spun around in the water, eyes darting everywhere in search of William.

He had never jumped. He was still with Mercy on the walkway above the waterwheel while the mill slowly crumbled beneath them. Anna saw him make a desperate lunge towards his sister, and realized why he hadn't jumped with her—he was buying her some time.

She swam hard to the riverbank, sputtering and gasping for

breath as she pulled herself onto solid ground. The mill loomed about a hundred yards away now. Water gushed from its empty windows as the river eviscerated it from within. Planks and stones tore loose from the walls as more of the structure collapsed under the relentless force of the raging flood. It was about to come crashing down any second.

Anna squeezed the Black Testament tightly as she sprinted along the river bank. She heard a strangled cry erupt from atop the waterwheel and glimpsed Mercy tightening a clawed hand around her brother's throat. Then her view was obscured by the hulking bulk of the mill itself as she skirted the dry land around it.

Upriver from the doomed mill, the water of the millpond lay tranquil and silent. Still sheltered by what was left of the mill dam, its surface gleamed like black glass under the pale moon as Anna skidded to a halt by the water's edge. Dripping and shivering with cold, she clutched the ancient grimoire, her heart racing as she closed her eyes and started chanting. She was dimly aware that William's hoarse cries had ceased as she lost herself in the ecstasy of her magic. Was he already dead? Did Mercy fulfill her own prophecy by killing him?

Anna's teeth chattered, her breath hanging in the frigid air, as she continued her ritual. The millpond stirred. Ripples disturbed the placid surface, emanating from a point at its center where an ominous vortex formed. Dark shapes moved beneath the swirling water, and an eerie mist rose from the water, shrouding the surroundings in a ghostly haze. Anna's heart pounded in her chest as fear and exhilaration coursed through her veins. She knew the risks involved. She was opening a door between realms, and while it was open, anything could slip through—including Rebecca Hale.

But she had no other choice. Banishing Angéle de la Barthe's evil spirit was the only way to save Mercy's life.

Just then, an explosive crack shot through the air as the weakened beams of the mill gave way. Anna stole a glance long enough to see the entire building lurch forward, its timbers splintering and buckling under the intense pressure of its own weight. With a thunderous roar, it succumbed to the river's relentless assault, collapsing into a mass of debris and splintered wood. The rushing waters swallowed the remnants whole, carrying them downstream in a chaotic whirl of foam and spray, until only ruins remained.

There was no sign of William or Mercy, but Anna knew the threat was far from over. The water of the millpond churned and spun before her in an ever-strengthening maelstrom. As the final words of her incantation left her lips, the pool erupted in a burst of otherworldly light. The Veil between the living and the dead wavered and strained like a thread stretched to its limits. A chorus of disembodied voices whispered from deep within the dark whirlpool, their words unintelligible but laden with ancient malice. Shadows danced beneath the water's surface, taking shape and form as they clawed at the edges of the swirling portal Anna had thrown open.

The temperature dropped further. Anna shivered uncontrollably now, her eyes fixed on the spectral gateway she had created. The air crackled with an electrifying power, and the ground trembled beneath her feet. She sensed the spirits on the other side, their ravenous gazes piercing up through the Veil into the mortal realm. Their forms were indistinct, like wisps of smoke given substance. Hollow eyes stared at her from the bottomless depths of the churning maelstrom. A chorus of voices spoke in unison, their words a jumbled roar of torment, sorrow, and longing.

A deafening bolt split the air, sending shockwaves through the surrounding woods. The Veil between the living and the dead tore open, revealing a swirling vortex that seemed to consume everything in its path. Ghostly wails and unearthly moans filled the night, a legion of lost souls yearning for release.

Anna felt the pulsing heat of the Black Testament against her chest. This was it. She had to do it now, before any of those bloodthirsty horrors came through the breach. She raised the grimoire high, ready to hurl it down.

And stopped.

She couldn't do it.

The Black Testament was her only chance of restoring her mother's mortality and saving her from Hell. If Anna cast the Black Testament down into that black vortex, it would disappear beyond the Veil forever. Any hope of seeing Abigail alive again would be lost with it.

The blackened pages of the grimoire fluttered in the wind like the wings of a trapped raven as Anna wavered. She couldn't give up her one chance of rescuing her mother. Not now, not when she was so close. There had to be another way.

The weight of a lifetime of sacrifice crashed down on her all at once. She was tired, exhausted from years of doing the right thing for others. This time, she wanted to do the right thing for herself. She would never have admitted it before, but she missed her mother terribly. She would give anything

—sacrifice anything—to get her back. And with Abigail returned from the dead, they could save countless more lives together.

And yet, they would never save them all. Anna had learned that lesson in Burlington when she had to choose between saving her mother or an innocent little girl. So if rescuing Abigail from Hell meant abandoning Mercy to her fate out here in this harsh and desolate land, then it was a price she was willing to pay. What was one girl's life compared to the multitude Anna could save with her mother by her side?

Walk in the light, my precious girl...

A sudden echo of Abigail's last words stirred in Anna's mind. Her dying wish had been for her daughter to resist the darkness in her nature. How could Anna ever tell her mother she had sacrificed an innocent girl's life to bring her back? How could either of them live with that guilt? Neither would truly have escaped Hell; they would carry it within them always.

Was that the Devil's plan for them all along?

A sudden rush of footsteps grabbed Anna's attention. She whirled around in time to see Mercy hurdling toward her, fingers elongated into claws and eyes blazing with unholy light. She felt the wind explode from her lungs as the possessed girl slammed into her with unnatural strength. They tumbled together, the Black Testament slipping from Anna's grasp as she hit the ground hard with Mercy on top of her.

Anna felt hot blood spill down her cheeks as the girl raked her face with her nails. She struggled and thrashed, but the spirit inside Mercy was too powerful, too ferocious to resist.

The girl's movements were no longer human, but a grotesque flurry of savage bloodlust. She kept Anna pinned to the ground by the throat while her free hand balled into a fist and came pounding down on Anna's face.

Pain exploded behind Anna's eyes. For a moment, time hung suspended as she teetered on the precipice of unconsciousness. Through the haze of pain and disorientation, she clung to her will, fighting against the darkness and clawing her way back from oblivion.

Mercy raised her fist again, fingers curled into a clawed hammer, ready to strike. Desperation flooded Anna's veins as she searched for anything, any way to protect herself.

Suddenly, Mercy erupted in a shriek of rage. Clinging to consciousness, Anna glimpsed William standing over his sister, the Black Testament raised high over his head.

With a visceral cry, he hurled the cursed grimoire deep into the bottomless vortex.

Mercy's frail body contorted in agony. The shrieks of rage emanating from within her echoed through the night before fading into an ethereal wail. One last convulsion wracked Mercy's frail body. With a guttural roar, she expelled the ancient spirit of Angéle de la Barthe—a vaporous figure in scorched black robes that hung like smoke in the air.

Mercy let out a soul-wrenching scream and collapsed to the ground.

De la Barthe's disembodied spirit wailed in agony. Her shadowy form writhed and coiled, pulled down, down, down by the dark forces binding her to the grimoire, into the swirling spectral energy at the maelstrom's epicenter. She clawed at the air; her form flickering, torn between the realms

265

of the living and the dead. Rage contorted her features into a grotesque mask of fury. Her screams echoed into nothingness as she vanished beyond the Veil, her venomous presence severed from the mortal realm.

But the danger still wasn't over.

Dark tendrils emerged from the watery abyss, snaking their way toward the surface with sinister intent. The ghastly figures that had been mere spectators now surged upward, their ghostly faces twisted in agony and rage.

Panic seized Anna as she realized the volatile balance she had disrupted. The line between the living and the dead had been erased, and the forces she had unleashed were about to overtake her. Bloodied and battered, she staggered to her feet and gasped the words to close the breach between worlds. Her voice resonated with power, weaving a barrier that surged forth, stitching the torn Veil back together. The malevolent tendrils recoiled, and the shadowy figures retreated into the darkness, their haunting visages fading into the abyss.

But not before Anna saw her mother's face, staring up at her from the other side.

"Mother!" she cried.

It was like gazing into a watery mirror. Abigail's image, so like Anna's own, wavered in the darkness, flickering like a flame caught in a gust of wind. Her lips moved, but Anna couldn't hear what she was saying. She saw something wistful creep into her mother's blue eyes as she reached out for her daughter from the abyss.

And then Abigail was gone, the dark water rushing over her as the portal sealed shut.

"*No!*" Anna shrieked, her voice a heartbroken wail that

echoed across the millpond. She staggered backward, her chest heaving, her body drained of energy.

Mercy lay still by the water's edge, her breaths ragged but undeniably her own. William wobbled to his weakened sister's side and cradled her in his arms. The moon reappeared from the shifting clouds, casting its gentle light upon the scene. Mercy's blue and red eyes, now clear and lucid, locked onto Anna.

"Thank you," she whispered, her voice a fragile echo of the girl she once was.

But Anna didn't hear her. Instead, she felt a profound despair settle over her, a grief that reached deep into her soul. She collapsed to her knees and gazed out over the now serene pond, the weight of what she had done settling upon her.

Abigail had seen her. She knew Anna had held the power to save her in her hands.

And she knew her daughter had forsaken her.

What had Abigail tried to tell her? What were those unheard words that never made it through the Veil? Were they words of forgiveness? A whispered echo of the love that transcended death itself?

Or a desperate cry for help?

Epilogue

Deep beneath the unassuming facade of her modest row house in Boston's Beacon Hill, Anna descended the winding stone staircase to her subterranean labyrinth of arcane knowledge and experimentation—her secret arcanium. The air grew cool and damp as she ventured deeper underground. The orange glow of her lamp danced across the walls, revealing passages hewn from ancient stone. Only the occasional drip of moisture from unseen crevasses broke the deep silence.

At the bottom of the stairs, Anna dispelled the wards on the giant wrought-iron gate. The sanctum of her arcanium stretched out before her, a vast expanse shrouded in torchlight, its ceiling lost in the shadows. Shelves upon shelves of ancient grimoires, their leather-bound spines cracked and worn with age, lined the uneven stone walls. Jars filled with bizarre specimens—preserved eyes of extinct creatures, dried roots, and vials containing shimmering liquids—occupied wooden tables arranged haphazardly throughout the space. Glass vials of luminescent liquids and powders of unnatural hues, filled the shelves. Esoteric instruments of silver and bone, etched with sigils and glyphs, stood ready for Anna's manipulation. Mysterious artifacts occupied the cabinets of curiosities, relics of bygone civilizations and forgotten religions, all cataloged with meticulous precision in Anna's Book of Shadows.

Deeper in the cavernous expanse, a large stone table served as Anna's primary workspace. It was here, under the dim glow of flickering candles, that she had assisted her mother in their arcane experiments and rituals. Connected by a series of winding passageways, smaller alcoves branched off from the main chamber, each devoted to a particular branch of esoteric study. One housed a peculiar array of crystalline structures, pulsating with an otherworldly radiance. Another held nothing but a collection of skulls and skeletons.

Dominating the heart of the arcanium was Anna's stone scrying pool. She paused by a cabinet to pour herself a glass of peaty whiskey before moving to stand by the pool's still water. The fiery heat of the alcohol warmed her chest as her fingers traced the intricate symbols carved into the ancient stone rim. The water within shimmered in response as she chanted an incantation under her breath, her lips forming the ancient words she had learned from Abigail as a child.

As her incantations reached a crescendo, the water in the scrying pool rippled, its surface distorting like a mirage. An eerie energy filled the air, sending a prickle down Anna's neck. The image in the water shifted, revealing the bustling interior of a tavern near the harbor. Wooden planks creaked under the weight of rowdy patrons, and the air was thick with the tang of ale and the sounds of laughter. The flickering candles and the hum of distant conversations were faintly discernible in the spectral image.

Anna sipped her whiskey, her eyes focused on a young man with tousled hair and a face that bore the wear and tear of a hard life—William.

More than a month had gone by since she kept her word and brought William and Mercy back to Boston with her. Since then, she had been preparing for this night and what she was about to do. With the moment at hand, she now felt the need to watch over the siblings one last time, like a guardian cloaked in shadows.

Finding them work at one of the harbor-front taverns had been a simple task once Anna called in a debt from a barkeep. William now moved with a practiced ease behind the bar, pouring ale and exchanging banter with the patrons. Mercy, her pale hair cascading like a waterfall around her shoulders, moved gracefully among the tables. The long sleeves of her blouse hid the ghastly scars on her wrists.

A mixture of relief and dread filled Anna's heart as she watched over the girl she had saved from damnation. She saw the haunted look in Mercy's strange eyes, the signs of trauma that would forever haunt her. The rogues and deviants of Boston's underworld would easily ignore and embrace her ghostly appearance, and she would be safe among them. It wasn't a glamorous life, but those rough sailors and tough barmaids had been like family to Anna since she was a child. Still, she wondered how long it would be until the girl's bloody past caught up to her. How would it shape the woman Mercy would become? Would Anna one day answer a knock at her door, only to find Mercy there, pleading to be initiated in the ways of witchcraft and the occult?

Anna inhaled a deep breath, the cool dampness of the underground air filling her lungs. Her gaze drifted to where the iron door to her Conjuring Chamber stood cloaked in shadows at the far end of the cavernous space.

Her whiskey was gone, and the witching hour had come.

It was time.

Anna felt her fear rippling up from her gut as she approached the massive portal and grasped the handle. The unyielding metal was freezing beneath her touch, and she wavered a moment. There would be no turning back if she went through with this.

Hardening her resolve, she pulled on the handle.

A whisper of cold air from within brushed her face and fluttered her hair. Designed for communing with the dead and safeguarding against their escape, the chamber beyond the door pulsated with an unearthly energy.

Abigail's body lay beneath a shroud in the center of the circular space, suspended in a state somewhere between life and death. The lines of a massive pentagram were chiseled into the bedrock beneath her. At each point of the pentagram, towering mirrors of obsidian hung suspended by thick, wrought-iron chains. The mirrors, framed in ornate black ironwork, captured and reflected the flickering light of the charmed torches that lined the chamber's periphery. Strange runes adorned the edges of the frames, shimmering with an eldritch glow, each mirror a window to a world steeped in shadow and mystery.

Anna's black hair cascaded over her shoulders as she strode to the center of the giant cell and stood over her mother's body.

Soon, the enchantment preserving her earthly remains will wane, and her flesh will wither and rot...

Cotton Barlow's words haunted Anna's thoughts. The memory of her mother reaching out for her from the abyss had tormented her ever since that terrible night in Sévérité. But was it already too late? Had Anna already waited too long?

A sudden unearthly chill flowed into the chamber, numbing Anna's flesh. She was no longer alone; Gideon was there with her. She felt the familiar's invisible presence by her side in the one place on earth to which he no longer required an invitation.

"I have become her, Gideon," Anna murmured as she gazed down at her mother's cold and bloodless features, now obscured beneath the shroud. "I have spent half my life dreaming of escaping her, and now I have become her— pursuing the same goal, driven by the same desperate need to be reunited with my mother again. I can't give up now. I refuse to abandon her, not when there is still a chance of saving her from Hell. The Black Testament may be lost beyond the Veil, but there is still someone there powerful enough to reveal its secrets to me."

"What do you intend, Mistress?" Gideon's hollow voice reverberated off the stone walls. There was an uneasy tone to it now, a fearful apprehension that Anna didn't know the undead spirit was capable of.

"You know what I must do, Gideon," she replied. "And I can delay it no longer."

She turned and started across the chamber toward the

mirror at the western point of the pentagram, that which stood in the direction of darkness and death.

Gideon's unseen force rocked her back on her heels with staggering strength.

Anna let out a startled gasp and caught her balance. Shadows crawled over the walls, and in the dim light, she saw him—a formless silhouette taking shape between her and the mirror.

"I cannot let you do this," Gideon intoned.

Anna fixed him with a furious glare. "*Let* me? Do you forget whom you serve?"

"I serve your *mother*, child. Even now and until the end of days. *She* is the one who bound me to you, to be your conscience and protect you... even from yourself."

"What have I to lose, Gideon?" Anna shot back. "My soul? I am already damned. You know that as well as I. You know what de la Barthe said. The Devil has already claimed me for himself. At least with my mother returned, we may save as many innocents as we can before Hell demands its sacrifice."

The air crackled with energy as the shadow slithered forward, tendrils of smoke stretching toward Anna like ghostly fingers. It coalesced into a humanoid form—a handsome young man with nothing but darkness for eyes.

But Anna had expected such a clash. And she had come prepared.

In her tireless search through the arcanium library, she had failed to find a way to revive her mother. But she did stumble upon the means by which to sever the spell that had bound her and Gideon since birth. Having sworn off witchcraft for fear of reviving Rebecca Hale's insidious hold on her, Anna had resisted carrying out the spell—until now. After tonight, it would no longer matter, and she couldn't allow Gideon to stand in the way of what she had planned.

Anna's palm found the vial in the pocket of her cloak, the tincture of her blood mingled with consecrated graveyard dirt and Gideon's own bone dust. With a flick of the wrist, she hurled the contents at her spectral guardian. In the same instant, she shouted his full Scottish name, that which gave her power over him.

Gideon recoiled, his ethereal form contorting in agony as the concoction seared through him. He seemed to ignite and come apart, disintegrating into smoldering embers that swirled in the air as if caught by a gust of wind. He let out a howl that echoed from the depths of a bottomless pit before vanishing into the ether with an unearthly shriek.

Anna took a deep breath and surveyed the chamber. All was still and quiet except for the faint hum of residual energy lingering in the air.

She *is the one who bound me to you, to be your conscience…*

Gideon's words echoed in Anna's ears. Yes, conscience was the missing piece in her soul. Abigail had sensed it in her at a very young age. She had initiated Anna into the ways of the occult in hopes that it would give direction and purpose to her daughter's heartless impulses. But beneath the facade of strength lay a darkness that consumed her from within. Anna had spent her entire life hiding from her own demons, haunted by the dead witch whose spirit was intertwined with her own. She had been a girl adrift in a sea of chaos, searching for something—anything—to fill the void within her. Abigail had hoped Gideon would be there to guide her daughter when she no longer could.

What would become of her now that he was gone, maybe forever?

After tonight, it wouldn't matter.

There wasn't a moment to lose.

Steeling her courage, Anna stood before the mirror and filled her lungs with air, exhaling deeply to clear her thoughts. There was no room for error in what she was about to attempt. One mistake would cost her life—and her soul. With one more deep breath, she closed her eyes and began to chant.

With each recitation of Anna's invocation, the mirror rippled like a pond disturbed by a stone, distorting her reflection until it transformed into a sinister silhouette. The air grew even colder as the temperature plummeted, and Anna's breath formed visible puffs of frost.

Suddenly, the torches extinguished. The chamber plunged into darkness.

Anna jumped. This wasn't supposed to happen.

Silence enveloped the space, broken only by her trembling breaths.

But amidst the blackness, a pair of fiery orbs pierced through the shadows, glowing with an unholy light.

Anna Jacobs, blood of my blood…

Anna heard the old, familiar voice echoing in her head, resonating from somewhere black and bottomless. It was a haunting rasp, chilling in its familiarity yet dripping with venomous disdain.

The flaming orbs drew nearer, revealing a shadowy figure materializing in the mirror. Its form was vaporous, a swirling mass of darkness and malevolence with eyes that burned with a hellish fire behind a dreadful black veil.

Rebecca Hale's dark presence coiled around Anna, tightening its grip with each passing second, making it hard for her to breathe.

"You knew it was possible," Anna said, her voice steady despite the tremor that threatened to betray her resolve. "You knew the Black Testament contained a spell that would restore my mother's mortality. Now you are the only one who can help me find and decipher it."

Rebecca's cackling laughter echoed through the darkened chamber, a blood-curdling sound that shook Anna's bones.

So, you have finally come crawling back to me. Why would I aid you, *treacherous wretch that you are?*

Anna swallowed hard and kept her icy gaze fixed on the baleful apparition within the mirror. "Because of the price I am willing to pay."

Rebecca's spectral form circled the confines of the mirror, the undying fire of her eyes never wavering.

Name it…

Anna tried to swallow again, but her mouth had gone dry. "For years, I have contemplated your hold on me, the strange and terrible union between us. But now I finally understand. I am your phylactery, the only earthly vessel binding you to the mortal realm… and I offer myself to you."

Author's Note

Thank you, dear reader, for the generous gift of your time and attention. If you enjoyed this book and would like to see more, please consider taking a moment to leave a quick review on Amazon and/or Goodreads. A kind word from a reader like you is one of the best ways you can support independent authors and is very much appreciated.

Until next time, look under the bed, close the closet door, and whatever you do, don't turn around...

**She was innocent of witchcraft when they arrested her.
She was guilty when they hanged her.**

Step into a world of dark magic, fierce women, and terrifying evil with *A Firebrand of Hell*, a short story prequel to the best-selling *Book of Shadows* series, now available absolutely free!

Visit www.michaelpenning.com to download your copy!

BOOKS BY MICHAEL PENNING

Book of Shadows Series

Novels:
All Hallows Eve
The Suicide Lake
The Wolf Society
The Black Testament

Companion Stories:
The Damnation Chronicles

Other Novels
Solitude

Michael Penning is a bestselling author and award-winning screenwriter of horror and dark fiction. He has been obsessed with all things dark and spooky since before he could finish his own sack of trick-or-treat candy. When he's not coming up with creative ways to scare the hell out of people, he enjoys traveling, photography, and brewing beer. He lives in Montreal with his wife and daughter. For updates and free giveaways, visit www.michaelpenning.com and follow Michael on social media @michaelpenningauthor.

Printed in Great Britain
by Amazon

55248962R00162